MW01139527

BOONE

&

CHARLY

Second

Chance

Love

MALLORY MONROE

Copyright©2019 Mallory Monroe

All rights reserved. Any use of the materials contained in this book without the expressed written consent of the author and/or her affiliates, including scanning, uploading and downloading at file sharing and other sites, and distribution of this book by way of the Internet or any other means, is illegal and strictly prohibited.

AUSTIN BROOK PUBLISHING

DEDICATION

To my beloved, God-fearing, wonderful husband of twenty-four years.

May you rest in peace.

This novel is a work of fiction. All characters are fictitious. Any similarities to anyone living or dead are completely accidental. The specific mention of known places or venues are not meant to be exact replicas of those places, but are purposely embellished or imagined for the story's sake.

DISCLAIMER: THE PHOTOS DISPLAYED ON THE COVER OF THIS BOOK ARE THOSE OF MODELS, NOT TRUE TO LIFE REPRESENTATIONS OF ANY OF THE FICTIONAL CHARACTERS DEPICTED IN THIS BOOK.

VISIT

www.mallorymonroebooks.com

OR

www.austinbrookpublishing.com

for more information on all titles.

TABLE OF CONTENTS

CHARLY'S PROLOGUE

The bell rang and students poured out of their classrooms and filled the hallways with hundreds of happy bodies. Charlene "Charly" Johnson, attempting to lock her office door, was as happy as they were. As the dean of girls at the school, and a P.E. teacher to boot, she was thanking God it was Friday too.

"Not so fast, Shaun!" she yelled at one student when he tore past her, bumping into her just as she locked her office door.

"Sorry, Mrs. Johnson!" the student yelled back, but did not slowdown in his mad dash to get away.

Charly smiled and shook her head. The wildness of youth, she thought as she picked up the thick briefcase that sat at her side. She maneuvered her way around hundreds of loud, lingering teenagers to make her way to her beloved Saab convertible in the back side of the parking lot. She was off until Monday, hallelujah! She couldn't help but be happy too.

She got in, put on her sunglasses, and sped off, shifting gears along the winding L.A. roads and back streets and made her way to her home on the lake. She couldn't wait to get home and take a soaking bath before her husband arrived and distracted her with his usual work drama. Friday evenings, before he made it home, were always her *me* time, and she was relishing it this time.

But when she drove onto the driveway of their home, her hope was quickly dashed. Her husband's truck was parked on the steep incline, barely leaving room for her as usual. He was home already.

For several minutes Charly sat behind the wheel of her car staring at his big truck, and then at their big, contemporary home. He admitted to cheating again. This time with one of his paralegals, which was so unoriginal to Charly she could hardly believe it. She should have left him then. Or the time before then. Or the time before that! But she didn't. Like all those other times, he put on that drop-dead charm, reminding her of why she married him in the first place, and she, like the fool she'd been, forgave him once again.

But now, as she sat in her car, she couldn't figure out the why anymore. Why did she keep forgiving a man like Darryl? Why did she keep putting up with his mess? It wasn't love. She wasn't sure if she ever really loved Darryl at all. He was more like a safe, stable landing for her rather than a love affair.

They met five years ago, when they both were in their upper-twenties and were already enjoying great success. He as a corporate lawyer. She as an assistant high school dean, one of the youngest African-American deans in the entire district. She knew he liked the ladies when she first met him, but he declared his love for her and devotion to their relationship and insisted his playboy days were over. A little less than six months into their courtship, she accepted his proposal and married him.

But now, five years later, she was thirty-two, he was thirty-four, and it felt as if time had stood still. Because he never really changed. His same old bad behavior from their dating days spilled into their marriage like a rude intruder and she knew, early on, that she had made a big mistake. But for some reason that she knew was her problem alone, she allowed him to treat her the way everybody in her life had always treated her: bad. And she could never push herself to divorce him.

Her parents left her.

Her siblings left her.

She wasn't letting her husband leave her too.

In her mind, he was all she had.

She grabbed her briefcase off of the passenger seat and made her way up the steps and into their home. She expected to find him lounging on the sofa with a glass of wine in his hand, complaining about this client or that partner the way he usually did whenever he beat her home, but he wasn't in the living room at all.

"I'm home!" she yelled out, expecting him to at least acknowledge her presence. But there was no response.

She sat her briefcase on the foyer table and tossed her keys in the key dish. Then she made her way further into their home. "Dare? Where are you?"

It was only then, when she asked where he was, did she hear what was some kind of noise and movement coming from upstairs. She couldn't tell what the noise was exactly, but she knew it was coming from their bedroom.

Their *bedroom*!

Her mind immediately flew to the gutter, and she focused on the last woman he had cheated with: the cute paralegal. He said it was over and she had been reassigned to work with a different law partner, but Charly didn't know that to be a fact. That was only what he told her. But the idea that he would bring his whore to their home just seemed like too low a blow to Charly, even for a man like him.

She made her way up those stairs with a quickness. Her heart was pounding because she really didn't want to have to deal with his nonsense. But she knew she had to. She had swept his lying and cheating under rugs too many times already. No more, she thought angrily.

She had been hoping for a drama-free weekend for a change. But the closer she got to that bedroom, and the louder that noise became, she knew peace and calm were out the window. She hurried to that room.

Their bedroom door wasn't closed, as she expected it to be, and when she made it to the doorway, as if to catch his cheating butt in the act once and for all, she caught him alright. Darryl Johnson, her husband, was in their bedroom. But there was no woman in the room. Which shocked her.

He wasn't even in bed. But he had a suitcase on top of the bed and was grabbing what looked like black plastic bags out of his dresser drawers and throwing them into that suitcase.

Although Charly was relieved that he hadn't stooped as low as she thought he had, she was perplexed too. *What in the world*, she wondered. "What are you doing?" she asked him.

"We have to get out of here," Darryl said quickly, without looking at his wife. He was a tall, handsome black man with a body to match his beauty. But he was in a super-hurry.

"What are you talking about?" she asked him.

"We have to get out of here," he said again. "We have to leave now!"

"But why, Darryl?" Charly had a fixed frown on her face. "Why do we have to leave? What are you talking about?"

But he didn't respond to any of her questions. His singular focus appeared to be getting those numerous plastic bags out of that dresser and into that suitcase.

"Dare, what's wrong?" she asked.

"We've got to go!" he yelled. "Didn't you hear me the first time, woman? We've got to get out of here!"

"But why? Tell me why?"

A sad look appeared in his eyes, and he stopped what he was doing for a second and actually looked at her. "I took some money," he admitted with what sounded like regret in his voice. But then his movements sped right back up again, and he continued tossing bags into the case.

But Charly's heart was pounding now. He took money? What did that mean? Did he mean he *stole* money? "What money?" she nervously asked him.

"This money!" he yelled as he opened one of those plastic bags.

Charly could see that it was filled to the brim with what looked like hundred-dollar bills. She could not believe her eyes. "Darryl!" she yelled. "Where on earth did you get all of that from?"

"I told you I took it," he said angrily as he continued to throw more bags into his suitcase. "Don't you ever listen to me ever?"

Charly wasn't about to argue with his nasty behind. Not at a time like this! "But where did you get it from?" she asked him again.

But he didn't answer. Like every human being that had ever been a part of her life, he was treating her as if what she thought, or what she cared to say, or what she needed to know didn't matter.

But that didn't stop her questioning him. "Whose money is it?" she asked him.

He mumbled something, but Charly didn't understand what he said. "What?"

"Mafia," Darryl said. "It's mob money, okay? I stole mob money!"

Charly's heart dropped. "Darryl, you didn't!" she cried. "You stole from the *Mafia*? Darryl!"

As if her reaction to his crime reminded him of the horrible trouble he had gotten himself into, he gave up with the packing and left some plastic bags still in his dresser. He flapped his suitcase close without zipping it up, placed it under his arm, and began hurrying out of their spacious bedroom. "Let's go," he ordered. "Let's get out of here!"

But Charly was still in a state of shock as he bumped by her and hurried onto the landing. Where did he think they were going to go? He stole mob money. *Mob money*! How in the world did he think he could ever get away with something that crazy?

Unless . . .

"Do they know you stole it?" she asked him as she hurried onto the landing behind him. She was hoping against hope that he had some sense left.

But her hope was, again, quickly dashed. "They know," Darryl said. Then he stopped and looked at Charly. "They've got a contract out of me."

Charly's already big eyes stretched larger. "A contract?" she asked. She'd heard of such a thing in the movies. It was when the Mafia paid a hit man to take you out. But this was no movie. This was her life!

But as usual, Darryl didn't seem to care about her part in his drama. He was out for self the way, if Charly were to be honest, he always was. He continued to hurry toward the stairs.

Charly felt as if she was floating. How could the day go so horribly wrong? But there was another thought too: why didn't she leave this fool when he first showed her who he was?!

But as soon as she thought it, she realized she no longer had a choice. Because as soon as Darryl began running down the stairs, and as she was hurrying to the top stair after him, their front door was kicked open and a white man with what looked like a pump-action shotgun, entered their home. His gun was raised and aimed at Darryl even as he bust in.

Charly screamed. Darryl stopped in his tracks as if he wanted to turn around and run back upstairs. Because as soon as that gunman entered their home, he didn't hesitate. He pumped that shot gun and shot Darryl right through the chest with a blast so loud Charly felt as if she'd been shot too!

The blast was so powerful that Darryl didn't just fall, but he fell over the railing and all the way down to the first floor, his unzipped suitcase flying open as it fell, too. All of that money that meant the world to him, that he was willing to risk his safety over and hers too while he was at it, spilled out like confetti in a parade. And Darryl died, Charly realized, with his eyes wide open. The way hers never was.

But she could only glance at her unfortunate husband. Her focus, instead, had to be on that gunman. She was certain he wasn't ready to call it a day. He killed his target. That should have been the end of it.

But she'd made the mistake of making eye-to-eye contact with that killer. He saw her clearly, and she saw him clearly. And he pumped that shotgun once again, and fired.

But Charly was already running for the bedroom. His shot tore a hole into the side of her wall, but he missed her.

But that didn't mean he gave up on her. Not a chance, and she knew it. She could hear him running up those stairs too.

Shaking nearly uncontrollably, she closed and locked their bedroom door and started nervously turning around in the room. What could she use to defend herself? They didn't have a gun in the room. They didn't believe in guns! There wasn't even a knife or a baseball bat in the room. Even her cell phone was still downstairs. There was nothing!

She had no choice, she realized, but to make a run for it.

She ran to the bedroom window and snatched those designer blinds so violently that they broke away from the window frame and fell to the floor with a hard crash. But Charly didn't care. She was fighting for her life and she wasn't about to give up.

But the gunman was at the door, and he was bumping against it to force it open.

She nervously started unlatching both of the window locks. But just as she did, the bedroom door gave way and the gunman barged in. He saw her when she lifted the window.

As soon as he broke in, he pumped that shotgun, aimed it, and fired again.

But Charly was one step ahead of him once again. Because she already knew what she had to do. That was why, as he was firing that shotgun, she was diving out of that second-story window as if she had wings. She thought she heard that bullet whizz right by her ear as she dived.

She landed on their well-manicured lawn awkwardly, and painfully, but she didn't delay. Because she knew he wasn't going to delay either. She could just imagine him running to that window and firing on her again. And if she laid there, she'd be a certain target.

She got up, threw off her high heels, and in her tight skirt started running and screaming from the top of her lungs. "Help me somebody!" she was crying. "Help me!"

She had neighbors, but the properties were vast and she had to run across nearly five acres of her own lot to get to her next door neighbor's expansive property.

The gunman ran to the window as she was running and screaming across her lawn. He smiled because he knew he had her. Even though she was running, she was still an easy target.

He pumped his shotgun again, aimed it directly at her, but something caught his eye. And he didn't fire. Because as soon as he was about to unload what was his next-to-last bullet, a car suddenly turned the corner and was driving down the street. Charly turned when she heard the sound of a car, and began desperately waving her arms. "Help me!" she was crying. "Please help me!"

The white woman on the passenger seat of the car recognized her. They were neighbors. She told her husband to slow down and she pressed down her window. "Charly, is that you?" she asked. Not because she didn't recognize Charly, but because of the usually calm, cool and collective Charlene Johnson just didn't behave so hysterically.

"Help me!" Charly was crying. "He killed Darryl. Darryl's dead. Help me! Please help me!"

"Get in!" her neighbor's husband said anxiously as both neighbors, now scared themselves, looked toward Charly's house. The gunman, seeing them, backed away from the open window and hid. The wife of his target already saw him. He wasn't about to have anybody else make a positive ID too.

Charly opened the car's backdoor and threw herself onto the backseat. Her neighbor's husband took off, not to their home, but kept driving to get her to the police station. His wife was frantically calling 911 as he drove.

Charly looked back, at her house, as they drove away.

She didn't see it, but the gunman was already running back downstairs to get into his own automobile and to get out of that neighborhood, and that town, altogether.

Charly turned back around, her heart hammering. She couldn't believe what had just happened to her.

Darryl was gone.

Her husband was dead!

And she saw his killer.

Life as she knew it, there was no doubt in her mind, would never be the same again.

BOONE'S PROLOGUE

"You took your pretty time."

Robert "Boone" Ryan ignored his girlfriend as he buckled their baby girl into her car seat. Courtney, their daughter, was flapping her legs and smiling her fat pink cheeks up at her daddy as he positioned her on the backseat of his SUV.

But Monica, his girlfriend, was getting on his absolute last nerve.

"What took you so long?" she asked as she stood in her driveway with her arms folded, as if she was his drill sergeant. "I called your cell phone five times and you didn't answer. Where were you, Boone?"

But Boone continued to ignore her. If he hadn't, he knew he'd get into another big fight with her melodramatic butt. "Had a good day, sweetie pie?" he, instead, asked his two-year-old as she grinned up at him. "I was thinking about you all day long."

"I thinking you, too, daddy," his daughter said in her broken, still-developing speech. He laughed, kissed her on her little button nose, and then closed the door. He began heading around to the driver side of his vehicle.

But the fact that he was there, and they were about to leave, wasn't enough for Monica. Oh no! She was still too upset to let it go. "You heard me, Boone Ryan," she said. "Why are you acting like you don't hear me?"

Boone got behind the wheel of his SUV. He wasn't trying to get into it with that woman tonight. But Monica flung open the passenger-side door demanding an answer. *Every man in this town wants me*, her beautiful eyes seemed to be saying to him. *How dare you treat me this way*! "Where were you, Boone?" she asked him again.

Every muscle in Boone's muscular body tightened. He knew he was only putting up with her crazy butt because of his daughter. But sometimes he wondered if even that was enough. "Get in the car," he said to her.

"Why can't you answer my question?" she said to him. "I could have had any man in Hemingway and I chose you. And you treat me like *this*?"

She was a rich, spoiled brat that Boone knew he should have never bedded. But he did. It was done now. "Get in, Monica," he said with little patience. "The reservation is for eight. We only have fifteen minutes to get there."

"If you would have been here on time that wouldn't be an issue. Now would it?"

He looked at her with anger he could no longer suppress. "Get in," he said to her with clenched teeth.

"But you weren't on time, were you?" she said, ignoring him. "And we both know where you were, don't we? We both know where you were!"

Boone rolled his eyes. That woman! "Monica, I'm not in the mood, okay? Get your ass in or close my door and keep your ass out. The choice is yours."

"You were with one of your bitches," she said as if it were a fact. " But which one was it this time, Boone? Which one this time?"

Boone shook his head. That woman was going to be the death of him yet, he could feel it in his bones. Why he was even bothering with her ridiculous behind was the question. He pressed the

Start button to crank up his SUV, and he put on his seatbelt.

But Monica would not let it go. "Which one was it, Boone?" she asked again.

"I have no idea," he finally said. "There are so many I can't keep count." He knew that was what she wanted to hear. "Now you either get in or stay out because I'm leaving."

He could see she was beyond angry, and hurt too, as her big blue eyes became filled with water. "You are such an asshole!" she screamed, wiping away tears. "I hate you!"

"Get in or stay out."

Monica became even angrier because of his dismissiveness. "I'll stay out, thank you. Me and Courtney will stay away from you forever, how about that?" And then she slammed the front passenger door. She hurried to open the back passenger door to get their child.

But Boone was fed up. She was always taking their daughter away from him as a way to punish him, when their daughter had nothing to do with it. But that was Monica's M.O. Every time they got in an argument, it was the same thing. He had to kiss her ass just to see his daughter, or take her to court for a drawn-out custody battle.

But not this time.

Because as soon as Monica slammed his door, and was about to open the back passenger door, he flung his gear in Reverse, laid on the gas, and sped backwards down her driveway. Courtney was as much his as she was hers, and he was tired of that woman treating him as if her rights were superior to his. They were supposed to try and be civil and go out to dinner for a change, to talk through their problems, but instead she was going on and on about him being a little late. He was the chief of police for crying out loud. Sometimes stuff happened and he ran late. She knew that. He was tired of her nonsense!

But Drama Queen Monica was tired of his nonsense too. He could hear her screaming from the top of her lungs as he sped out of her driveway. And even when he shifted gear into Drive and sped down the street, through his rearview mirror he could see her running out into the street still screaming at him. And she had her cell phone out. She was probably calling 911, like she usually did, as if he was kidnapping his own child. As if he, the chief of police, didn't know his own damn laws.

But she wasn't calling 911 that time, he quickly realized. She was calling him. And as soon as he pressed the button on his steering wheel to answer the call, and before he could get a word in edgewise, she was screaming in his phone. "Bring my baby back, you bastard! Bring my baby back or I'm calling the FBI!"

Now Boone was as angry as she was. "Call'em then, bitch!" he yelled. "Call'em! Who do you think you are? Call'em!"

He was yelling so hard, and was filled with such rage, that he forgot about the stop sign. As he blew right through it, another SUV was blowing through the intersection too. Only that SUV had the right-of-way. Only that SUV slammed into the side of his SUV with such violence and force that before Boone knew what hit him, his SUV was flipping sideways over and over and hitting down so hard each and every time that he was knocked out long before the SUV slammed down for the final time.

Monica, who saw the crash, had dropped her cell phone and ran all the way to the end of her street. When she saw just how far that SUV had flipped, and just how mangled it was, her heart dropped through her shoe and she ran as fast as she could to the wreckage.

"My baby," she kept crying as she ran. "My baby! My baby's in there!"

The people jumping out of their cars to assist saw that the lady in the SUV that had hit Boone's vehicle was wearing a seatbelt. She appeared dazed, but was alright. They, instead, ran with Monica to Boone's SUV. But everything was so mangled, nobody could even begin to pry open any door or break any window. It was that bad.

It would take the arrival of cops and paramedics, and the Jaws of Life working feverishly to pry open the smallest part of Boone's SUV. But even before anybody told her so, Monica knew the news couldn't be good. Not in that mangled wreckage!

The rescue workers knew it too. Both father and daughter were in horrible shape, and the daughter more so than the father. And it was their chief of police too? They worked like mad to get them out of that wreckage.

By the time father and daughter were pulled out and rushed to the hospital, and even though the paramedics were speeding well over a hundred miles-per-hour to get them there, only one of the two would make it out of that hospital alive.

Only one would be beaten down by Monica and called a murderer despite his own wounds.

Only one would never be the same again.

CHAPTER ONE

Three Years Later

No hitting. I'll send you right back in if you don't play fair.

Jason, tie your shoes before you trip and fall.

Stop bothering that girl, Mikey. Can't you see she doesn't want to be bothered?

Charly Johnson, in the courtyard of Sacred Hearts Daycare Center making sure the four-year-olds got their recess time in, grabbed yet another kid who was running wildly and redirected him too. Three years ago she was the dean of girls at one of the largest public schools in L.A. The trajectory of her career had no downside. But now she was working at a daycare, making twelve bucks an hour and almost never making ends meet. She had fallen far.

After surviving the horrific shooting that claimed the life of her husband, she was arrested as an accomplice in his crimes. After they realized she had nothing to do with it, and the suddenly missing money was not something she had the opportunity to take, the charges were eventually dropped and she was allowed to identify his killer from a police mugshot book. The man, a contract killer for the mob named Meeker Tabloski, was tried, convicted, and sentenced to Life in prison. He was killed in prison within days of his arrival. That part of her nightmare, she thought, was over.

But because Darryl had stolen money that remained unaccounted for, although she insisted that the cops or the killer took it when they arrived at her home, the Feds seized that home, their bank accounts, their cars, Darryl's boat, everything. They left Charly with nothing but the clothes on her back. She kept her job, initially, until the parents complained vociferously about having what they declared was a mob-connected thief on staff. She wasn't convicted of anything, had never had ties to any mobster in her life, but they still declared her guilty. She was let go by the school district.

She fought it at first, insisting that she had done nothing wrong and was being wrongfully terminated. But she wasn't tenured. She could be dismissed summarily, and was. And although her only crime was that she married Darryl Johnson and Darryl had stolen money from the mob, no lawyer would take her case. And nobody else wanted to hear it either. By association alone, her employer and almost every single one of her friends, wanted no parts of her.

And when all was said and done, and Charly was broke and so broken she could barely see straight, the Feds had the nerve to consider filing charges on her again.

"For doing what?" she asked them repeatedly. They never answered, just kept threatening her with charges as if they just knew she was lying about that money.

She and Darryl had intermingled their lives so decidedly, the way most married couples did, that they figured his loss was her loss, and his gain had to be her gain. But there was no gain. It was just a loss all around. Because Darryl, her husband, was gone too. It was a lot.

"How's it going?"

Charly looked over her shoulder and saw that Rhee Daniels, her friend and the owner of the daycare, had walked up behind her. She glanced at Rhee, and then looked back at the hyperactive kids. "It's going," she said.

Rhee looked at the kids and shook her head. "The wild bunch. It's as if every parent with a bad child wants them to come to my daycare."

But Charly wouldn't go along with that. "They aren't bad," she said to her boss. "They're just full of life. They're rambunctious. That's a good thing."

Rhee laughed. "Yeah, okay. If you say so," she said.

Charly rubbed her forehead. Rhee Daniels, an old friend from college and the only person willing to give Charly a job when she needed one the most, was a lot of positive things. She was loyal. She was fun to be around. But treating the kids in her daycare with the kind of respect they should be accorded was not one of her positive attributes.

And as if to prove Charly's point, Rhee screamed loudly at one of the kids. "Mikey, leave Amber alone with your stupid butt! Boy, you hear me? Leave that girl alone!" Then she yelled at him in even more frustration, even though he was no longer pulling on Amber's hair: "You so stupid!" she yelled.

"Come on, Rhee," Charly said, feeling for the kid.

"What?" Rhee asked. "I didn't call him bad."

"You shouldn't call him stupid either." Charly knew the job Rhee had given to her was her only lifeline, and losing it could render her homeless again, but that didn't mean she wasn't going to tell her friend how she truly felt.

Even if her friend wasn't trying to hear it. "Child please," Rhee said to Charly. "Some kids are bad, and some kids are stupid. I happen to have both kinds in my daycare. You can bury your head in the sand all you want and pretend we got the future Barack and Michelle Obama up in this bitch. I can't do that. The truth is still the truth."

"It's not true," Charly objected, "but if you keep calling them such negative names long enough it can become true. And the last thing these kids need is for the Pygmalion Effect to infect them."

Rhee looked at Charly. "The Pig-*what*?"

Charly looked at her friend. Sometimes she forgot that Rhee partied far more than she studied in college. "We don't want to put all of those negative labels on our kids that later becomes a self-fulfilling prophesy for them," Charly said. "That's what."

"Then they need to stop acting like zip-dang fools," said Rhee. "They stop acting like they don't have any home training, then I'll stop treating them like they don't have any home training. I don't play with these kids." Then she handed Charly an envelope. "This came for you," she said.

Charly looked at the envelope, then took it from Rhee's hand.

Because Charly was often forced to move whenever the area she was living in became too violent even by her now low standards, and she therefore wasn't living in what she'd call a permanent residence by any stretch of the imagination, Rhee allowed her to use her home address on all of her business correspondences. Since Rhee knew she couldn't pay Charly very much money, which meant Charly had to live in those low-income, tough areas to survive, she had no problem letting her old friend use her address.

The fact that Charly was arrested, too, when Darryl first died, kept her standards low as well. Because the arrest itself was still on her record. It required an explanation whenever a background check was pulled on her. And despite her explanation, it always got her a rejection. Why should they hire somebody who had to explain their involvement in a theft and murder when they could hire somebody who didn't have that baggage?

Charly looked at the state the letter was coming from, and tried to remember just what job she applied for in Kentucky. But she couldn't remember. She'd been applying, for almost three years running, for far too many jobs to remember exactly.

Besides, she knew what a letter meant. If a potential employer sent a letter rather than called her on the phone, she knew it meant a flat turn down or a *we selected a more suitable candidate* even when they didn't so much as give Charly an interview. She was never excited when a letter arrived.

But like always, she opened it anyway.

"I know you applied everywhere," Rhee said as Charly opened the letter. "But Kentucky? Come on, girl," Rhee said with a grin. "You and Bluegrass music? You and Appalachia? No way. I can't see a prim and proper sister like you anywhere near a good ol' boys state like that."

Charly would have smiled at Rhee's little observation, but she was too busy staring at the letter. Because it wasn't a rejection. And it wasn't an interview request, either. She looked at Rhee.

"What?" Rhee asked, worried. "What is it? Another rejection?"

Charly shook her head. "No. They want to hire me."

Rhee was shocked. "Really? To do what? What's the job? A full-time teacher?"

Charly, still in shock, shook her head again. "No."

"Then what?"

"A full-time dean of students," she said.

Rhee, stunned, took the letter from Charly's hand. "You lying," she insisted as she grabbed the letter. Then she read the letter for herself. "The board of directors of Saint Christopher Academy in Hemingway, Kentucky wishes to extend an invitation for you to join our faculty as our new dean of students."

Rhee smiled, happy for her friend, but kept reading. "If you accept our offer, please phone us at your earliest convenience. The contract is standard for all of our senior staff, including a five-hundred-dollar signing bonus and a paid apartment for the first year of your tenure." Rhee began happily hitting Charly across her shoulder as she read about the bonus and apartment part. "We look forward to hearing from you. And again, congratulations on your selection!"

Rhee looked at Charly, unable to stop smiling. She knew the struggles her friend had gone through after Darryl died. She knew all about her loneliness and that damn arrest. She was thrilled for her friend. "They want you, Charly," Rhee said. "They want you!"

Charly was smiling too. "They want me," she said, agreeing with her friend.

"Are you shocked?"

"Yes!"

"Are you happy?"

"Very!"

"But it's Kentucky, Char."

"I know."

"Aren't you scared?"

"Scared? No. Petrified? Yes!"

"Then why are you smiling?"

"Because they want me!" Charly said again, smiling even greater. "They want me! Thank you Jesus, they want me!"

And then both friends laughed and hugged as if they were college kids again. It was the best news Charly had received in three long years, and she couldn't stop celebrating.

Until Mikey pulled Amber's hair once again, causing Amber to cry once again. They both stopped hugging and laughing and began yelling for that rambunctious, full-of-life, bad and stupid boy to quit.

CHAPTER TWO

The redhaired woman was still asleep when Boone Ryan eased out of her bed. He removed his condom and dressed quietly and expertly, because he was well-accustomed to those early-morning getaways. He looked at her as he buckled his belt. She slept so peacefully, he thought, as if she'd just had the time of her life and was completely content. But what was her name? Maureen? Was that it? Or was it Loreen? Or Doreen? Or was it *Kate*? He couldn't remember for the life of him. They met at a bar. They both had too much to drink when they got back to her place. Her name never came back up.

Not that it mattered. Because it didn't. He got what he came to get. She got what he came to give her. They weren't kids mixing emotions into it. They were two older, lonely grownups hoping to not be lonely at least for one night. They had no illusions about it.

And now he was tipping out, not like a gentleman because he wasn't one. But exactly like the bastard everybody knew he was.

He made it downstairs, out of her front door, and into his white, shiny Ram pickup truck in no time flat. As he cranked up to leave, he caught a glimpse of himself through his rearview mirror. His thick brown hair was piled high in terrible need of a comb. His big, brownish-green hazel eyes were bloodshot, with spider lines of age beginning to form along the sides. And on top of all of that, he needed a shave. He looked so bad he looked away. He was too old for this crap. It wasn't even fun anymore. But he kept doing it anyway.

He threw his gearshift in Reverse, sped backwards, and then turned and sped away. He was out of her neighborhood and into downtown Hemingway in no time flat too. And as quickly as he had left her home, she had left his mind.

His plan was to head to his house first, to shower and shave, and then head into work. But his phone rang. And it was the station.

"Sorry to disturb you, Chief."

"Not sorry enough apparently," Boone responded to his officer.

"Sorry, sir, but we just got a disturbing call I knew you'd want to know about. Seems Dalbert's got another one of his goons around the high school again."

Boone frowned. "Slinging?"

"That's what the principal believes, yes, sir."

"Dammit! We toss him in jail, that bleeding-hearted judge gives him a slap on the wrist, and now he's at it again. Who does he have over there this time?"

"Billy Ray Rogers, based on the description we're getting. Want me to send a squad car over, or you want us to haul Dalbert in instead?"

"Both," said Boone. "Send a squad car to get Dalbert. I'll handle Billy Ray." And with that order, Boone made a swift U-turn in his big pickup, and sped to Hemingway High.

When he arrived on Firestone Road, drug dealer Billy Ray Rogers was just coming out of the high school gate. He and Boone locked eyes. And Billy Ray, like any guilty man knowing the legend of Crazy Boone Ryan, took off running, his long, blonde hair flying as he ran.

Boone slammed on brakes, backed up as fast as he could, and then turned his wheel and drove his big truck across the sidewalk, between two buildings where Billy Ray had run, and out into the open field. The students that were late for school and were walking across that field were startled, but not surprised. They knew about Boone's legend too.

Billy was fast, but he wasn't fast enough to outrun a truck, and Boone caught up to him easily. His bumper was on Billy's tail as Billy kept trying to outrun the truck. Billy even stopped running in a straight line, and ran side to side in a deliberate zigzag. Anything to get away from Crazy Boone.

But he was only making matters worse for himself. Because Boone was angry now. And all of that zigzagging Billy Ray was doing was getting on his nerves.

So he put a stop to it.

Literally.

As soon as Billy Ray zagged back into the path of his truck, Boone rammed into the back of Billy Ray's legs with just enough of a tap that Billy Ray flipped into the air like a GI Joe doll and landed, with a heavy thump, onto the hood of Boone's truck. Boone then slammed on brakes so hard that Billy Ray slid off of the truck and onto the ground with another heavy thump. He screamed out in agony.

But Boone was in agony too. He was agonizing over those fools who thought they could poison the kids of his town and get away with it.

That was never going to happen on his watch.

"Still wanna run?" Boone was angrily asking Billy Ray as he jumped out of his truck and hurried to the drug dealer. "Still wanna zigzag your ass away from me?" He grabbed Billy Ray up from the ground by the catch of his long, dirty-blonde hair. "What you got to say, Billy Ray? I can't hear you? Why aren't you running now, Billy Ray? Why aren't your ass running now?" Then Boone slammed Billy Ray's hurting body against the side of his truck.

And it was only then did the suspect find the strength to speak up. "You tried to kill me," he said.

"You'll live," said Boone as he began searching Billy's pockets.

Billy, realizing some of those late-arriving students were recording the incident on their cell phones, started milking his pain for all it was worth. "Help!" he started screaming. "Somebody go get help! He's trying to kill me!"

It was only then did Boone realize, too, that they were being filmed. But it didn't matter to Boone. He kept searching the suspect's pockets.

But when those students were smiling as if it was some kind of a joke, Billy Ray became irate. "Go get some help, you idiotic kids!" he yelled.

"This ain't no freakin' joke. Put those phones down and go get help!"

But nobody was about to tell on Boone Ryan.

Billy Ray, knowing it too, forgot about them. He, instead, looked at his captor. "You tried to kill me, bro," he said again. "You don't go around hitting people with trucks. I could have died!"

"And it would have been exactly what your ass deserved for selling that poison to kids."

"What selling? What poison? I wasn't selling anything! I was just taking my baby sister her lunch money."

But Boone was already pulling dime bags of opioids out of Billy Ray's pockets. "And what's this supposed to be?" he asked him as he tossed the bags onto the truck's hood. "More lunch money for baby sis? Or is it for somebody else's baby sister? Or their baby brother?" He shoved a bag into Billy Ray's face. "Is this the lunch money you're talking about, you worthless pile of trash?!"

He then grabbed Billy Ray by his collar and dragged him to the cab of the truck. "What are you doing to me?" Billy Ray cried out. "I need a doctor!"

"I got your doctor," Boone said as he lifted the drug dealer, using the strength of his muscular arms, and tossed him into the cab. The students went wild with laughter when Billy Ray cried out again.

But Billy wasn't playing. He was in terrible pain. He contorted his body and kept screaming out in pain. "This police brutality!" he was crying. "What you doing to me is police brutality, bro!"

"This is not police brutality," Boone responded. Then he reached into his truck's cab and punched Billy Ray in the face as hard as he could. "But that is," he said.

Billy Ray started crying like a baby. "This so wrong, bro. How could you do this to a citizen? This so wrong, bro!"

"And what you're doing to destroy those kids' lives isn't wrong?" Boone asked. "Selling that poison to kids is okay? Give me a break!"

Then Boone got into his truck, spun around, kicking up dirt as he did, as a few of those students kept filming his departure for their Facebook pages. But it wasn't as if Boone Ryan cared. He didn't, not one bit. He headed for the police station.

As he drove, he shook his fist to shake off the pain. It was swollen from the punch he gave to Billy Ray. But he'd do it again in a heartbeat, and all day long if he had to. Those damn drugs killed his kid brother. He wasn't letting them kill his town too.

CHAPTER THREE

"Our hands are tied," the chairman of the board of directors said to the seven-member group as they all sat around the conference table. The chairman, Fritz Hollingsworth, didn't like the idea either. Neither did the vice-chairman, Les Pataki. But there was nothing they could do about it.

"But who is this person?" board member Margaret Ackroyd asked. She was the heir to the Ackroyd Mining Company and was one of the wealthiest landowners in the county. And she was in the *don't like* category too.

But what she also didn't like was the way the leadership was caving. "And what do you mean our hands are tied? This is our school, not Freddy's. My father and yours, too, Fritz, started Saint Christopher's as a great, private school for the elite in this county to attend. It was bad enough when we were shamed into allowing some of that trailer park trash over around Appalachia to enroll. Now we have to hire somebody not even from this area?"

"This area?" asked Les. "She's not even from this region. From what I recall, she's from California!"

There was a collective sigh of outrage at the very thought!

"She probably doesn't even know how to get to Kentucky," Les added.

"But why was she selected?" asked Margaret. "She doesn't have a graduate degree, which I thought was always preferable."

"Preferred," said Fritz, "but not required."

"And her bachelor's degree," continued Margaret, looking at the resume she had in front of her, "is from some school I've never heard of before in my life!"

"It's a tiny, historically black college," said Les. "Before I was given her resume and looked it up on Google, I'd never heard of it either."

"And the bachelor's degree she received from that school," said Margaret, "is in something called Physical Education. What in the dickens is physical education?"

"It's PE, Margaret," said Mark Kerchup, another board member. "We've been out of school too long. She trained to be a gym teacher."

"A *gym* teacher," Margaret said, shaking her head. "Why I've never! A gym teacher is about to become our dean of students. A gym teacher. Honestly, Fritz! This is absurd!"

"She did work as a dean of girls before," Mark said. "So, it's not entirely out of left field, keeping to the PE analogy."

"Regardless," Fritz said again, "our hands are tied. Freddy has demanded that this city and all of its' institutions change their images. He wants diversity and he wants it now."

"And it's purely political," Les said.

"Of course it's political!" said Margaret. "He looks in the mirror every morning and thinks he sees a president of the United States someday, and our lack of diversity will hurt his chances. Forget what all of this diversity will do to our heirs and to this great town. But does Freddy care? Of course not! The blacks put him over the top when he ran for mayor, and he feels he has to give them something. At our expense," she added.

"I agree with everything you just said, Maggie," Fritz said. "But I say again, and I will continue to say until the cows come home: our hands are tied. Freddy will pull our school's charter, and he has the power to do so, too, if we don't comply."

"But why *her*?" Margaret asked again. "She's only thirty-five years old, her experience is minimal at best, and she doesn't even possess an Ivy League degree when our goal is to get each and every one of the graduating seniors at Saint Christopher's into Ivy League schools. There has to be far more qualified candidates than her!"

"She was the only person of color to apply for the position. Freddy wanted this done a long time ago. A person of color has got to be in a senior position on our faculty. He said our time was up and he wanted this done and done now. Our hands are tied."

Margaret sat back, and everybody exhaled. Then Les thought of something. "Has the school staff been notified?" he asked Fritz. "There are members of the senior staff that had been waiting in line for their chance at that promotion. They've been here for decades. Have they been told of this appointment?"

Fritz shook his head. For the first time, they all could see his frustration too. "No," he said. "And I know already so don't remind me. They're going to be pissed."

"And rightly so," said Margaret, as she slammed that resume onto the table.

CHAPTER FOUR

The old but reliable Nissan Sentra she purchased a few months back pulled into the gas station and stopped at the pump. Charly sat behind the steering wheel and fumbled through her purse in search of some gas money. She'd driven all the way from L.A., filling up repeatedly, and was now on the outskirts of Hemingway, Kentucky. But she wasn't sure if the quarter of a tank of gas she had left would be enough to take her all the way there.

But she found no ready cash. A few ones here and there, but no twenty dollar bill as she thought she'd still had.

If it had not been for the job also providing her with an apartment, and a small signing bonus, she'd be in trouble.

She'd been applying for teaching or administrative positions across the country, whenever a position arose. When she was offered the position of dean of students at a small, private, Christian school in Kentucky, she accepted without hesitation. She was grateful to be working at

Rhee's daycare center, but she was barely making ends meet. She jumped at the chance.

She left California with everything she owned stuffed into the trunk of her car. She left in the middle of the night.

Now it was day, she was in Kentucky, and her new life was about to begin.

But again, like almost every day since Darryl's death, she was broke.

She grabbed her credit card. It still had four or five hundred bucks in the available balance column. But she also knew credit cards had to be paid back. And she was behind in payments already. At least her contract called for the school to give her a signing bonus on her arrival, which she hoped would tie her over until her first paycheck, where she could catch up on her bills and finally get back on track. But she never liked uncertainties. What if they didn't come through with the signing bonus? What if she had to make her own living arrangements? She threw the card back into her purse.

She, instead, scoured the glove compartment and between the seats of her car until she managed to gather up eight bucks. Hoping it would pay for enough gas to get her to that school, she grabbed it and got out.

Men were looking at her hard, and with angry faces despite her smile, as if they'd never seen a tall black woman before. But she didn't let it get to her. She'd been through hell and back again. A few angry faces meant nothing to her. She, instead, ignored them royally and made her way inside the gas station.

But for the Kentuckians she encountered, she was a sight to behold. Not because she was tall and African-American, as she had assumed, but because she walked with such confidence and grace that it made them wonder if she was somebody special. Like a movie star. Or a rich person. And they all gave her an extra look.

But it wasn't as if Charly looked back.

She didn't.

The last thing on her mind was getting a man's attention. It wasn't even on her radar screen. She was hoping and praying that this new gig would be the last job she would ever have to apply for. She was hoping and praying that she would finally find some peace and contentment and, most of all, *stability*, in this most unlikely place.

That was what she was thinking about as she walked into that gas station, plopped down her eight bucks, and paid for her gas.

Her three whole gallons of gas.

CHAPTER FIVE

The Hemingway Police Station was filled with laughter. A group of veteran cops were standing around Sarge's desk watching a video that a student posted on his Facebook page the day before. They were laughing because, on the video, their chief had been recorded hitting Billy Ray Rogers with his truck and then tossing him into the back of his truck's cab. When he punched Billy Ray, the cops nearly fell out laughing.

"We're working for a mad man!" said one of the cops.

"Talking about arresting that drug dealer," said another one. "We need to arrest that chief!"

"You arrest him," said Sarge. "I'll pay your mortgage if you do it." And they all laughed at that too.

"Nothing's gonna happen to him," said yet another cop. "Not as long as his cousin Freddy is mayor."

They knew how it worked in Hemingway. The chief would get reported for excessive force. The complaint would go all the way to City Hall and end up on the desk of the chief's boss and cousin, Mayor Freddy Ryan. But Freddy didn't mix it up with Boone either. He'd scoff at the chief's unethical and illegal actions, and order him to stop it and stop it now, but take no further action himself. The Hemingway PD was now a three-ring circus, and Boone, not Freddy, was its ringmaster.

And the laughter continued as they kept re-looping the video. Until Dontay Culpepper, the African-American rookie whose desk was near the front window, saw a familiar sportscar speed into the parking spot beneath the flag pole. You'd think a kid was driving the way he sped in so recklessly. Dontay was a rookie, but he knew that car already.

The chief, it was said, had many automobiles, but he primarily drove two: his big, white Ram truck, and his red Ferrari. It was the Ferrari today.

"Chief just drove up," Dontay announced to his fellow cops, and everybody stopped with the laughing and scrambled back to their desks to at least look as if they were busy at work.

Morley Davenport, who sat at the desk directly in front of Dontay's, didn't attempt to look busy at all. He looked out of the window, too, as Boone Ryan, already out of his Ferrari, was reaching back into the car to grab his suit coat. His very expensive suit coat.

Morley shook his head. "I'll bet that suit alone cost more than every one of us makes, combined, in a month."

"Jealous much?" another cop, further over, asked Morley.

"Is your mama jealous?" Morley said back to him, and the other cops laughed.

But Dontay was shaking his head, too, as Boone stood at his car, leaned his head back, and with a small bottle of Visine put eyedrops into his tired, bloodshot eyes. "He parties more than I do," the twenty-two year old rookie said, "and I'm half his age!"

"I still can't get over that suit," Morley responded.

"It's just clothes," said Dontay. "It's not that serious, though."

"And why is he even here?" Morley asked. "I still can't figure that out either. That guy's damn-near the richest man in town, and comes from the richest family in the whole county, yet he still comes to work every single day. To a job like this. That sounds like an ailment to me."

Dontay looked at the older cop. "It is an ailment," he said. "It's called having a work ethic. But you wouldn't know anything about that ailment, now would you, Mor?"

The other cops laughed. "You let that rookie get over on you like that?" one of them asked Morley.

But before Morley could respond, the door flew open, their chief walked in, and the entire squad room plunged into the sounds of computers typing and papers shuffling and quiet, efficient, busy work.

"Hello, Chief," said Morley as Boone walked past his desk first.

"I'm still waiting to get Dalbert in one of those cells," Boone shot back. "Where is he?"

That was what Morley got for speaking, the other cops appeared to be thinking. But Morley only nodded. "We're still looking for him, Chief. It's only the second day. We'll find him."

"You'd better," Boone said.

"Good morning, Chief," said Dontay as Boone continued walking and walked by his desk.

Boone glanced at Dontay. He was the youngest cop on his force, and the only African-American. "What's so good about it?" he asked him.

Dontay had not expected that response. He gave him a normal greeting. It wasn't as if he told the chief to go play with himself or something equally rude. All he said was good morning for crying out loud.

But Dontay was always singled out by the chief that way. Most would say it was because of his race, especially since Chief Ryan was never considered to be *a friend of the Negro*, as some black residents loved to joke. But Dontay didn't think like that. The reason didn't matter to him. He was determined to not let that reason define him. "I'm sure there's a lot that's good about it," he shot back, "but I can't think of one single thing right now."

Morley could see a slight lift of the chief's lip as he continued to walk by. Boone liked Dontay, although most of the other cops wouldn't believe it. But Morley had been working for Boone the longest. He knew him.

He also knew that the chief would ignore all the other *good mornings* and *how you doing* greetings, would enter his office without looking back, and would slam the door behind him. And Boone did just as Morley expected him to do.

There was a collective sigh of relief in the whole of the squad room when that door slammed shut.

And then the phone rang. Dontay, as the grunt on the force, was tasked with answering all calls that the switchboard operator sent back to the squad room. "Hemingway PD. Officer Culpepper at your service. How may I help you?"

There was a look of surprise on Dontay's youthful, handsome face. "At Saint Christopher's?" he asked as if there had to be some mistake. "Are you sure?"

Morley looked at him, as did the other cops.

"Behind it? By the cafeteria? Yes, ma'am," Dontay said over the phone as he grabbed a small Post-it note and wrote down some information.

"Okay. Yes, ma'am. I'm going to let him know right now." Then Dontay hung up the phone.

"What is it?" Morley asked as Dontay ripped the yellow Post-it note from the pad, got up, and hurried toward the chief's office.

"Dontay, what is it?" another cop asked too.

But Dontay didn't even hear them. He hurried to the chief's office, knocked only once and then, to the surprise of the veteran cops who wouldn't dare take such a liberty, hurried on in.

They looked at each other. All they knew was that something had happened at Saint Chris Academy. And for normally cool Dontay to act the way he did, they also knew it had to be something bad.

CHAPTER SIX

Charly exhaled when she turned onto the street that housed Saint Christopher Academy. She had so much excitement in her heart she could hardly contain it. This wasn't going to be just any old job to her, like all of those other jobs she'd held since she was fired or, as the district put it at the time, since they decided not to renew her contract. She was getting back on her career path. She was grateful to have been given a second chance.

And oddly enough, the position, as the dean of students at a tiny, backwater but prestigious school, was considered by her to be her best assignment to date. Not because Saint Christopher was larger than her previous school: it wasn't. She was dean of girls previously at a big, sprawling public school. And although Saint Christopher was ranked among the best schools in Kentucky, she was certain it wouldn't hold a candle to any school in L.A.

But she considered it her best assignment because of the timing. She needed this gig like she needed air to breathe. In her previous life, she could pick and choose what jobs she took or didn't take. Those days, she knew with a certainty, were gone. Now this job was the only game in town. It was her new lifeline.

It was a lifeline if she ignored the fact that it was in Kentucky of all places, in a town called Hemingway that wasn't even on most maps, and that it was at a school, according to her internet search, that was literally all-white. But regardless of all of that, she was pumped. Her life, after all of that terribleness, was finally getting back on track.

She felt that way until she pulled into the parking lot of the beautiful school and saw what appeared to be a dozen police cars, with their sirens still twirling, in the back part of the school. It looked like more police cars than she thought would be in the whole of a town that small. Even the parking space reserved for the dean of students, her new position, had a red sportscar backed up into it. Something was happening. And it was something, if the show of force was any indication, horrific. Charly's excitement took a significant dip.

She was praying for peace and calm and this was what greeted her? What looked like an active *crime scene*?

Her heart now pounding, she grabbed her purse and briefcase and got out of her Nissan. Although the action appeared to be in the back of the school, Charly was, by nature, a cautious person. She didn't run to trouble, although it always seemed to find her out. She, instead, headed inside the brick building, across the marbled hall, and into the main office.

The entire front office staff appeared to be on the phones reassuring nervous parents when Charly walked in. As soon as the secretary, or the clerk, or the administrative assistant hung up the phone they were on, another call came in, forcing them to pick right back up. It was maddening.

But Charly waited patiently. She saw those police cars. She'd not only be calling, but would be making an appearance at that school if her child was there. But since she had no children, thanks to Darryl's desire not to be a father, that was not an issue.

Finally, after several more hang-ups and pick-ups, the secretary, Minnie Fennel, made her way over to the long counter that kept her and her staff behind the desk, and visitors in front of it. "May I help you?" she asked.

"Yes, thank you. My name is Charlene Johnson," she said with a smile and with her hand extended. "I am the new--"

"Oh," Minnie interrupted her. "It's you."

Charly could feel the animus, but she didn't let the secretary's refusal to shake her hand shake her smile. "Yes, it's me," she said, and placed her hand back by her side.

"The chief told them to wait in the conference room," Minnie said. "Go down this hall and take a left." Her phone began ringing again. "It'll be the first door on your right." She answered her phone. "Saint Chris Academy, may I help you?"

Charly, still unsettled by such an odd instruction, but too curious about what was going on to delay, did as she was told. She made her way along the hall beside the long counter, took a left, and then walked over to the door on the right. It was open, and she could hear voices, so she walked on in.

The conference room was filled with the executive staff of the school, along with a few of the board members who saw the police heading for Saint Chris and headed over there too. They all were Caucasian and much older than Charly. Decades older. And as soon as she walked in, the conversations ceased and she could have heard a pin drop.

"Yes?" board member Margaret Ackroyd asked Charly with a frown on her face. "Who are you to barge in here like this?"

Charly didn't stutter. "I'm Charlene Johnson. The new dean of students."

They all seemed shocked to Charly. Did they not know she was coming? The secretary did. Why wouldn't they?

But they knew. All of them knew. They were just surprised by what they saw. They expected Charlene Johnson to be some big, fat woman in runover shoes for some reason even they could not legitimately verbalize. That was how their less-than-liberated minds had envisioned her.

But Charly, to them, looked like a tall, attractive model. Not a thin one by any stretch, but not a fat one either: at least not to the men around that table. But a very shapely, big-bosomy one. Certainly nothing like the dean of students any of them were used to!

But if Charly were to be honest, their unfriendly faces was a huge letdown.

It was Amos Yerkson, the vice-principal, a man in his late-fifties, who was the first to show any politeness. He smiled, rose from his seat and made his way to Charly, extending his hand as he came. "Welcome to Saint Christopher Academy, Miss Johnson," he said to her. "We are so honored to have you join our faculty."

A friendly face finally, Charly thought. "Thank you," she said with a smile of her own, and shook his hand.

"I'm Amos Yerkson," he said. "And please forgive me. I planned to greet you out front. It's just that this business today has all of us off our game, I'm afraid."

"What business is that?" Charly, never afraid to pry, asked.

"The principal would have liked to be here today, too," Amos said instead of answering her question, "but as it happens he's on vacation. But I'm your direct supervisor, anyway, so it works out in the end."

"Yes, it does," responded Charly. "What business are you referring to? I saw the police cars out back."

They said black women were tough, Amos thought in a way he knew was stereotypical, but she was proving the point. And he was about to answer her. But when he looked and saw that all eyes of those obnoxious, overbearing board members were on the two of them, he placed his hand on Charly's upper arm and escorted her into a file room off from the conference area, closing the door behind them.

Charly was super-curious now. She stared at Amos with big, concerned eyes.

"There's no easy way to say it," Amos said, his own eyes filled with what Charly could only describe as dread. "But a dead body was found in the back of the school this morning."

Even though Charly assumed the worse, as she usually did, she did not assume *that*. "A dead body?" she asked, shocked. "Oh my goodness! Do they know who it is?"

"They may," Amos said, referring to the police, "but they aren't sharing that information with us."

"But what happened? Was she or he shot or --"

"Still no information," Amos responded. "But if you knew Boone Ryan, you wouldn't be surprised."

Charly had no idea who Boone Ryan was, and at that point she didn't care. "Who discovered the body?"

"The head cook," said Amos. "She went to throw a pot of water out of the backdoor, which we told her time and time again to stop doing, but she did it again this morning, and that was when she saw the body. Nearly drenched it, she said. The police are with her now. I just arrived, so that's all I know. I don't know who, what, when, none of those things."

He seemed almost out of control, Charly felt. It was understandable, he was the vice-principal of the school and the death apparently happened on his watch. But he was also a leader at that school. He needed to pull it together.

Not that Charly had it altogether herself. She didn't. She thought she was getting away from drama when she left the west coast. She thought she would find peace and redemption here. But to find more killing? It astounded her.

"But please, don't let it upset you," Amos said as he squeezed her arm, as if he could feel her anxiety. But the way he placed his hand on her made her uncomfortable. He, apparently, sensed that too and removed it. "It's an awful way to begin your tenure here, I know it is, but I assure you this doesn't happen to us every day."

Charly looked at him as if he was crazy.

"Or not even every other day," he quickly corrected himself.

When she continued to stare at him as if he was still mad, he made himself clearer. "This is the first time something like this has ever happened at Saint Chris, is what I'm saying," he said.

Charly was relieved, but still unsettled.

But then the door was opened and a uniformed police officer peered inside. "Sorry to disturb you, Amos," he said, "but the chief wants all of the senior leadership in the cafeteria."

"Finally," Amos said with a touch of obnoxiousness himself, and then he motioned for Charly to go first.

They both headed out of the file room, and made their way to the chief.

CHAPTER SEVEN

They all sat up front, with the members of the board of directors, Fritz Hollingsworth, Les Pataki, and Margaret Ackroyd, seated on the front row. Amos and Charly sat just behind them. The head cook, Zelda, the woman who discovered the body, sat behind them. It was the pecking order in Hemingway. The members of the board hailed from among the wealthiest families in the county, families that ran that whole town. They always took the choice seats.

A small group of plainclothes detectives, along with a larger contingent of uniformed cops, were in the front of the cafeteria leaned against the stage. One man in particular, Charly noticed, seemed to be at the center of it all. He was on his cell phone, in what appeared to be a heated conversation with somebody, although she could not hear what was being said. But his face made it clear it wasn't great.

Amos leaned toward her. "That's Boone Ryan," he whispered in her ear with breath that smelled like eggs. "He's our infamous police chief.

He is the sort of person you shall want to avoid at all costs," he warned.

Although Charly nodded, Amos's warning only increased her curiosity and she found herself staring at the "infamous" chief.

He appeared to be in his forties, if Charly had to guess, and he wore a very stylish suit that looked rather rumpled considering how much he had to have paid for it. Either he was up all night in that suit, she concluded, or he wore rumpled clothing and just didn't care. But by the look of the very well-polished, expensive dress shoes he wore, she knew it wasn't the latter.

The police chief ended his phone call and tossed his phone in his pocket, still upset by what apparently had been discussed. But when he looked up and saw that the school leadership had assembled, he put on a smile and walked over to where they were seated. He stood directly in front of them.

Charly had already decided that he was a ladies man, with probably more women than he could handle or that was decent for any one man to have, and that devastatingly attractive smile proved it for her.

"I know Dr. Dorsett is still on vacation," he said. "Who's in charge on his absence?"

Charly would have thought he would know that, being the chief of police, but he apparently did not.

But then he continued. "And if you say Jesus," he added, "I'll pull out my revolver and shoot you on the spot."

The board members, who'd had it up to here with Boone Ryan and his antics to begin with, recoiled at his politically-incorrect joke, but Charly couldn't help it. She smiled.

Boone noticed her smile at the same time that he noticed the oddity of her presence. He purposely didn't know much about Saint Christopher nowadays, although his parents had forced him to attend it in his youth. But even then he found the place to be a stuffy, closed institution that never had a black face in sight. Or, until recently, a poor white one. She had to be new in town.

Although Amos stood up after he asked who was in charge, Boone kept glancing over at the woman beside him.

"The principal is on vacation," said Amos, "as you rightly stated. Therefore, I am in charge, sir."

"And you are?" asked Boone.

Amos found it insulting that Boone didn't know who he was, but it wasn't surprising. Boone never bothered to get to know the law-abiding residents. From what Amos saw, he seemed to prefer to cast his lot with the law breakers. "I am Amos Yerkson, the vice-principal," Amos said.

"And the lady beside you?" Boone couldn't help but ask.

Amos knew exactly why that rascal asked. "I want to introduce you to our brand new dean of students, Miss Charlene Johnson."

At first Boone was surprised. And then he smiled. "I'll be damn," he said. "Who would have *thunk* it? A woman dean at Saint Chris."

"And a black no less," Charly volunteered before she realized it, a remark that caused the whole of the front row to turn and look at her with disdain. And their old eyes said it all: it was one thing to think such a thing, but utterly rude to proclaim it!

Chief Ryan, however, laughed out loud. His men, including Dontay Culpepper, didn't hold back either.

"Yeah," Boone said to Charly, "that too."

Charly gave another sweet smile and a lift of her eyebrows that made Boone feel as if he had an ally. Why he felt that way made no sense to him. But he felt it.

Now she had his attention. His tired, brownish-green eyes traveled down the length of her body the way they always did when he was sexually curious. She was a tall, voluptuously curvaceous, elegant-looking lady, he thought. And although she possessed a dramatically beautiful face, he was willing to bet she was one of those women who didn't see herself that way.

He drew that conclusion, not because he was clairvoyant, but because of the ill-conceived clothing she wore. It was a nice-fitting, conservative skirt and blouse with a cardigan sweater to round out the package. It didn't hide her boobs, they were too sizeable, but the blouse was buttoned up to the throat and the skirt nearly covered her calves. I mean really, he thought. She was a woman in her mid-thirties, if he had to guess, not some fifty year old. What on earth was she trying to hide?

"Are you new to Hemingway, Miss Johnson?" Boone asked her.

"Just arrived," she said.

"Some welcome."

"Yes," Charly agreed. "And here I was expecting a tickertape parade."

Boone laughed again. "I'll bet these blue-haired old ladies in this joint are gonna love you," he said snidely.

But Charly, for that brief moment in time, *loved* him, because his little reply caused those disdainful eyes on the front row to finally shift away from her, and back to him. Not that she was intimidated by those board members. She wasn't in the least. But it was just that she was tired of being judged and deemed unworthy no matter where she went. Or what she said. She was tired of it. She was hoping this time would be different.

And like his assessment previously, he now had her attention too. He was a tall man. She was five-seven, but she believed him to be at least six-two, with a big, muscular body bordering on becoming slightly overweight; thick brown hair with touches of gray; hard, brownish-green eyes with a hazel look, and an interesting mouth. But his eyes, though attractive, weren't kind, even when he was laughing. There was an overall unapproachableness about him to Charly.

"If you're the VP," Boone said to Amos, "and this lady here is the dean, who are the rest of these people?"

"You know exactly who we are, Boone Ryan," Margaret said. "Don't you dare insult us."

It was true. Boone's family wasn't among the richest in the county, they were *the* richest in the county. He knew all of those board members very well. They were his family's social circle.

"I didn't say I didn't know you, Maggie," Boone responded. "But I have no idea what your role at Saint Christopher's is."

"We're members of the board of directors," Fritz said. "I am the chairman. Les is the Vice Chairman. And Maggie is, well, Maggie. She's a board member. We run this school."

Boone rolled his eyes. The members of his social circle ate up power like ordinary citizens ate their lunch, and it was repulsive to Boone. "You may run this school from the board perspective," he said to Fritz, "but I need the day-to-day runners. I need to meet privately with the vice-principal and Miss Johnson."

Margaret was shocked. "*Her*? What do you need to meet with her for? She just got here, literally, and she wouldn't be here at all had it not been for your cousin's insistence that we diversify our faculty."

Boone knew which cousin she meant. Freddy, the mayor, was the cousin she meant. He was all of their bosses in a manner of speaking.

But for Charly, it was an eye-opener. She was, if Margaret Ackroyd was to be believed, an experiment in diversity. Like a token. Like somebody hoist upon them. Which, translated, meant that they were looking for her to fail.

She already knew, but knew even more starkly right then and there, that failure was not an option.

"Come with me," Boone said to Amos and Charly despite Margaret's protestations. Then he looked at the head cook. "You, too, Zelda," he added, as he looked at the large white woman with big, pink, jowly cheeks.

Amos, Charly, and Zelda followed Boone and Dontay, one of his plainclothes detectives he also ordered to come with him, all the way up front to the main office. The main office was overcrowded with parents when they made it up front, and every parent was gravely concerned. They all were shouting for answers from Amos as he entered the office, and from Chief Ryan, too, but they both ignored them and continued walking. But Boone looked back at Dontay.

"Tell your fellow officers to get up here and control this crowd," he ordered. "And don't let anybody else in the building."

"Yes, sir," said Dontay.

"This entire school is a crime scene until I say it's not. Got it?"

"Got it," Dontay responded, and hurried to do as he was told.

Boone and his guests went into the principal's office. Boone closed the door behind them.

But when Amos, Charly, and Zelda sat in the chairs in front of the desk, and when Boone leaned against the desk with his feet outstretched, it was as if he only had eyes for Amos. He didn't ask Charly, nor even Zelda, a single question.

"How well did you know Rita Mae Brown?" he asked Amos.

"Excuse me?" responded Amos. "I don't know any Rita Brown. What are you talking about?"

"Rita Mae Brown was the young lady found dead behind your school this morning. Now I need to know how well did you know her."

Charly looked at Amos. He knew the victim?

But Amos, again, denied knowing the victim. "I told you I don't know any Rita Brown."

"Rita Mae Brown."

"Her either."

Boone stared at the vice-principal as if he was disappointed. But when he crossed his legs at the ankle, Charly couldn't help it. She looked down mid-way. Not surprisingly given the sensual aura that seemed to encompass him, she could see where he was very well-endowed.

"Let's try again," Boone said to Amos. "How well did you know Rita Mae Brown?"

Amos frowned. "Why are you still harping on that? I told you I don't know the girl."

"A couple of the kitchen workers told me earlier that they saw you arguing with *the girl*, as you call her."

"Arguing with her? When?"

"Yesterday."

"Here?"

"Behind the Walmart. Now does her name ring a bell, suddenly, to you?"

Charly could see a change in Amos's demeanor. He suddenly looked stricken, as if he didn't realize somebody had seen him. "Now that you mention it," he said, "yes, I do recall some knowledge of her. But only fleetingly."

"What were you two arguing about?"

"We weren't arguing," Amos said.

"All I have to do is go to Walmart and get the tape," said Boone. "Do I need to do that, Mr. Yerkson?"

Amos exhaled. "Okay, there might have been a slight argument," he said.

Charly looked at him again. Why was he lying, she wondered?

It certainly crossed Boone's mind, too, as he questioned him. "What was the slight argument about?" he asked Amos.

"I don't even remember," Amos responded.

When Boone uncrossed and then crossed his legs again, he continued to just look at Amos, without saying another word. It was tortuous enough that Amos finally came clean. "She wanted to borrow money," he said.

"Why on earth would she need to borrow money from you?" Charly found herself asking. She couldn't help it. This man was the vice-principal of a Christian school. Why did he originally lie about his knowledge of her?

Boone glanced at Charly when she got in on the questioning. He'd been questioning suspects for damn-near twenty years. He didn't think he needed any help.

"It's what I do," Amos responded to Charly's question. He liked her as soon as he first saw her. "I help people in the community out. Especially my GED students."

"GED?" Boone asked. "They teach GED classes at Saint Chris? That has to be a first!"

"Not here," Amos said. "I teach a GED class at the rec center in Low Town." Low Town, Charly would later learn, was the name for the poorest side of town. A place where poor blacks lived in apartments and row houses, and where poor whites lived in trailers.

"Was Rita Mae one of your pupils?" Boone asked Amos.

Amos nodded. "Yes, I believe so. But I had no idea she was the body behind the school."

"I also heard," Boone said, "that you had an affair with Rita Mae."

Charly didn't even look at Amos that time. She knew that couldn't be right.

But unlike previous comments by the chief, Amos wasn't quick with his denial on that one.

Boone was staring at him. Even Zelda looked at him. "Is it true?" Boone asked him.

Amos seemed defeated to Charly. He just shook his head. "No," he said with little fight in his voice. "It's not true."

"So you're saying my sources are lying?"

"If they claim I had an affair with Rita, yes, they're lying. I barely knew her. I volunteer at the recreation center. I teach GED class. That's how I know her. We had no kind of relationship whatsoever outside of that class."

"But yet you lent her money?" Charly asked. Charly was stuck on that money-lending part. In her world, you just didn't do that willy-nilly.

"I told you I lent many poor people money. Life had been cruel enough to them. I gave them a helping hand."

"And argued with them about it?" Charly asked.

Boone smiled. That was exactly the question he planned to ask. But Amos didn't bother to answer her.

"It's a good question," Boone said. "Why argue about it if giving away cash is what you do?"

"She kept coming back for more," Amos said. "I didn't think that was right. That's what the argument was about."

Charly could relate to that. People knew a good thing when they saw it and some abused it.

But Boone had too much information to fall for that line. "If you had no contact with her beyond lending her money," he said, "then why did she have your cell phone number and your house number in her phone? Why did she call you nearly forty times after that argument, and eight times early this morning?"

That was shocking to Charly, especially when Amos didn't seem to have an answer. He, in fact, looked completely defeated.

Boone stood up, pulled a pair of handcuffs from the small of his back, and moved over to Amos. "Stand up," he said to him.

Amos stood up.

"Amos Yerkson, I am arresting you for the murder of Rita Mae Brown. You have the right to remain silent."

As Boone began reading Amos his Miranda warning, Charly stood up too. She was shaken. The only man that showed her an ounce of kindness in that whole school, her direct supervisor and the man responsible for showing her the ropes, was now being arrested for murder? For *murder*? It was as if this was some kind of a cruel joke. She thought she left that kind of craziness behind with Darryl's lifeless body, only to come all this way to Kentucky of all places to find craziness here too? It was unbelievable to her.

And the way Amos didn't fight the charge, or try to break free from those handcuffs when an innocent man, it seemed to Charly, would be shouting from rooftops. She was stunned.

Amos finally spoke, but it was barely a whisper. "I didn't do it," he said.

But Boone wasn't listening. The evidence was the evidence. He, instead, glanced over at Charly as he continued to recite Amos's rights. He could feel her anxiety and could see the sadness in her eyes. For some strange reason, her sadness bothered him. It pricked at him. "You okay?" he found himself asking her. He wasn't a caring man. Nobody in that town would ever confuse him for sensitive. But he hated, for some reason, to see *her* hurting.

"You okay?" he asked again, when she didn't respond the first time.

But Charly was looking around, as if she didn't know which way was up.

"Hey?" he said.

It was only then did she look at him.

"You okay?" he asked yet again.

"Yes," she finally responded to him, but he could tell her mind was a million miles away.

Charly was in a state of shock and couldn't conceal it. She couldn't stop thinking about her plight, the school's plight, poor Rita Mae Brown's plight, Amos's plight! She came all this way for more pain? For more craziness?

And it was suddenly too much.

Tears welled up in her big, golden-brown eyes, and it was a remarkable sight to Boone. She presented as such a strong woman. But right at that moment, he saw just how vulnerable she really was. And it bothered him!

He wanted to reach out to her, and wanted to ask again if she was okay.

But she didn't give him the chance.

"Excuse me," she said, and walked swiftly out of the office.

CHAPTER EIGHT

She sat behind the desk of the office Minnie the secretary said was designated for her. As a midsized office tucked away and further down the hall from the principal's and the vice-principal's offices, it was okay. The office wasn't the problem. It was the feeling of dashed expectations that Charly couldn't manage. She had hoped her move to Kentucky would signified something special, like a new beginning for her. Like a fresh start. Something different. But she'd only been in town less than an hour, and already it felt too much like more of the same.

Tears reappeared in her eyes as she sat behind that desk. Was it ever going to turn around for her? Or was upheaval and drama and sadness and despair going to forever be her norm? Now a young lady was dead right on the campus of the school that hired Charly. And the young lady was killed no less! It was a lot.

Charly grabbed tissues from the box of Kleenex on her desk and began wiping her eyes. Her new life could not have gotten off to a rockier start.

Her cell phone rang as she was blowing her nose. She pulled it out, looked at the Caller ID, and then hesitated. It was Rhee, her friend and day care owning former boss. Rhee had such high hopes for Charly's new life too. Charly knew she was just about the only person on earth rooting for her, but that didn't give her comfort either. She hated to have to disappoint her too.

But she knew she had to answer. Rhee was good to her and deserved an answer. With her phone still on her desk, she placed the call on Speaker.

Just as she did, Boone appeared at her open office door. He couldn't say what led him, after Amos Yerkson was arrested and hauled away by a couple of his uniformed officers, to walk down that hall to her office. But he felt a strong need to check on her. To make sure she was okay.

But she had just answered a phone call, and she was blowing her nose and wiping tears away.

"Hey, Rhee," she said on the phone. "How you doing?"

"That's my question exactly," the lady he heard her call Rhee said over the phone. "How's your first day in Blue Grass country?"

"It's . . .," Charly said, and Boone stared at her. Poor kid couldn't pull herself to lie, apparently, to whomever that Rhee person was.

"That doesn't sound very promising," Rhee said. "What happened?"

Charly pinched the bridge of her nose. "It's a long story," she said.

"Oh, boy," said Rhee. "Don't tell me those white folks reneged and didn't give you that signing bonus? What about the apartment? They didn't give you that either? Don't tell me you went all that way and you're homeless again."

Homeless, Boone thought, as he stared at Charly. She'd been homeless before? Her life story was apparently far more dire than he had assumed.

"I knew going to Kentucky was a bad idea," Rhee continued.

But Charly stopped her. "That's not it. They haven't reneged. I just got here. But listen, let me call you back. It's a little hectic right now."

"Is that what you call mistreatment? Make sure you call me back, too, girl, I don't care how late it is. I want to know the tea, and I want to know all of it."

"Okay. I'll call you back," Charly said, and then ended the call. A tear escaped her eye after ending the call, and she quickly wiped it away. A good time, Boone felt, to knock.

As soon as Charly glanced over and saw Boone at her door, she quickly turned away from him, wiping her eyes vigorously. The last thing she expected was to see him, or anybody else, way back there.

Boone began walking in. "Hope I'm not disturbing anything," he said as if he hadn't just eavesdropped on her conversation.

"No," she said, although she wasn't looking at him. "You aren't disturbing me."

He walked further in and stood parallel to her desk. He didn't look at her, and because her eyes were undoubtedly red from all of that crying, she was avoiding eye contact with him too.

But when he just stood there, and didn't say a word, she looked at him. "May I help you?" she asked.

He hesitated, and then he spoke. "Not quite what you expected, hun?" he asked, and then looked at her. Her huge, watery eyes hadn't turned red. She was one of those rare people who could cry a river and her eyes still look crystal clear. But they looked to Boone to be so sad.

Charly almost looked away. She didn't want to make eye contact with him! But when he looked his hard, hazel eyes at her in such a sympathetic way, she couldn't turn away. "A dead body?" she asked. "Definitely not what I expected in my first hour on the job."

She tried to smile at her own little attempt at levity, but he wouldn't dignify it. He knew she didn't mean it. "You're tough," he said to her instead. "You'll be okay."

Charly found that an odd thing to say. He knew nothing about her whatsoever. How would he know how tough she was? How could he declare that she was going to be okay? But for some reason she appreciated his confidence, even if she didn't feel it herself. "I guess so," she said.

"I know so," he said as if he knew her like that, and the two of them locked eyes. But it was Boone who felt the most exposed, and looked away. "Anyway," he said, "I'd better get to the station. I've got a suspect to interview. See you around, Dean," he said.

"Sure," said Charly.

Boone stared at her again and he suddenly had an irrational desire to pull her into his arms and assure her everything was going to be alright, when he didn't know that for a fact at all. He didn't know her for a fact at all! But that was how he felt.

But that was too crazy even for him.

Without saying another word, he left her office.

She was about to exhale. Something about being around that man made her uneasy for some reason. But to her surprise, he suddenly returned. "Yes?" she asked.

"What about dinner?" he asked her.

Charly felt as if she had missed something. Dinner? "What about it?" she asked him.

"How about dinner? Having it with me, that is."

"Oh!" Then she realized what he was actually asking. "Oh," she said with less enthusiasm. She wasn't about to go out with a man like him. He was all wrong for her. Good looking. Great body. Too alpha for his own good, just like Darryl. He was the last man on earth she needed to even contemplate going anywhere with.

Boone, sensing her rejection and now feeling totally exposed, quickly cleaned it up. "As the chief of police, I can give you some insight into which members of your student body are on my radar screen. I don't know if you know this, but we have an opioid crisis in this town. A major-league one. As the dean of students, you might want to know which kids are aiding and abetting that crisis."

Charly knew that wasn't his original intent. But he cleaned it up too well for her to reject his offer. Mainly because she really did need to know all about the drug epidemic facing her students, and the police chief was the best person who could tell her. "Yes, of course," she said. "And yes, dinner will be fine."

Boone relaxed, although he knew she was only going out with him to aid her students. But by the way he was feeling, he'd take her however he could get her. Why he was willing to take her that way he couldn't say. Women usually took him however they could get him, not the other way around. But apparently he wanted to bed her just that badly. "Good," he said.

Then, at the exact same time, she asked, "where?" and he asked, "tomorrow night okay?"

They both smiled. Boone took charge. "Tomorrow night okay?" he asked again.

She nodded her head. It wasn't like she had something to do tomorrow night. "That'll work, yes," she said. "But I was asking where. Where would you like to meet for dinner? Which restaurant?"

"Oh, I see. But no, you don't have to drive. I can pick you up."

"That won't be necessary," Charly said firmly. He might have been the chief of police, but he was still a stranger to her. "I'll meet you there."

"Ah. Okay. That's different." He wasn't used to a woman quite that independent around Hemingway. They were usually thrilled to drive around with Chief Ryan in one of Chief Ryan's fancy cars. But he knew she didn't know him like that. "It's a place called Danley's," he said. "Get on Main Street and keep going north as if you're heading out of town. It'll be to your left. You can't miss it."

"What time?"

Boone ran his hand through his already messy hair. He really didn't have time for a dinner with anybody, if he were to be honest. Why in the dickens was he asking her out? "Eight?" he said.

Charly nodded. "Eight will work. I'll see you tomorrow, Chief."

Boone smiled. He was suddenly looking forward to seeing her again. "Good. See you tomorrow," he said, glanced at her again, at her breasts mainly, and then walked out.

Charly waited to make sure he didn't return yet again, and then she leaned her head back and exhaled. The last thing she knew she needed was to have dinner with an interesting guy like Chief Ryan. But she agreed anyway.

The story of her life, she thought.

CHAPTER NINE

Early the next morning was dead quiet in Low Town as the stuffy van slowly turned into the Brickenbrack Trailer Park and made its way toward the single-wide trailer at the end of the street. Sarge was the driver of the van, while Boone, Dontay, Morley, and five additional cops all rode in back of the van. All of them held fully loaded rifles in their hands. All of them, with the exception of the chief, wore battle fatigues. None of them, with the exception of the chief, wore shades.

And Boone wasn't just wearing shades. He was shielding his light-sensitive eyes with those shades. And it wasn't because he had an eye condition. He had no such thing. But because he was nursing a hangover from too much partying the night before.

"Kinda early to be wearing sunglasses, don't you think, Chief?" Morley asked Boone. The other men in the van smiled. Boone was hungover again, and they all knew it. To all of them, they had a really cool chief. To Dontay, who was by far the youngest, it was kind of crazy. That man partied more than he did, he thought again, as he watched his chief.

"Don't you think so, Chief?" Morley asked again. He was usually the only one who could get away with needling Chief Ryan that way.

But Boone wasn't in the mood. He ignored him.

Morley, smiling, elbowed Dontay, who was smiling too and shaking his head.

But when the van stopped three doors down from their target trailer, all smiles were gone.

"We're here, Chief," Sarge said.

Boone finally opened his eyes and looked around at the scene, sat erect, and then looked at his men. "We go in on my count," he said. "Everybody stay behind me. If a bullet is fired as we're making it in, I take the bullet, not any of you knuckleheads. Got it?"

"Yes, sir," they all said. They all were glad to know that their chief not only had their back, but their front as well. And that kind of leadership was why every one of them, to a man, respected Boone Ryan. They feared him far more than they respected him, but they respected him too.

"I don't want anybody going rogue on me," Boone continued. "I've been a cop for over twenty years and I've seen these raids go sideways in a moment's notice if you deviate from the plan. I want everybody to focus on their area. Morley, you and Dontay cover the right side. You two," Boone said, pointing at two other officers, "cover the left side. The rest of you bring up the rear. I'll cover the front. Nobody gets in front of me. Treat my body like your shield. Got it?"

They all said that they did. But Boone continued to stare at them. He felt as if each one of those policemen were his responsibility and he was determined to make sure they all went back home to their families that morning and every morning they were under his watch.

Satisfied that they got the message, he nodded. "Let's go," he said.

Dontay grabbed the battering ram, and they all hurried out of the van.

Inside of the home, you could hear a pin drop. All of the men were sleeping on their respective beds, or on the sofa, or on the floor, with their women beside them as if all was right with the world. Until one of the men felt a mosquito on his neck and slapped his neck, causing his old lady to stir. And that was when their front door was knocked down.

They all jumped up, with the men grabbing for their guns and the women screaming in terror. But Boone and his men were already in, and their rifles were drawn.

"Everybody down!" Boone was yelling as he entered the home. "Get down, *got*dammit! You think I'm playing with you? Everybody down or nobody gets out of this bitch alive! Get down!"

And like soldiers surrendering on the battlefield, every one of those drug dealers, along with their women, dropped their weapons and fell on their knees.

But as his men began frisking and cuffing their suspects, Boone wasn't satisfied with the bust. Because he still hadn't found the one man he came to get. He still hadn't seen hair nor hide of the prize that entire raid was premised on.

With his rifle still aimed, he moved like a panther throughout the trailer, looking from room to room, cubbyhole to cubbyhole, in search of Dalbert Lee. Dalbert was the ringleader. He was the filth Boone had been searching for ever since he arrested Billy Ray Rogers, one of his minions, near Hemingway High. When the tip came in that Dalbert was holed-up in that particular trailer, Boone jumped on it.

But there was no sign of Dalbert Lee. None.

"Chief, in here!" It was Dontay.

Boone, hoping that he'd missed Dalbert's hiding place and Dontay, who was sharp as sharp could be, had found it, hurried to the opposite end of the trailer. He hurried into a tiny bathroom. Dontay and another officer were standing over a tall waste basket.

"Look," Dontay said when Boone walked in. "They got a nice little stash up in here."

Boone looked inside of the waste basket. Dime bags of opioids half-filled the container.

Dontay was smiling. "This is a good bust, Chief," he said.

"Yeah, good," Boone said with little enthusiasm because he knew, without the leader, desperate lives would continue to be destroyed on the streets of Hemingway. "Would have been better if Dalbert's ass was here," he added.

Then he ordered Dontay and the other cop to bag it up.

As for Boone, he knew he couldn't dwell on another failed attempt to find that rascal. He had a murder in his town to investigate, and the well-respected vice principal of the most prestigious school in town in his jail. And his men were right: he was hungover from too much partying the night before.

It was early morning, the sun was breaking into a magnificent shine, he was set to have dinner with that interesting new dean later that night, and he was already having a bad day.

CHAPTER TEN

He got there first: a first for him. He parked his Ferrari, entered the restaurant, and made his way to the table against the window he had reserved. It wasn't a fancy restaurant: they didn't have fancy restaurants in Hemingway. But it was the best they had.

But as Boone looked around, he still wished it was better. That dean had a classiness about her. Like she was used to nice things, although she had apparently fallen on hard times since. He meant to do some digging into her background, to see what those hard times were about, but there wasn't enough hours in the day. He was too damn busy running a police force that was systematically being blamed for not doing more to stem the tide of the town's growing drug problem.

But he got there first. He still couldn't believe it. He was accustomed to women waiting on him. But, instead, he was waiting on her! It kind of angered him, if he were to be honest. Especially when he looked at his Rolex and saw that she was actually late. He was a little late. She was *really* late. Who did she think she was?

But when she walked through that door filled with such confidence and grace, he realized who she was. In a skin-tight little black dress that highlighted her curves, a red scarf tied expertly at her throat, and red heels, she had the kind of all-woman body a man with big equipment loved. He could do her all night long, he knew it. And that face, that face, that magnificent face with her smooth brown skin, and her high cheek bones, and that undeniable elegance about her. He stopped with the *why did I get there first* nonsense almost immediately. Because he knew, right then and there, she was the kind of interesting that made her well worth it.

Other men in the restaurant seemed to find her interesting, too, Boone noticed. He saw how their eyes gave her assessing looks as she was being escorted to his table. One guy, a tall black man, even spoke to her loudly, as if they were long, lost friends and he actually turned around in his seat to watch her body as she walked by. That angered Boone too. What was he looking at so hard? It was downright disrespectful!

Then Boone had to catch himself again. She wasn't his woman. What was his problem? He didn't even know her!

But then why, he wondered, did he feel as if he did?

"Sorry I'm late," Charly said as Boone stood up and she sat down across from him at his table.

He sat back down too. "Couldn't find the place?" he asked her.

She seemed to have to think about it as she sat her big purse in the empty chair. "No, I found it okay. I left home later than I planned." She actually had spent far too long trying to figure out what to wear. But that wasn't his business.

"May I take your drink order, ma'am?" It was the waitress. Boone had already ordered and was sipping on a glass of wine.

"A martini would be nice," Charly said.

"Yes, ma'am," the waitress said, and left their table.

"So, how do you like it?" Boone asked her.

She began looking around at the restaurant. That wasn't what he meant. He meant how did she like Hemingway in general, and her new job in specific, but he didn't correct her. He, instead, watched her as she looked around.

Up close, she wasn't as well put together as she presented. He could see stress in her huge eyes, and a tightness around her small shoulders. And even physically, he could see she had some age on her. Nowhere near his age, but he had taken her for a woman in her early thirties. Now he figured she was more mid-range thirties. Thirty-five, thirty-six, thirty-seven. Something like that. Which only intrigued him more. He never was a man who liked really young women, although he dated plenty of them. But in his dream world of a dream woman, she would be a woman with some maturity about her. Somebody he felt he could talk to. Somebody like the woman right in front of him.

He caught himself again. *Dammit, Ryan, what's your problem? Somebody like her? Seriously? Since when did you go for the academic types? Get a grip!*

"It's nice," Charly finally said in answer to the question she thought he was asking. "It's a larger restaurant than I thought it would be." Then she looked at him. "Come here regularly?"

"Not really," he said, as his cell phone, that sat on the table beside him, rang. He turned it over and looked at the Caller ID as he continued to answer her. "It's a little stuffy for my taste."

Charly smiled. "But not too stuffy for mine, eh?"

Boone laughed. She was quick. "Something like that," he said, and then answered his phone. His smiles were gone, and he was serious, as he answered.

And it was Charly's time to give him an assessing look. What immediately popped out about him was how expensive his clothing were. Darryl was a slave to designer suits, too, so she knew the high-end brands when she saw them. She also knew quality in material. Boone's suit had both. Compared to how he looked yesterday, he appeared freshly shaved, scrubbed, and just conveyed an air of freshness all around today.

And even though he wasn't the most handsome guy in the world: he was too hard-edged and stern to be pigeonholed into any *gorgeous* category, he could definitely give a run for his money to the sexiest guy around. He had sexy in spades. Even a woman like her, who wasn't looking for a man like that, could see it.

Which brought her back to the point of her decision to have dinner with him: the kids. "You said there was a drug issue in Hemingway," she said when he ended his phone call.

Boone glanced at her. He hadn't expected to launch right into it. He had hoped to get to know her a little better. But she was right. It was a business dinner and he needed to realize that. "It's a big issue," he said. "Kids are overdosing and the parents are up in arms and the mayor, who happens to be a cousin of mine, is getting on my case."

"Your case?" Charly asked. "Why?"

"They all figure I should be doing more."

"More to stop kids from doing drugs? How can you, as a cop, do more?"

"They want me to lock up every drug dealer in this town."

"And those same kids will go to another town and buy their drugs. Or another doctor. Or whatever the case may be. If they want it, they'll find a way."

Boone looked at her. He understood that, too, but for so long he felt as if he was the only person in town who understood that. He nodded his head. "I agree with you," he said. "But try telling that to scared parents or to a mayor who just got elected on a promise to win that war on drugs. And I'm the guy that's got to ensure that victory."

The waitress brought Charly her drink, took their food orders, and left again.

"You seem really passionate about this crisis."

"I am. My kid brother, Peyton, died of a drug overdose. Ever since then, I knew what I hated most in this world. Drugs. I am very passionate about it."

Charly could feel his passion. "Sorry to hear about your brother."

Boone nodded. Charly could tell it was still a hard pill for him to swallow. Which was probably why he moved on. "But as much as you try to tell these parents around here that there's precious little the police can do to stop their kids from using drugs, even if we lock up every drug dealer around," he continued, "they still want results. Not actually results. But feel-good results. So does the mayor's office. They all want to claim how we arrested this many people this week, and this many people that week. It's . . . I don't even know the word," Boone said.

"It's insanity," Charly said. "But I've been there. My husband ran for public office once and he was making crazy promises too. It was a good thing he lost."

Boone's heart actually sank. He couldn't believe it. "You're married?" he asked her, unable to shield his surprise. Why did he assume she wasn't? He felt like an idiot!

"My husband died three years ago," Charly said.

And Boone was so relieved he even smiled. "Oh," he said. Then, realizing how inappropriate it was to be smiling, his look turned serious. "Sorry to hear that," he said.

"No, you aren't," Charly said, smiling too. "But go on."

Boone laughed. He liked this girl! "Anyway," he said, and she laughed too.

She felt far more comfortable around him than she thought she would. Certainly more comfortable than she felt around him the first time they met. But maybe the fact that a murder had taken place had something to do with that.

Boone pulled out and put on a pair of reading glasses that made him look even sexier to Charly. Then he pulled out two sheets of paper and looked them over as he spoke. "These are the names of the students I want you to be on the lookout for," he said to her, looked over his reading glasses at her, and then handed those papers to her.

Charly took the papers. "Oh my gosh," she said, looking over both sheets. "This many students are selling drugs at Saint Christopher's?" she asked, and then looked at him.

"Not just selling," he said. "That first sheet are the names of the people suspected of selling," he said. "I say suspected because we don't have enough evidence to pull them in. We damn near have to catch them in the act to pull them in."

"Oh, I see now," Charly said, reading the top of the page. *Suspected Dealer List* was its heading. There were what appeared to her to be about twenty or so names on that list. Then she looked at the second list. *Suspected Users List* was its name. It was full, front and back. "Oh my," she said. "There are a lot of users."

"Suspected users," said Boone.

"Knowing you," Charly said, "they wouldn't be on the list if you didn't have more than just a suspicion."

When Charly realized what she had said, they both exchanged an awkward glance.

For Charly, she felt exposed. She didn't know him well enough to say what she said!

For Boone, it was the first confirmation he had that she might just find him interesting too. He smiled. "You're right," he said. "I have more than a sneaking suspicion about all of them. But as a cop, I have to always preface my knowledge."

Charly smiled. "When I was dean of girls in California, I had to be careful too. I understand."

"What shall I call you?" Boone asked out of the blue.

Charly was, at first, a little taken aback. Where did that come from? But then she rallied. "Charly will do," she said.

"You really need to be careful at Saint Chris, Charly," Boone warned, rallying too. "Even more so than you were at any previous job you've ever had."

Charly was now intrigued. "Why would you say that?" she asked. "I would think L.A. had more of a drug problem than this small town."

"And you would think wrong," said Boone. "Not because there's more people involved in drugs. But everything is supersized at Saint Chris. The parents are the elite of the county. You'll become the wicked witch and they will ride you like a broom if you implicate their little angels in any way. They're riding me and they know me. I know they'll ride you. And then there's the board of directors."

"The board is who really hired me," Charly said.

"Right."

Charly could feel an undercurrent. "And they can fire me," she said.

"Right," Boone said, nodding his head. "And they won't hesitate if you displease them. So don't," he said. "We want to keep you around."

Charly smiled. "Who's we?" she asked. "That's news to me."

Boone smiled. "*I* want to keep you around," he admitted.

And he didn't seem embarrassed after he said it, either. Charly was impressed. It was a very nice thing for him to say. Perhaps the only nice thing anybody had said to her since her arrival in Kentucky.

Which reminded her. "How's Vice-Principal Yerkson?" she asked Boone. "Are you going to release him until you can compile more evidence?"

Boone looked at her with a hard look. "I've compiled enough evidence already." When he realized he was turning back into his usual gruff self, he softened his tone. "But we'll see," he said.

But Charly had already seen that hard look. And that brought her back down to earth too. This man would break her heart just as sure as she was sitting across from him. She wasn't about to go down that road again.

A popular Blake Shelton tune came over the restaurant's stereo system, and some couples started getting out on the dance floor. Charly decided to turn her attention away from Mister Heartbreaker and focus, instead, on the dance floor. She had never even heard the song that was playing, but she was digging it.

Boone felt as if he had blown it somehow and wasn't digging a thing.

But then, to make matters worse, two women, back to back, came to their table.

The first one, a beautiful blonde in her late twenties, was quick about it. "How are you, Boone?" she asked as she walked up.

Both Boone and Charly looked at her. "How are you?" Boone said to her. He knew her. He'd spent a night or two with her not that long ago. But he couldn't remember her name.

"I see you like Danley's too," the woman said.

"Apparently," Boone said.

"You never brought me here on a date," the woman said.

Boone glanced at Charly. Charly was staring at the woman because she was now staring at Charly. Then the woman smiled. "Lowering your standards, I see," she said to Boone.

Boone frowned. "Now? No. I'm not lowering my standards. But I was when I was with you."

The woman's smile left, as if she was surprised he didn't allow her putdown of Charly to stand.

She also, to Charly, seemed just as hurt as she was angry. "You are such an asshole, Boone Ryan!" she said to him, and then left in a huff.

But just as Boone and Charly were just adjusting to the dynamic that first one had brought to their table, another woman walked over. As if she was just standing in the wings, Charly felt, waiting for the first one to leave. Both Boone and Charly looked at her too.

"Hello, Boone," the woman said. She was even younger than the first one, barely in her early twenties. But just as attractive.

Boone, it seemed to Charly, apparently had a definite type of woman: small, white, and blonde, and extremely attractive in a way that seemed to suggest their looks were all they had going for them. A type, Charly knew, she most certainly was not.

Boone didn't recognize the younger lady, but was willing to bet she was another one of his one-night stands. To his shame, he had so many. "Hello," he said flatly to the woman, hoping that his lack of enthusiasm would be enough to get her to move on too.

But it wasn't. "How have you been?" she asked him.

Charly could see his uneasiness. Was she his girlfriend? She certainly was acting like it. But she only proved to Charly that Chief Ryan apparently had an additional type: young. He apparently liked them young. Nearly half his age. Which felt like a letdown to Charly. But the fact that she felt letdown, when dating younger women was absolutely his prerogative and absolutely none of her business, made her uneasy.

"I've been good," Boone said, answering the young lady's question. "And you?"

"Still waiting for that phone call you promised me."

Boone glanced over at Charly with a look of embarrassment in his eyes. As if those women were exposing faults he didn't think she'd already picked up on. It was a telling look to Charly.

"How about that," Boone finally said to the woman, and sipped from his glass of wine.

"Yeah, how about that," the young lady said with bitterness in her voice. "But my bad believing a bastard like you." Then she looked at Charly. "You've obviously been busy," she added, and then left their table. Like the previous lady, she was in a huff too. But she was able to shield it better.

Boone looked at Charly. The little respect she had for him, if she had any at all, probably just flew out the window. But if she was disappointed in him, she didn't show it. To his surprise, she actually smiled.

"You get around, don't you?" she said.

Boone smiled too. He really liked this girl! "I plead the fifth," he said, and sipped more wine.

Charly laughed. And their evening was back on track.

After dinner, he walked her to her car. He followed slightly behind her, staring at her butt. He wanted to follow her home and spend the night with her desperately. He could only imagine what being with her would be like. Besides, he was never a fan of sleeping alone. Usually any woman would do. But not this time. He wanted Charly beneath him.

But she extended her hand. She apparently didn't want him on top of her, he thought.

"Thanks for the info, Chief," she said so formally it surprised him. "I'll pay close attention to the students on your lists, although I will not judge them simply because they're on a list. I won't do that. But I'll keep my eyes open."

Her hand was lingering out there momentarily, and then Boone shook it. "Thanks," he said. "That's all I ask."

But even as she was about to pull her hand away from his, he continued to hold her hand. "Call me if you see anything at all. Even if it's minor. Let me decide how important it might or might not be. Understood?"

Charly nodded. That was a reasonable request. "Yes."

"I don't want you playing cop on me," Boone said. "They may be kids, but the people they work for aren't. The people they work for aren't above violence."

That brought a shiver to Charly's spine. And she nodded again. "I'll be sure to contact you," she said.

He patted her small hand with his other large hand and continued to hold her hand. He wanted to be with her that night. He wanted her beneath him so badly he could taste it!

But he knew she was not the hit and run type. And even if she was, he wasn't hitting and running on her. Not her. He released her hand.

Charly smiled again, got into her Nissan Sentra, and drove away.

Leave her alone, Boone had to convince himself as he made his way to his Ferrari. There were too many fish in the sea. Why get all in his feelings over her when all he had to do was get in his car and go get whatever woman he wanted, even one of the two that came to their table earlier. Despite their big talk and bitterness, he was a man very comfortable in his abilities in bed. They'd go with him lightening quick, and he knew it.

But when he got in his car, ready to go bag him a fish, he kept thinking about Charly. She was the one, he realized, he wanted that night, not some random female.

That was why he didn't go fishing at all.

He just went home.

CHAPTER ELEVEN

"How did it go?"

Charly didn't understand what she meant. It was Saturday morning, she had just entered the main office at the school and was making a beeline for her own office when Minnie Fennel, the school's secretary, stopped her. "Sorry?" she asked Minnie.

"Your first week on the job," Minnie said. "You've been here over a week. How would you rate it?"

"Oh!" said Charly. For some irrational reason, she though Minnie was inappropriately asking about her dinner date with Chief Ryan. Although that date occurred nearly a week ago. Although he hadn't bothered to so much as pick up a phone and ask how she was faring. But he was still on her mind.

"And I'm not trying to pry into your business," Minnie added before Charly could answer her question. "It's just that it's a small town. You've got to get used to that. People are going to talk and tell all day long."

"People are talking?"

"Yes, they are."

Charly knew Minnie expected her to ask what those people were saying, but Charly wasn't about to. She didn't care what they were saying. She had a job to do and she aimed to do it.

But Minnie told her anyway. "They're saying you're having a rough go of it. That you don't know what you're doing. That you're in over your head."

Charly smiled. They would say that, she thought. "Did the alternative placement list come in yet?" she asked instead.

Minnie appeared surprised that Charly didn't defend herself. She would have if they were talking about her like that! "No, ma'am," she said to Charly. "But I'll call the school board and see what's the hold up. They aren't open on Saturdays, as you know, but I'll check on Monday."

"Okay, thanks," Charly said and was about to head to her office.

"Have you seen Amos yet?"

That was an odd question to Charly. "Me? No. Why?" She didn't even know the man. Why would she be the one to go and see him?

"I don't know if he's going to plead guilty or innocent," Minnie said. "Parents are calling and asking that question."

"He said he didn't do it," Charly said. She knew that much. "Tell them that."

"But that's what they all say," Minnie said. "Everybody in jail says they didn't do it. But anyway, don't you have better things to do on this gorgeous Saturday than to come to work?"

"You're here," Charly said with a smile. "Don't you have better things to do?"

"Absolutely," said Minnie with a grin. "But duty called. Principal Dorsett ordered me to come in today to answer any phone calls from still-nervous parents. It's been a week since they found that body, but some of them are still thinking about pulling their kids."

"Is he going to cut his vacation short and come back?" Charly asked. The situation certainly warranted it in her eyes.

But Minnie was already shaking her head. "Not on your life," she said. "Dr. Dorsett goes to Europe every year. It's a tradition for him. It's in his contract. He's not changing his vacation for anybody."

Charly didn't understand that kind of commitment. But it wasn't for her to judge. "Anyway, I've got some paperwork to do."

"Oh, that's why I asked about Amos," Minnie said. "Chief Boone finally allowed him a phone call, although he should have been allowed it long ago. He told me that before you arrived in Hemingway he had put together an orientation packet that explains your duties and responsibilities. He said you'll find it in that small, blue file cabinet in your office closet."

Charly had seen that cabinet, but couldn't find the key.

"Here's the key," Minnie said, handing the key to her.

"Thanks," Charly said. "If you hear from him again, tell him I appreciate it. That packet should help my transition tremendously."

Minnie nodded. "Yeah, he's really good about helping people out."

Charly looked at her. "Then you believe he could be innocent?"

"I don't know anything about that," Minnie said quickly. "Besides, Chief Ryan wouldn't have arrested him if he was so innocent."

"Innocent people get arrested all the time, Minnie," Charly said.

"Not in Hemingway, they don't," said Minnie. And then the school's phone rang.

As Minnie answered the call, Charly made her way down the back hall that led to the Dean of Students office, an office just beyond the Principal's office and the Vice-Principal's office. To her relief, the packet was in the bottom file cabinet, exactly where Amos said she'd find it. She was glad to have it.

But as soon as she got behind her desk, ready to devour the information, Minnie walked into her office with new news.

"What is it?" Charly asked.

"That was Fritz Hollingsworth."

Charly frowned. "Who?"

"The chairman of the board of directors of Saint Chris. The man who hired you?"

"Oh, right. What did he want?"

"He says he wants you to get over to Rita Mae Brown's house asap."

Charly frowned again. "The victim's house? Why?"

"He feels you should offer the school's condolences to the Brown family, given that the child died on our property."

"*I* should offer the condolences?"

"Yes. Why not you?"

"I would have thought a member of the board would have already paid their respects to that girl's family. It's been a week since it happened."

Minnie laughed. "I'm sorry," she said. "But you must be joking! Rita Mae Brown's family lives in Low Town."

"Yes, and?" Charly asked.

"Those uppity mucks aren't going anywhere near that area," Minnie said.

Charly nodded. Those uppity mucks had no problem putting her up in an apartment in that area, and they wouldn't even visit it? If she didn't know who she was dealing with in that school's leadership, she knew now.

But she didn't go there. That wasn't Minnie's business. "I would have thought they wouldn't want anybody from the school going to visit the family anyway," she said.

Minnie didn't understand. "What do you mean?"

"Given that one of our faculty members has been arrested for her death, I would think they wouldn't want me, as a member of the faculty, to contact the family at all."

"Ordinarily, that's probably true. But Chairman Hollingsworth seems to think you'd be perfect for the job."

"Why?" *Because I'm black*? Charly wanted to ask.

"Because you're new," Minnie said. And then she added: "And black."

Charly smiled. Minnie lacked any kind of warmth, but at least she was honest. "The chairman said that?"

"Didn't have to," Minnie said.

"Yeah, well, until I get that order directly from the chairman, I'm not about to intrude on that grieving family. But thanks," Charly added, and looked at Minnie.

Minnie understood. She was being dismissed. "Fine," she said, and then left Charly's office.

And Charly, anxious to find out just what Amos's orientation packet contained, opened it, put on her reading glasses, and began studying all that he prepared.

But then her office phone buzzed. After a second buzz, she tore away from the packet and pressed the button. "Yes?"

"Chairman Hollingsworth on Line 2," Minnie said.

Charly, surprised, immediately answered the call. She didn't know much, but she understood the chain of command. And Fritz Hollingsworth, as chairman of the board of directors, was at the top of that chain. "Hello?"

"Dean Johnson?"

"Yes, this is she."

"This is Fritz Hollingsworth. I understand you needed to hear my directive straight from the horse's mouth."

Charly swallowed hard. "Yes, sir," she said.

"You're hearing it. Get your tail over to the Brown house. Minnie will give you the address. They aren't planning to bury the girl until next Saturday, which is crazy in my opinion, waiting that long, but that's how they do it. Pay your condolences on behave of Saint Chris."

Charly knew she could get fired summarily during her year-long probation, which meant the chairman needed no cause to get rid of her, but she also knew if she didn't stand up for her beliefs now, nobody was going to be listening later. "I would have thought the attorneys wouldn't want school officials to have any contact with the Brown family. At least not until Amos Yerkson's situation was resolved," she said.

"Nonsense," said Fritz dismissively. "Her body was found on our property. The least we can do is pay our respects."

"Then wouldn't it be more advisable, sir," Charly said, "for you or another member of the board to pay those respects?"

"Are you defying my order, Johnson?" Fritz asked with an undertone of anger in his voice.

Charly knew she had stepped in it. "No, sir," she said. "But--"

"There's no but," Fritz said. "Then again, yes, there is. Get your *butt* over to the Brown house and extend our condolences. That is all, Dean Johnson," he said, and then hung up the phone with what even Charly could feel was force.

She exhaled, and hung up too. And that feeling of dread, of drifting, of being a woman alone in this brutal world, reemerged. And she knew, if she was smart, she'd better add another chore to her to-do list: to start looking for another job. Her days in Hemingway, Kentucky, she was now convinced, were numbered.

But then she realized what was being asked of her, and that now that she had a direct order she had no choice but to obey that order, closed the folder, got up, and took off.

CHAPTER TWELVE

The same red Ferrari that was parked in her parking space at Saint Christopher's when she first arrived in town was parked in front of Rita Mae Brown's family home when Charly drove up. She now knew, after seeing it at the restaurant he took her to last week, that it belonged to Chief Ryan.

To her own shock, she felt an odd surge of excitement at the thought of seeing him again. Odd because of his lack of contact with her since they met up at that restaurant. She therefore rationalized her joy, knowing that being "excited" was too strong a word. She decided that she was pleased to know that he might be at the Brown house, too, because he had been so kind to her. She rationalized that to be the case, rather than any misplaced affection she might think she had for a man she hardly even knew.

Besides, maybe somebody else owned a red Ferrari in that town.

But when a young lady answered the door and invited her in, the first face she saw, sitting on the sofa beside an older African-American woman, was Chief Ryan himself. And although inwardly she couldn't deny that she was glad to see him, she could tell on his face that the feeling wasn't mutual. To her surprise, he, like everybody else in that town so far, looked upset by her presence.

All the other eyes of the African-Americans staring at her, from the various family members sitting around in the crowded living room, to those sitting around the dining room table in the adjacent room, weren't exactly friendly eyes either. They looked upset by her presence too. But Charly had a duty to perform, and she aimed to perform it.

Boone saw her when she first walked in, and she was right in her perception: his anger did flare. What on earth was she thinking, he wondered? Didn't she realize the last person on earth those people wanted to see was a dean from Saint Chris?

But somehow Boone knew Charly would not have made that move on her own. She was a smart girl. She knew better than that. He'd bet the farm those clowns on the board put her up to it. They wouldn't do it themselves, but they gladly put her in the line of fire. It angered Boone that they weren't looking out for their brand new dean better than that.

"I'm here to see Rita Mae Brown's mother," Charly said after entering the home.

Stephanie Brown, Rita Mae's mother and the woman seated next to Boone, looked at Charly. "Yes? May I help you?"

Charly smiled and walked over to the woman. "My name is Charlene Johnson," she said, extending her hand.

Although the mother seemed leery of Charly, she shook her hand anyway. "Did you know my daughter?" she asked her.

"No ma'am," said Charly. "On behalf of Saint Christopher Academy, I want to extend my condolences to you and your family for your tragic loss."

A collective sigh of disbelief filled the room all at once. Apparently there were many in the room who knew where she worked, but many others who didn't. "Are you for real?" a young man with dreadlocks asked her: one of the ones who apparently didn't. "You're from Saint Chris? Are you *kidding* me?"

Charly looked back at the young man. He was one of the ones seated at the dining room table.

"Why would you come here?" asked a young lady seated at that table too. "The vice-principal of that school killed Rita Mae, and you have the nerve to offer condolences?"

"Is there no shame over there?" asked yet another young person. "We don't want you here. We don't want to have anything to do with you!"

Boone could hear the pain in their voices, but he could see the pain in Charly's eyes. He rose to his feet, buttoning his suit coat.

"You're so wrong for even coming here," said the guy in dreads. "You're just another sellout!"

"Okay, that's enough!" Boone said with force. All eyes turned to him, including Charly's. But when Boone spoke, with those intense eyes and deadly serious look on his face, nobody said another word. It was one thing to pile on a school dean. It was another thing altogether to take on the head of what they viewed as a racist police department that could harass them no end if they disrespected the chief.

"She's a brand new hire," Boone continued. "She had nothing to do with what Amos Yerkson did. She was ordered to come here," he added, although he didn't know that for a fact. "You're jumping all over the wrong person, so cut it out!"

It was obvious to Charly that the family members were upset, and wanted to lash out at the chief too. But they didn't. And although Charly appreciated the fact that the chief stood up for her, she felt she needed to make her intentions clear to the family herself.

Instead of addressing the young people who had addressed her, she turned her attention back to the mother. "I didn't come here to add to your grief and pain," she said to her. "And I do apologize if my presence has done that. That's not my intention. I wish you well. I wish your family well. And I will leave you alone."

"Are they afraid?" the mother asked her.

Charly didn't understand the question. At first she glanced at Boone, but then she looked at the woman. "Afraid?"

"Are they afraid I'm going to sue Saint Christopher's?"

Boone stared at Charly as if her answer would answer a lot of questions for him. Would she come clean, he wondered, or recite the company line?

"In a word," Charly responded to the mother, "yes," she said. "That is probably their concern."

Boone inwardly smiled. *That's my girl*, he thought. Then he frowned. *His girl*? *What in the world was he talking about?*

The others in the room looked at Charly, too, as if she could give them some insight on the enemy.

"Do you think I have a good case?" the mother asked her pointblank.

But before Charly could say a word, Boone intervened again. "She's not answering that," he said.

"If the vice-principal did what the police has accused him of doing," Charly answered despite Boone's comment, "then yes. You have a very good case. If he didn't do what he's been accused of doing, then your case, I imagine, would be most difficult."

The mother stared at Charly, and then nodded. And then she extended her hand. "Thank you for your condolences," she said.

Charly smiled and shook her hand. "You're welcome," she said, and then made her way for the exit.

She hadn't even made it all the way to her car before a young man from inside the house, the one with the dreadlocks, had apparently come through the backdoor and around the side of the house.

She was at her car door by the time he walked over to her.

"Dalbert's the man you need to be checking out," he said to her.

"Excuse me?"

"If you want to really know what happened to Rita Mae, you need to talk to Dalbert."

"Who's Dalbert?"

The man gave her a hard look. "Dalbert Lee, lady. Don't you know anything?"

"But who is he?"

The man shook his head, as if she was some kind of idiot for not already knowing who the man was. One week in town? She should know everything apparently! "Your boyfriend will know," he said to her.

Shocked, she started to ask what boyfriend did he mean, but caught herself. The chief did come to her defense inside of that house. They did have dinner together once and undoubtedly people in that town were talking about that too. It was easy to conflate facts with fiction.

But she did have questions about the man standing beside her car, and why would this Dalbert person know something about Rita Mae's death. But before she could say another word, he took off. She turned as he headed back around the side of the house where he had, presumably, come from.

Charly wondered why he suggested she check out Dalbert Lee rather than telling it to the chief. But that town was filled with oddities.

And speaking of the chief, the young man had barely left before Boone came out of the house, too. He made his way toward her.

"Stop letting them use you like that," he said to her.

Did everybody in Kentucky begin sentences as if they were already in the middle of a conversation? "Excuse me?"

"Fritz and that board," Boone said. "Stop letting them use you like that."

"They aren't using me," Charly said. "I work for the school now. The school felt somebody had to do this."

"Why you?" Boone asked.

"Because Rita Mae Brown was a black woman, her grieving family is black, and, in case you haven't noticed, so am I."

Boone smiled. "I thought you were going to say you did it because they made you do it."

"That too," said Charly, and Boone laughed.

Then he looked down the length of her, and back up into her soft eyes. There was something about her that gave him a sense of longing every time he saw her! But why, he wondered? "Be careful out here," he warned her. "I don't want you fired before you get a chance to make your mark."

Charly appreciated his concern. She managed to smile. "I couldn't agree more," she said.

Boone caught an undertone there. He stared at her. "You think there's a chance of it happening?" he asked her.

Charly couldn't believe she was discussing her private thoughts with a man she barely knew. But she answered him anyway. "It's possible, yes," she said.

"Despite the fact that you did what they told you to do and came here?"

"From what I'm hearing around the school, the board felt they were forced to hire me. Apparently the mayor insisted on diversity or something to that effect, and I was the only person of color to apply. I doubt if my following their orders is going to change that harsh reality."

Boone agreed with her assessment, and he liked the fact that she, like him, didn't sugarcoat the truth. He continued to stare at her. "Just don't let'em see you sweat, kid," he advised her. Then he frowned. "No matter what."

Charly nodded. She understood. Then she found herself staring at Boone.

"What is it?" he asked her.

"A guy from inside Mrs. Brown's house came up to me just before you came out."

"Oh, yeah? Tried to hit on you, did he? I'll set him straight. You aren't that kind of girl."

Charly frowned. What was he talking about? "No, it wasn't about that," she said. And if it was, she thought, she wouldn't be bringing that up to him. And he was going on and on about it, despite what she said.

"You aren't that kind of girl," he was saying. "I'll make sure they get the message. You're hands off," he added, which was an odd declaration for him to make, she thought.

"No, Chief."

"Call me Boone."

"Boone," she corrected herself. "It wasn't about me. He told me that if I wanted to know who killed Rita Mae, that I needed to check out somebody named Dalbert Lee."

Boone was embarrassed that he had gone in that personal direction, but was too surprised by what she said to worry about what he'd said. "Wait a minute," he said. "Who came up to you and told you about Dalbert Lee?"

Charly wasn't sure if she wanted to expose the young man. "Just some guy."

"Describe him."

Charly hesitated. "I don't want him harassed, Chief."

Boone frowned. "I don't harass people," Boone said. "Describe him."

"He's not the issue," Charly said.

"You don't know that," Boone said with a harsh tone to his voice. His eyes were big and staring at her, as if she was defying him and he didn't like it. "Describe him," he ordered.

But Charly would not be bullied. "He came to me in what I felt was confidence. I'm keeping his confidence. He is not the issue."

Boone was unaccustomed to being forced to back down. But he backed down. "And he said to check out Dalbert Lee?"

"That's the name he gave me," Charly said. "You ever heard of him?""

Had he? "I know him. Been looking for him. But why would that person connect Rita Mae to Dalbert?"

Charly shook her head. "I have no idea."

"I would have an idea if you told me who he was," Boone said.

"Who's Dalbert Lee?" Charly asked.

"A drug dealer. The biggest we have in town. I've been searching for his ass all week."

"So he's a problem?"

"He's a problem," Boone said, nodding his head.

"But if that guy is to be believed and there's a connection," Charly said, "then he seems to be suggesting that Rita Mae Brown was on drugs maybe?"

"That would be the implication, yes," Boone said.

"Were any drugs found in her system?"

"We don't have the toxicology report back yet. The medical examiner's office is backlogged bad with so many drug overdoses lately. But it's coming. I put some fire under his ass. I'll find out."

"If it's true, that certainly would exonerate Amos Yerkson," Charly said. "I don't think anybody would accuse the vice-principal at Saint Christopher's of dealing drugs."

"I don't know about all of that," Boone said, "but we'll see."

"Thanks," said Charly.

"I'm not thanking you until you tell me what was the name of the guy who stepped to you."

Charly smiled. "I don't know his name."

"Describe him."

"Here we go again."

Boone moved closer to her, invading her personal space. "Describe him," he said to her with a look so hard she almost buckled.

But she didn't. That look might work on the locals, she couldn't let it work on her or he'd lose all respect for her too. "I've got to get back to the office, Chief," she said.

Boone stared at her. They were so close she could smell his cologne and he could smell her sweet perfume. A smell, he knew, that would remain with him. "You don't snitch, and that's good," he said. "But not when it comes to me."

He was too close to her. But oddly enough, she didn't feel trapped. She felt warmed by his nearness, as if he was a blanket to the coldness of the town around her. And she needed that comfort. "I don't know his name," she said again, "but he was one of the young people inside."

"The one with dreadlocks?" Boone asked.

Charly was surprised he got it right off the bat. "Yes," she said.

Boone nodded with a look of satisfaction on his face. She was willing to help him. *That's my girl*, he inwardly found himself saying again. And then admonished himself again.

"You know him?" Charly asked him.

"I know him. He told me something to that effect earlier in the week."

"Oh. So you already knew about the Dalbert Lee's connection?"

Boone nodded. "Don't know if I believe it, but yes, I know about it."

"Is the guy with the dreads related to the Brown family?"

"Malcolm is his name, and no. He's a friend of Rita Mae's."

"Oh, okay. That would explain it then."

"Explain what?"

"Why he would point the police away from Amos and toward a drug dealer when, if Amos is found to be the perp, the family could stand to make a lot of money from Saint Chris."

Boone nodded. "Good point," he said. "I thought about that too."

"He must have been more than just a friend to her, though."

Boone nodded. "He was."

"That would explain it then. When you care about somebody, you shouldn't care about the money. You should care about them. Maybe he just wants justice for Rita Mae."

Her words cut Boone short, and he found himself staring at her again. Her saying that a person shouldn't care about money when you care about somebody, echoed in his mind. Because every woman he'd ever dated cared deeply about the money. *His* money. But this dean was different.

Or was she?

He wanted to ask her out again, to test the theory. But he was worried that he could fall hard for her. That she could break his heart. He decided against going there.

"I'd better let you get back to your office," he said. "And thanks for telling me," he said to her. "The sooner you realize I'm not the boogey man, the better."

Charly smiled. She was already beginning to realize that.

Boone stood back and she opened her car door.

"And Charly," he said just as he was about to head to his own car.

Charly looked at him. "Yes?"

"The next time I say you aren't going to answer a question, you'd better not answer it."

Charly couldn't believe he'd just said that to her.

Until he said this: "They're going to use your answer against the school you work for in a court of law. You will be called to testify against the school, I guarantee it."

Charly was shocked. "To testify?"

"Oh, yeah."

Charly had to testify against her deceased husband's killer. It was a horrible experience. She never wanted to see the inside of a witness stand ever again. "But I didn't say anything amazing," she said. "What I said was obvious. It was common sense."

"You said they will have a good case because of Amos's arrest."

"That's not what I said. I said if he was found to be guilty, they had a good case."

"All that matters," Boone said, "is that you said they have a good case. That's all the plaintiff's attorneys in the civil suit to come wants the jury to hear. And they're skilled enough to make it happen." Boone gave her a hard look. "I know what I'm doing, Charly," he said. "For your own good, you need to start realizing it."

Then he left her side, walked over to that Ferrari, got in, and then sped away.

Charly got into her own car. But she sat behind the wheel. She was upset with herself. Because the chief was right. She should not have given any opinion whatsoever about that situation.

But her big mouth couldn't shut up. She wanted to be honest with the grieving mother. Now that same grieving mother, she knew, was going to turn her words against her.

Great, she thought. Another reason for them to get rid of her. It was just a matter of time before her black behind was in the unemployment line once again.

She cranked up, disgusted with herself, and was about to shift her gear to Drive, until there was a knock on her window.

Startled, she turned quickly. Another young person from inside of the house, this time a young lady, was standing at her car door.

She rolled down her window (they were not electric), but not enough for somebody to get a fist inside of that window and harm her. "Yes?" she asked her.

"You need to check out Dalbert," the young lady said.

Charly felt as if she had missed half of the conversation. "Excuse me?"

"If you wanna know who killed Rita Mae," she said, "check out Dalbert." Then the young lady left, too, and went the same way Dreadlocks had gone.

MALLORY MONROE

CHAPTER THIRTEEN

Pauley Manchin looked at his watch again and then shook his head. "What's taking so long?" he asked Bellows. They were seated in Bellows car, just outside of the correctional institution, waiting patiently for the inmate release. "They said be here at nine am. We got here *before* nine am. Now it's damn near eleven and he's still not out yet."

"They're never on time," Bellows said. "And they do it on purpose, too. They never wanna give these cons a break even when they're getting out."

"But it's been two hours. Two hours! This is ridiculous!"

"Like I said, they're never on time," his partner said again. He was about to say more, but then the gate opened and the man they both had been waiting for began heading their way.

Pauley smiled. "There's the man of the hour." He unbuckled his seatbelt and began getting out of the car. "There's my boy!" When he stepped out of the car, he lifted both hands with his arms open wide. "What's up, Tabloski?"

Romney Tabloski grinned and ran across the
busy street with his pants sagging the way they had
when he first walked into that joint, as if he
couldn't wait to get away from there. When he
made it to the car, he and Pauley embraced.

"You took your sweet time," Pauley said.

"Yeah, right," Tabloski said. "Like my release
was up to me. Get out of here!"

Pauley laughed as Tabloski got in the front seat
while Pauley got in the back. Tabloski and Bellows
gave a handshake/hug combo.

"What's up, Tab?" Bellows said as they
hugged.

"Glad to be out, that's what's up," Tabloski
said as Bellows cranked up and drove off.

They small-talked, about what had been
happening on the streets of L.A. since Tabloski was
locked up, but then the conversation shifted as
both Bellows and Pauley knew it would.

"So, where is she?" Tabloski asked. "I wanna
go there first."

Bellows glanced at Pauley through the
rearview. Neither man answered the question.

"What's with the deaf and dumb act?" Tabloski
asked. "Where is she? I'm not resting until that
bitch is dead."

"Think that's a good idea, Tab?" Pauley asked him.

"What do you mean?" Tabloski asked him.

"You just got out. Something happens to her on the same day you get out ain't gonna look too good to the authorities."

"Who gives a damn about the authorities? And I don't care how it looks! We got a plan. We're sticking to the plan. Besides, don't forget who you're talking to. I know how to dress it up to look like an accident. I know how to have my alibi in place. Don't forget who you're talking to. Now where is she?"

Bellows looked at Pauley, again, through the rearview.

Pauley exhaled. "We don't know," he said.

Tabloski looked back at him. "What do you mean you don't know? I ordered you to keep tabs on her. I ordered that!"

"And we did keep tabs on her," Pauley said. "Didn't we, Bells?"

"We kept tabs on her," said Bellows. "Every so often we checked her out. After Darryl got iced, she moved around a lot. But we always found her. She was always around L.A."

"So what happened?"

"She changed locations again. She just took off. You know how dames are. But we're on it."

Tabloski shook his head, and then punched the dashboard with his fist. "We got to find that bitch!" he said angrily.

"Don't worry," said Pauley. "We're already on it. We're find her. We always do."

But that was little comfort to Tabloski. From the moment he walked into that prison to the moment he walked out of it, his entire existence was focused on handling her. His old man was convicted and died in prison, thanks to her.

Now it was her turn.

CHAPTER FOURTEEN

Two months came and went. During that entire time, Boone was singularly focused on beating back the drug epidemic that continued to infest his town. Young people were still dying. Old people were still angry. Rival dealers were killing each other over turf and it was becoming more than a small town should have to handle.

Boone was doing all he could. He arrested drug dealers and users alike, and he didn't care who they were. Which didn't endear him with community leaders nor his cousin the mayor. Everybody insisted that he should arrest the dealers, and that he needed to go easy on the users. The users, they insisted, needed medical attention, not jail. That was the pitch.

But Boone struck back. Where was all of this concern for users, he asked them, when Hemingway had a crack epidemic? Everybody insisted back then that he arrest the dealers and users alike. Lock'em all up and throw away the key, was the pitch back then. Look at the crime and destruction *those people* were bringing to their beautiful town. But now that the opioid crisis was infecting *their* young people and not all of those people of color, they suddenly wanted sympathy and treatment, not jail, for the users? And they expected Boone to go along with that?

Not Boone Ryan.

He didn't go easy on crack-heads during that epidemic. He wasn't going easy on opioid-heads during this epidemic.

And, as if he didn't have enough on his plate to worry about, he still couldn't take his mind off of Charly.

He picked up that phone to call her every single day since their dinner date. But he knew it was the wrong thing to do. She might have been the kind of woman he needed, somebody mature and stable and smart and fun. But he wasn't the kind of man she needed, somebody still having one-night stands and still partying like it was nineteen-ninety-nine and he was some frat boy, not a man in his forties. He was all wrong for her. That was why he didn't call her.

But that didn't mean she wasn't on his mind. She was. Almost constantly. But he was a busy man. Work consumed him.

At Saint Chris, Charly was busy too. After two months on the job, she was feeling it now. She felt she was in a groove and in a good place jobwise. She was, as her mother used to say, getting the hang of it.

She'd also admit that she was a little disappointed that there was never any further "dates" with the chief. And she knew, on his end, it could have been any of a number of reasons why he decided against pursuing her: she didn't give him any on that first date when he obviously wanted some. She wasn't his type. He'd rather eat nails. It could have been any reason.

But whatever the reason, she knew she couldn't dwell on it. On the one date they did have, two different women came to their table, with both bitter that he wasn't taking them out to dinner, either, and Charly wasn't about to become like them. She knew from the moment she saw Boone Ryan that he was the last man on earth she needed. His decision to stay away from her was exactly what *she* needed. She wasn't mad at him. He was showing her who he was, a man not interested in commitment, and she was going to believe him.

For a solid two months straight, they only saw each other in passing. And always in a public place. Always in a situation where they'd speak and keep it moving. Like at her first faculty meeting.

The faculty assembled in the teacher's lounge, with bodies leaned around the wall, as Fritz Hollingsworth, Boone Ryan, and the school's principal, Dr. Paul Dorsett, were talking amongst themselves in front of the group. Charly had been on the job for a little over two months and she had her hands full. But unlike her first few weeks where she'd been inundated with policy books and regs, with learning the campus buildings and the executive officers, it was almost exclusively now all about the kids. Dealing with the less-than-saintly student body was her main task. And if she thought public school kids had issues, she had to think again. They had nothing on the kids at Saint Chris!

But because Amos was still incarcerated, and because the principal returned from his vacation insisting that he needed to get up to speed on all that had happened while he was away before he could help her learn the ropes, she relied on her previous tenure as a dean and did her job. But she knew it wasn't the best that could be done because she lacked too much information. Many times, she was flying by the seat of her pants.

But when she walked into the teachers' lounge for the mandatory meeting and saw that Chief Ryan was one of the three men up front, and despite the fact that he hadn't tried to hook back up with her at all, she still was glad to see him. She knew it sounded crazy, but he represented a friendly face to her. Like a breath of fresh air. The only friendliness, other than Amos Yerkson on her first day, that she had experienced during her entire time in Hemingway.

When she entered the faculty lounge, Boone was still up front talking to Fritz and Dr. Dorsett. But as Fritz continued to talk, Boone's eyes moved to Charly immediately on her arrival. He couldn't stop taking peeps at her as she sat at a table midway from the front. He noticed how the talkative faculty members at that table suddenly stopped talking altogether when she sat down, as if she was somehow intruding. Some of them wanted the job she had, and Boone knew that was partly the reason for their coldness. But others were just plain rude to any outsider anyway, Boone also knew. Her first couple months in town, he decided sadly, were apparently still rocky.

"Okay, faculty, listen up," Principal Dorsett said, attempting to quiet the room. "Teachers, listen up!" But they kept on talking. "Teachers, show some manners. Teachers?"

Boone, irritated that they continued to ignore their principal, took matters into his own hands.

He had to get back to the station. He didn't have all day. "Shut the hell up!" he yelled at the noisy teachers.

And that one request worked. They all shut up.

"Thank you, Chief Ryan," Dorsett said to Boone, and then turned his attention back to the faculty. "Before we get started with our meeting, and since this is our first official meeting since I returned from vacation, I want you to please join me in welcoming Miss Charlene Johnson, our brand new dean of students. Miss Johnson, please stand up and take a bow."

Charly smiled as she stood up. There was a very light splattering of applause as she stood, with the vast majority of staff not applauding at all, and Boone could see the disappointment in Charly's eyes. But she continued to smile, God love her, he thought, despite their rudeness. And then she was about to sit back down.

But Dorsett stopped her. "Before you take your seat, Dean Johnson," he said, "why don't you share with the faculty what you shared with me on yesterday. I think it was a very good idea. Dean Johnson," Dorsett said to the other staff members, "believes that we should streamline referrals out of her office. Tell them about it, Charly," he said.

Boone saw the apprehension in Charly's big, beautiful eyes, as she knew like he knew that those teachers didn't want to hear a damn thing she had to say. But she remained standing and spoke up.

"I was telling Principal Dorsett that we are ill-serving our students when we write multiple referrals on them for what actually was one offense with multiple violations. Students are being written up on a main office referral if their violation involves structural damage. They are being written up on a Guidance office referral if their violation involves mental abusiveness. They get a referral to the athletic director if their violation was physical in nature. Sometimes one office doesn't even know that the other office has a referral on the kid. What I suggested to Dr. Dorsett is that all referrals are written to the Dean of Students office, to my office, with a list of the various violations on that one referral if it all happened at the same time. That way, the student only has the one referral on his or her record, which is only fair, rather than two or three for the same offense."

"And I think it's a very good idea," Dorsett said. "Any questions on that?" he asked the staff, and some hands actually did go up.

Charly was surprised. But Boone was suspicious. He knew that group too well. "Yes?" Dorsett said to one of the teachers whose hand was up.

"We want to know how she got that job," he said.

Charly looked at the teacher. She shouldn't have been surprised by such a question, but she was. It seemed to be none of his business, if you asked her. Boone was watching Charly.

Fritz expected outrage when they hired Charly. He was getting it now. "She applied for the job," he answered. Dorsett, the principal, let him answer it.

"I applied too," said another teacher, "and I have twenty-eight years of experience."

And then it was a free-for-all:

"I applied too. I've got nearly twenty years' experience myself."

"I applied with my thirty years of experience."

"What's her experience? What are her qualifications? Are you telling me she has more experience than all of us?"

Boone looked at Fritz. He should have told them that she was selected, she's the new dean of students, end of story. But no! He turned to the dean herself. "Miss Johnson," Fritz said, "would you care to respond to your colleagues?"

Boone wanted to kick his ass. He or Dorsett should have handled that, not leave it to her! Why weren't they protecting her?

But Charly, Boone realized, could handle herself. And she didn't stutter. "I previously worked as a dean of girls at a large high school in California," she said.

"For how long?" asked one.

"Well, I started out as a teacher," she said.

"A gym teacher," said one of her colleagues in a dismissive tone.

"I was a physical education teacher, that's right," said Charly. "But I was promoted to Dean," she added.

"And how long did you work as dean?" asked yet another teacher.

"I was an assistant dean for four years."

"How long were you a full-fledged dean," asked one teacher. "Not an assistant."

"I was dean for a little over two years," Charly said, and the room went ballistic.

"Two years? That's all?"

"Are you kidding me?"

"How could somebody with just two years of experience get a prestigious job like dean of students at Saint Chris? How is that possible?"

If it had been Boone, he would have told every one of them what they could do with their outrage, and walked out. But Charly's toughness, he realized as he watched her, was nothing like his. Her toughness was in her ability to sustain. To take a licking and keep on ticking.

And she responded to her critics while she was at it. "You are correct," she said in answer to one of the teachers. "My experience as a dean isn't vast at all. But at least I was a dean," she added. "An assistant dean is still a dean. I have over six years of experience as a dean."

The teachers stared at her, wondering if she would dare insult them. Boone stared too, hoping she could pull it off.

"You all quoted your experience," she said. "And it's impressive. But all of you, if I'm not mistaken, have years and years of experience as teachers. I have experience as a dean. There's a difference."

Boone smiled. She pulled it off, by gum!

But the teachers took a different road. "I have an Ivy League education," said one teacher.

"So do I," said another.

"I don't," said Charly. "But I have an excellent education."

"From a black school."

"From a historically black university, yes," said Charly. "A university created because people like me were ordered to pay taxes that paid for state universities, but we were not allowed to attend those universities."

"It's not that way anymore."

"No, it's not," said Charly. "But they didn't want to tear down the state schools and send everybody to the historically black colleges. And the historically black colleges didn't want to get torn down either."

Boone smiled. She was pulling it all, doggonit!

"We don't believe in quotas and set-asides," said yet another teacher.

"Neither do I," said Charly. "I think it's unfair that people like you get ninety-percent set aside, while people of color, who are nearly, if not in fact, the majority in this country, have to scrape the bottom of the barrel for the meager ten percent that's left."

Boone's smile became even more obvious, especially as the teachers looked at each other as if they were trying to figure out if she'd just insulted them. Then he couldn't help it. He laughed. He laughed long and hard. The teachers, and Fritz too, failed to see the humor.

And then Charly sat back down.

"Moving right along," Fritz said, giving Boone an angry look.

Dorsett wasn't as unforgiving, but he was a little pissed too. "Anyway," he said, "before Chairman Hollingsworth and I discuss in-house matters, the chief has a few words to say to you. That is, if he can stop laughing long enough."

Charly smiled at that.

"But we are pleased to have him with us today, and we want to give him our undivided attention. He didn't have to break away from his very busy schedule to talk to us, but he has agreed to do so. Let's listen up!"

Then Dorsett moved over slightly and Boone took center stage. He was dressed to kill, Charly thought, in his well-made suit, but there was still something oddly frazzled about him, as if he was together, but not quite altogether. As if, the way she saw it, he was hanging on by a thread.

And as he spoke, she noticed, he kept ruffling his hair, as if he was trying to be delicate to his delicate audience when there was really no delicate bone in his body.

"As I'm sure you are all aware," Boone said, "we have ourselves a major league drug problem in Hemingway. This opioid crisis is hitting us particularly hard and it's not getting any better. And what's making matters worse is that the participants are more likely than not our school-age kids."

"Surely you don't mean *our* kids, Chief," a teacher said to him.

"Excuse me?" Boone asked that teacher. "What do you mean?"

"Shouldn't you be preaching this sermon to the faculty at Hemingway High?" asked another teacher.

Boone frowned. Above everything, he hated people who would put themselves above other people simply because of their station in life. "Why would you think that you don't need to hear this?" he asked.

"Because the children who attend Saint Chris are not addicts," the teacher said.

"You don't know what the hell you're talking about," Boone shot back and some teachers gasped at his rudeness. Charly stared at him.

"Five high school kids almost died of drug overdoses just last week in our town. Five kids. And yes, you're right: none of them attended Saint

Chris. But guess how many kids who've already graduated nearly died of a drug overdose in this town?"

"More than five," said one.

"More like twenty-five," said Boone. "Twenty of which," he added, "attended Saint Chris."

The teachers were astonished. As were Fritz. "Where are you getting this information from, Chief?" Fritz asked. "There's been no news reports of that many alumni having drug issues."

"And there won't be any news reports. Their parents are well-connected, as you all know. They know how to keep their family horror stories out of the news. But that doesn't mean it's not happening, because it is. Pretend it's just those other people all you want. But that won't help a single kid at this school. Besides," he added, "there's plenty of addicts at this school already."

"I don't believe that," said another teacher.

"Neither do I," echoed another.

"Then don't believe it," said Boone.

They waited for him to say more to convince them, but he didn't bother. He knew that crowd too well.

"What do you want from us, Chief?" Dorsett asked.

"I need the staff here to do a better job at recognizing a kid in trouble. Those twenty kids didn't all just graduate and become dope addicts. It started before they graduated, but the cues were missed. I gave a list to Dean Johnson," he added. "I expect all of you to familiarize yourselves with that list as well. But of course you won't. But you should."

Then Boone exhaled. "Another kid nearly overdosed last night," he said, "and another one's on life support. This is a major-ass issue."

"I hear you haven't been able to find Dalbert Lee," a teacher said. "Don't you think *you* should be doing a better job?"

Boone exhaled. They knew how to push his buttons, Charly noticed. "It's just a matter of time," he said.

"You aren't exactly in position to lecture us," the teacher said. "That's all I'm saying."

"And I think your statistics are overblown, Chief," another teacher said. "Just because Peyton put a stain on our school's record, doesn't mean our current kids will do the same."

Everybody seemed shocked that the teacher would go there. They all looked at Boone. Charly knew who Peyton was. Boone had told her, on their one date, that Peyton was his kid brother, and he had died of a drug overdose.

But Boone was staring at the teacher. "Watch yourself, Gordy," he said.

"I'm just telling the truth," said the teacher. "Because your kid brother wasn't worth a damn, doesn't mean our current kids are going to follow in his footsteps."

But as the teacher said the words *wasn't worth a damn* in relation to Boone's kid brother, Boone was already coming for him.

Boone shocked the room when he jumped over a desk, grabbed the teacher by the catch of his collar, and jerked him up from his seat. "Say it again!" he yelled at the teacher as he slammed the teacher's back onto another desk while still holding his collar. "Say it again, you bastard!"

Many of the teachers had stood up and hastily moved away from Boone, including Charly. And like all of them, she was in shock too. Like all of them, she was staring at Boone too.

"Chief!" Fritz was yelling. "Stop this at once! Your behavior is intolerable!"

"Disrespect my brother again," Boone said to the teacher, ignoring all else, "and I'll tear you apart limb by limb. Do we understand each other, Gordy?"

"Yes, sir," the now-humbled teacher said. "We completely understand each other. I didn't mean it like that, Boone. I apologize, man. Just let me up!"

Boone stared at him for a few moments longer, and then he removed his hands from the teacher's collar with such a forceful push-away that the teacher fell onto the floor.

But nobody dared say a word. Even Fritz knew to stay out of the eye of the storm when Boone Ryan was raging.

But to Charly's shock, Boone actually glanced at her with a look of regret, she thought, and then he left the room.

Nobody noticed that little glance at all, and certainly not that look of regret in his eyes. But she did.

And as if nothing had ever happened, as soon as Boone left the room, chairs were put back in place, faculty sat back down - Gordy included, and Dorsett and Fritz continued the meeting. Their seeming unwillingness to so much as acknowledge the chief's unprofessional behavior, to Charly, was telling.

But after the faculty meeting, as she was leaving, a teacher whose name she did not know, passed her a note. She opened it.

Amos Yerkson needs you to come and see him, it said.

Charly looked after the teacher, to see if she could clarify, but the teacher was gone. Why in the world, Charly wondered, would Amos need to see her?

CHAPTER FIFTEEN

She woke up, the next morning, to the sound of rap music outside her window. It was the apartment, per her contract, that the school had selected for her. When she first arrived at the place, she was shocked that it was located in the heart of the hood. When she asked Minnie Fennel, the school's secretary, if there had been some mistake, Minnie made clear that there had not been any mistake. "You have every right not to stay there," Minnie had said, "but the cost of a different location would be incurred by you."

Since Charly was in no position to incur any such cost, she was staying right where they put her.

Even if it was in Low Town.

Even if it was in a complex once deemed, according to an old news article she saw online, to be ground zero in the town's growing crime wave.

It wasn't lost on her, either, as she made her way to the bathroom and turned on the shower water, that no other dean of students that had previously worked for the school had been assigned an apartment in Low Town. And she didn't even have to ask anybody if her theory was in fact true. She just knew it was.

But she wasn't going to let that bother her either. She'd lived in far worse places in her life after Darryl died. She could handle it.

Besides, she had a plan. She would stay right where the board placed her, let them continue to pay the rent as per her contract, and she would save her money. If she lasted in Kentucky, and was able to keep her job after that first probationary year, she'd take her nest egg and put down on a home of her own. In an area of town of her choosing. But she wasn't making any long-term commitments, or spending any big money on anything, until she had more to work with. It was still too iffy in Kentucky for her to feel completely at home.

But if that board thought that she was going to up and move right away and save them money - money she knew they didn't want to spend on the likes of her anyway, they didn't know her at all. The fact that they would put her up in such a place told her all she needed to know about their intentions. She wasn't going to let them know a damn thing about hers.

After showering and dressing, she made herself a hot cup of coffee. At least the place was clean and furnished, and supplied with all the creature comforts she would need. At least they did that right.

But she still felt some kind of way for how they weren't giving her the kind of respect her position accorded. But that would change, at least she hoped, once she proved her worth. And if it didn't, so be it. She'd, sadly, move on once again.

It was Saturday, she had slept later than she'd planned, and the complex she now lived in was humming with activity. She sat at the small kitchen table and opened her blinds. Young men were washing their old but well-maintained cars. Young ladies were parading around like peacocks in skimpy outfits. And children were running around as if life was theirs to have and hold. Charly smiled. Put the black lady in the black area of town around her people. That was what they did. But this seemed to be a happy place, filled with happy people, unlike that drab school that had been, on her first day on the job, a crime scene. Charly wasn't mad at all.

But she also couldn't stop thinking about that crime, and the fact that her supervisor had been accused of committing it.

And the fact that he had asked some teacher to give her that note. He wanted to see her.

She also couldn't stop thinking about his last words before he was arrested. *I didn't do it*, he said to Chief Ryan, although the chief didn't believe him.

But what if it was true, Charly wondered? What if Amos Yerkson was telling the truth?

She considered herself a good judge of character. And she'd seen in Amos Yerkson, when she first met him, a decent guy. A little too flirty for his own good? Yes. She saw that too. But a decent guy. Why would he kill that girl? But she also had to wonder why would he have lied about so many aspects of his relationship with that girl? He even lied about knowing her!

And Chief Ryan, she thought, as she sipped her coffee and looked out at her neighbors. There was something about him that she liked, if she were to be honest, but there was something about him that repulsed her too. His bossiness or arrogance or something. And the way he jacked up that teacher at the faculty meeting yesterday was a sight to behold. That man had a terrible temper. He was the absolute last guy on earth she needed to show any interest in.

And how he seemed so convinced of Yerkson's guilt right away defied logic to her too. Yes, Amos lied. And yes, it didn't look good for him. But surely it didn't look worthy of arresting him immediately. He tried to paint Amos as some conniving womanizer who'd kill another human being because she asked for more money. He didn't say she was blackmailing him. He only said she just wanted another handout. Charly knew bad men in her past, with her deceased husband being at the top of that list. Amos didn't appear to her to be that kind of person.

Besides, her parents always taught her to make up her mind about people for herself. They disavowed her when she took up with Darryl because they knew he was no good, and she refused to see it, but her upbringing stayed with her despite their abandonment. She had to make up her mind about Amos for herself. And it wasn't going to be based on the fact that Chief Ryan had arrested him.

And he did ask to see her.

And two people were already pointing the finger at somebody else, although she had no idea if the chief had already found that Dalbert Lee person and ruled him in or out as a suspect. He wasn't keeping her abreast of his investigation, and why should he?

But still. There were enough *what ifs* to intrigue Charly.

She got up, poured the last of her coffee down the drain, and grabbed her purse and keys. It was Saturday. There were a number of things she could have been doing and going to see Amos Yerkson, and Chief Ryan by default, wasn't supposed to be on that list. But it was.

CHAPTER SIXTEEN

Boone Ryan had a hangover. He was in his office and didn't want to be bothered. Leaned back in his chair, with a cold compress on his forehead, his bloodshot eyes were looking straight up at the ceiling. It needed a paint job.

He had been out at a pal's bachelor party in Lexington Friday night, and the wine, women and song went on throughout the night. His *not-so-young* body was now screaming for an aspirin. "Culpepper!" he yelled. "Dontay!"

Knocks were heard on the office door, and then Dontay Culpepper hurried in. "Yes, sir?" he asked as he entered. It was a fast response, but Dontay had been standing at the door, about to knock anyway, when the chief yelled his name. "You called?"

"Of course I called!" Boone said with a frown on his face. "Where's those aspirin I told you to bring to me? My head feels like a sledgehammer pounding on it!"

"I sent Betty over to Ethel Lynn's," Dontay said, "but she hasn't gotten back yet. But she's on her way. Any moment now she'll be here. And also, you have a guest."

Boone frowned again. "A guest? Who? Get rid of'em!"

"That's not possible, sir?"

"Why not?" Then he looked down from the ceiling at his officer. "Is it Freddy?"

"No, sir, it's not the mayor. It's the dean from Saint Christopher's."

Boone sat erect. Just to know that Dean Johnson was anywhere near him made him feel oddly excited. "The dean?" he asked. "She's here? What does she want?"

"I want to see Amos Yerkson," Charly, who was standing right behind Dontay, said as she moved from behind him.

When Boone saw her, he removed his compress and embarrassingly stood up. He could have killed Dontay for not warning him beforehand! "Dean Johnson," he said. "Come in!"

Charly walked on in.

Boone gave Dontay such a chilling look that Dontay almost ran away from the door. But his boss dismissed him before he could dismiss himself. "That'll be all," Boone said to him.

Dontay, happy to get out of there alive, quickly turned to leave.

"And Culpepper?" Boone said.

Almost a clean getaway, Dontay thought. "Yes, sir, Chief?"

"Next time I tell you to do something for me, you'd better do it yourself and not send somebody else. Get me those aspirin and get them now!"

Yes, sir! Right away, sir," Dontay said and stepped out, closing the door behind him.

Boone exhaled and motioned toward the chair in front of his desk. "Please have a seat," he said to Charly.

He stared at her as she sat down. She wore jeans that highlighted her curves and a tucked-in L.A. Raiders t-shirt that highlighted her sizeable breasts. Boone felt the heat as he sat behind his desk. There was no denying it, he thought. She gave him a rise every time she came near him.

"How can I help you, Miss Johnson?" he asked her. Then he smiled that charming smile Charly knew he used on all the ladies. "Or should I call you Charlene?"

She was surprised he didn't remember her nickname. And again, she felt unsettled. "Charly will do," she said.

He nodded. "Charly Johnson. Okay. Alright. I guess I can live with that," he added, which made no sense to Charly. "What can I do for you?" he asked her.

"I wish to see Amos Yerkson," she said again.

"Yeah, I know you do. But unfortunately, no. You can't."

"May I ask why not?"

"Because he's a murder suspect. I don't allow that."

Charly didn't understand. "You don't allow what?"

"My suspects to get too comfortable. They aren't on a picnic. They're in jail. Nobody's visiting Amos Yerkson except his lawyer. And since he doesn't have one, nobody's going to be visiting him any time soon."

"But how is that fair?" Charly asked.

Boone felt a little pissed that she would question his fairness. Who did she think she was? "It's not supposed to be fair," said Boone as he leaned back in his chair and began rocking. "But who said life was?"

"It should be," said Charly.

"But it's not," he said.

"But it should be."

Boone stared at her. Nobody got the last word on him. "But it's not," he said again, and with such finality that Charly knew not to push it.

She understood the type. Alpha male who would never be subservient to anybody. Which, she felt, was just a sign of his own insecurity. Which, she knew, was a sign for her to stay clear of him. But she left it alone. She was in no position to psychoanalyze anybody.

"As you know," she said, "I'm new in this town, and at Saint Christopher's."

"I heard," Boone said with that killer smile again. He continued rocking. He continued staring at her.

"Amos is my direct supervisor," Charly continued. "He was supposed to be the person to show me the ropes. I need to get some guidance from him."

Boone could see her frustration, but he also could tell she wasn't *that* frustrated. She was trying to manipulate him. She was savvy, which was a good thing in this dog-eat-dog town. She needed to be. But he was savvy too. "Come back on Monday after his hearing. If he's released, you can see him then."

They already refused to grant him bail. "And if he's not?" Charly asked.

"Then you can't."

Charly exhaled. This man was so hard! "What about Dalbert Lee?" she asked him.

Boone frowned. "What about him?"

"Two people came to me and said he might be involved with Rita Mae's death. I would have thought you'd investigate that."

"I haven't been able to find that joker to investigate anything."

"Oh," Charly said, and then rose to her feet.

But her sudden movement surprised Boone. "Where are you going?" he asked her.

It was a nonsensical question to be asked, she thought. "Home probably," she said.

"So you found a place?"

The questions this man asked! "The school found a place for me, yes."

"Oh, yeah? Where?" Even Boone didn't understand why he was so interested. Yeah, she was cute and had a slamming body. But so what? Around that town, he could get a piece of tail any time he wanted. What was the big deal about hers?

He didn't know. But something about that face even more so than her body kept him interested. It was as if he *needed* to know all about her.

Charley didn't understand his level of interest either. But at least he cared to ask, which was more than she could say about anybody else in this world. "On Rowe Avenue," she said. "At the Scotland Arms Apartment complex."

Boone's hard face frowned. Because he couldn't believe it. They put her up *there*? They put their dean of students in that hellhole? A classy lady like her? Those bastards!

His anger flashed all over his handsome face, surprising Charly. "You know the place?" she asked him.

He nodded. "Oh, yeah. I'm very familiar with that place."

Charly knew what that meant. It was a hotbed of crime over there. But it was what it was. "Anyway," she said, "I apologize for taking up any of your time."

"You aren't taking up my time. Sit down," he ordered.

Charly looked at him. Who did he think he was to order her about? No thank you, she thought. She turned to leave. "Have a nice day," she said.

Boone glanced down at her as she turned, and he found himself standing up himself. "Don't you want to see your supervisor?" he asked her.

Charly, surprised, turned back around. "I thought you said it was out of the question."

"Have a seat," he said. He didn't know why he was so bent on keeping her near him, but there it was. As obvious as the nose on his face.

If it would get her in to see Amos, Charly was game. She sat back down.

Boone sat down too. "Next time I tell you to do something," he said to her, "I expect you to do it."

Charly stared at him. The nerve he's got! "And why would you expect that?" she asked him.

"Because I told you to," he responded.

"You're not my boss, Chief Ryan."

Ryan glanced down at her, and then back up into her soft, golden-brown eyes. "Not yet," he said.

It wasn't just odd to Charly, it was downright crazy. Since she wasn't interested in anymore crazy in her life, she didn't even pursue it. "Are you saying I can see him now?" she asked.

Boone was rocking and staring at her. What in the world would possess him to change his rules for her? He still didn't understand it. But he stopped rocking and stood to his feet. He walked from around his desk and motioned for her to rise and, apparently, follow him.

Hopeful that it meant she was about to see Amos and not only get clarity on his situation, but clarity on her job duties, she stood to her feet ready to follow his lead. But he, instead, motioned again. This time for her to go in front of him. But when she moved away from her chair to do just that, he had invaded her personal space and was too close. They brushed against each other. And then looked into each other's eyes.

Boone saw a sadness in her eyes. She saw pain in his.

Two broken people did not need to ever hook up, and they both knew it.

Boone backed up just enough for Charly to safely get around him.

Boone and Charly didn't know it, but as they were meeting in his office, they were the hot topic of conversation in the squad room. And all of the guys, except for Morley and Dontay, were betting on her complete and utter failure to ever convince their irascible chief to let her anywhere near his prisoner.

"Pigs will fly," Sarge said, "before Boone Ryan allow that woman to visit with a murder suspect."

"But that's why she came," said Dontay.

"I know why she came," Sarge shot back. "But I'm telling you it's not going to happen."

"She does have big boobs," Morley said. "You know how chief loves those big women."

"The word is voluptuous women," said Dontay. "She's not big."

"Back in my day," said Sarge, "women had a little meat on their bones. At least the good looking ones did. It was expected. But nowadays, if you're not thin as a rail, you're fat. It's insane."

"I still say," Morley said, "that her boobs will get her that visit she wants with Amos Yerkson. If I know Chief, and I think I do, she'll get in."

"I know him too," Sarge said. "I may not have worked for him as long as you have, but I know him. You're as wrong as the day is long, Morley," he said.

"Wanna bet?" Morley asked.

"Hell yeah," said Sarge. "How much?"

"Lunch tomorrow."

Sarge laughed. "That's nothing!" he said. "I say a hundred bucks. Put your money where your mouth is."

"Okay, okay," Morley said. "You wanna play the big man, go right ahead."

"That's a lot of money," Dontay warned his mentor Morley.

But Morley was smiling. "I got this, little one," he said. Then he said to Sarge: "You're on. A hundred bucks it is."

Sarge laughed. "That's going to be one payout I'm really going to enjoy," he said.

Until the door to Chief Ryan's office opened again, and the chief and Charly walked out. "Let Dean Johnson see Amos for a few minutes," Boone said to Sarge.

Morley and Dontay grinned. Sarge couldn't believe it. "But sir, I thought you said nobody was allowed--"

The chief gave him that chilling look.

"Yes, sir," Sarge said, understanding he'd crossed the line, and rose to his feet. "Right this way, Miss," he said.

Charly looked back at Boone. "Thank you," she said to him.

Boone actually smiled at her, which shocked the daylights out of his men, and then Sarge escorted her towards the cells.

But every man in that squad room kept their eyes on Boone. They watched him as he seemed to lustfully watch her body make its way down the hall with Sarge.

When they turned a corner and the view was gone, and Boone turned to head back into his office, it was only then did he realize his men were staring at him as he had been staring at Charly. His smile disappeared, and he frowned. "What the hell are y'all looking at?" he asked angrily, and every one of them got back to work.

Boone then realized Dontay was still in the squad room, and his headache that had subsided while Charly was around, had returned monster-style. "I thought I told you to get me some aspirin," he said to him.

"I called Betty and she said she has the aspirin and is heading back. I didn't see the point in me going to get more aspirin too."

"You didn't see the point? Who the hell are you?" Then he pointed at Dontay. "If Betty isn't coming through that door in thirty seconds, you're fired!" Boone yelled, and walked back into his office, slamming the door behind him.

The squad room laughed as Dontay jumped from his desk and ran out of the squad room. His goal: grab those aspirin from Betty and rush them upstairs himself.

But Morley wasn't laughing at Dontay. He was a good kid, and he knew Boone liked the kid. Morley was shaking his head at Boone. "He's got another hangover," he said. "What a disgrace."

"Tell it to his face," another officer said.

"No thanks," said Morley, and they all laughed again.

But inside Boone's office, after he had slammed the door, it wasn't a laughing matter for him. Mainly because he had exposed himself so completely. Not just to his men, which was bad enough, but to Charly too. What on earth was he doing? He didn't even know her, but was so quick to give her anything she asked for. Even breaking his ironclad rule against allowing outsiders to see murder suspects. She must think of him as some pervert with a hard-on who'd do anything for a piece of good looking tail. Which wasn't true.

But something more was bothering him too. There were perfectly fine people living in Low Town, but there were all kinds of crooks and cons and even convicted murderers living there too. It wasn't a safe environment by any stretch of the imagination. And that so-called prestigious school put her up in a place like that? A good girl like her?

Then he had to catch himself. What was so good about her? He didn't really know her from a hole in the wall! What was wrong with him?

And then his head began pounding even more, reminding him he had his own problems. Why was he trying to take on hers?

But as soon as he got back behind his desk, and pulled out the file of another cold case he was trying to clear, her fresh, pretty face flashed across his mind yet again.

And the fact that those bastards put her up in a place like that.

He was angry all over again.

CHAPTER SEVENTEEN

The drive back to the office, to retrieve the file Amos had set up for her, was a slow drive on a lazy Saturday afternoon. To her shock, the chief had allowed her to spend nearly two hours with Amos. They talked, mainly about the school and her duties there. And when Amos told her that he had set up an entire orientation file for her, she was elated. She knew she liked him for a reason.

But they didn't hardly talk at all about Rita Mae Brown, which she thought was the reason he wanted to see her.

But Amos said he didn't kill her, and left it at that.

Charly wanted to know why he didn't come clean with the chief from the get-go. That if he would not have lied he might not have been arrested. But Amos would have none of that.

"He was going to arrest me regardless," Amos had responded to her. "There's no evidence that I did a thing to that young lady, because I never laid a hand on her, but you can't tell people like Boone

Ryan anything that doesn't comport with what they already believe."

"But what if the jury doesn't believe you?" Charly asked him.

"It won't get to that," Amos said. "Don't worry about me. Worry about yourself."

Charly frowned. "Then why did you ask me to come see you?"

"I wanted to tell you where you could find the orientation packet I put together for you. And I wanted to answer any questions you might have about your job responsibilities."

Charly was surprised. It was all about what he could do for her. She told him that Minnie had already given her the key to the file cabinet, but she did ask him lots of questions. For her, it turned out to be a very productive couple hours. Not so much for him, however. But that was his choice.

But as she drove slowly back to the office, along the long stretch of backroads that small towns always seemed to have, and Hemingway was no exception, she also couldn't stop thinking about another man at that police station.

Robert Boone Ryan.

The chief of police.

The sergeant who took her in back to see Amos Yerkson said he'd never seen anything like it.

When she asked him anything like what, he said the chief never allowed anybody from the outside to see his prisoners. Attorneys only, he'd said. But the chief not only allowed Charly to see Amos, but he allowed her to spend two hours with him!

And when her two hours were up, it was the chief himself, not his sergeant, who walked her back up front and, also, to her car.

Not that it meant anything profound. She knew it didn't. But it just made her feel . . . special? Different? She couldn't really describe it. But she did appreciate it. Despite the fact that Amos had warned her off of Chief Ryan the first day they met, and despite the fact that she already could tell he was a hardcore womanizer from way back, she appreciated his kind gesture toward her. He didn't have to allow her two minutes with Amos, let along two hours.

"What is his problem?" Charly found herself asking as she looked through her rearview mirror and saw a car tailgating her. There was another lane right beside them. A completely empty lane, and he could easily go around her. But he chose to ride her bumper.

She decided to speed up a little. But that didn't help. He sped up too and continued to ride her bumper.

She decided to slow down. Maybe he'd go around then.

But that didn't help either. He slowed down too.

And when she decided to move over into the fast lane, and allow him to drive on, she became worried when he moved over into the same lane she had moved into, and continued to ride her bumper.

They were the only two cars on that particular stretch of backroad. And just like that, the man she had been thinking about, Chief Ryan, came to mind. He believed he was the kind of man who would straighten that character out, or at least send a squad car to do so. She immediately grabbed her cell phone.

But just as she was about to dial 911, the car behind her suddenly moved back over into the right-hand lane and sped up.

But as he sped up, he swerved toward her, causing her to swerve away from him with the reckless swerve of a person surprised. Her car ran off of the road in a fast dash and sped onto the gravel as she tried with all she had to correct her overcorrection and avoid losing total control of the wheel. It was an epic battle as she had to rise out of her seat to maintain control. But it was a battle she was losing badly.

Her car kept veering further along the graveled path as it lifted and leaned onto two wheels. But then, just as she thought she was steering it back toward the street and back onto all fours, her Sentra slammed broadside into what felt like a steel pole to Charly, but was actually a sweetgum tree.

The red sedan that had caused the kerfuffle to begin with waited until it was all over, and then drove away at an unrushed speed, as if nothing had ever happened.

Back at the station, Dontay was answering a call and Boone was interrogating his sergeant, who, once again, approved yet another sick leave.

"And what did you say?" Boone asked his second-in-command, as he stood beside Sarge's desk.

"I told him I hope he feels better," Sarge said.

"You hope he feels better?" Boone responded angrily. "Are you out of your mind? You tell him to get his skinny ass in here and get in here now! We're already undermanned. Having a stomach ache is no excuse for not bringing your ass to work."

"People get sick, Chief."

"So what? Looking at the lot of you make me sick every day." His men laughed. "But I come to work. I do my job. You call him back and tell him either he get his ass into this station or don't bother to show his face around here ever again!"

Dontay hung up the phone at his desk, grabbed the manifest writeup and hurried to Sarge's desk.

"I can't tell him that, Chief," Sarge said.

Boone looked at him as if he was nuts defying him.

"What I mean is," Sarge said, realizing he might have overstepped his bounds, "we don't wanna lose him. He's a good cop."

"He's an average cop still on probation. Call him," Boone ordered.

Dontay handed Sarge the manifest. "What's the call?" Sarge asked him.

"Car wreck," Dontay responded. "One car accident from the reports I'm getting. That new dean was the driver."

Boone was about to continue his argument with Sarge, when he heard what Dontay said. He looked at Dontay. "The new dean?"

Dontay nodded. "Yes, sir. They say she was the driver."

Boone's heart began to squeeze. "Is she alright?"

It was an odd question to Dontay. He didn't even ask the uniforms on scene. "I don't know, sir. I didn't think to--"

"Where did it happen?"

"On Bassett Road, over by the Granger Farm. I'm heading over there right now."

"I'll take it," Boone said, moving away from Sarge's desk. "You get back to work." And then Boone began walking hurriedly, and then he began running, out of the squad room.

Dontay, shocked, looked at Sarge. The chief had never taken a car wreck call before.

Sarge shook his head. "Don't look at me. I ain't never seen nothing like it," he said, "and I been working for that man a very long time."

CHAPTER EIGHTEEN

She was sitting in the back of an ambulance when Boone's Ferrari sped onto the scene. The uniformed officers already there, and the paramedics too, were surprised to see the chief show up. But Boone didn't care about any of that. He parked his car behind the ambulance, got out, and made his way toward Charly without taking his eyes off of her.

Charly was still dazed, but okay, as she allowed the paramedics to check her vitals and ask her numerous questions. She didn't know the town's protocol or common ways, so she wasn't as surprised as the others to see Boone arrive. She was glad to see him.

"Hey," she said when he walked up. The paramedics spoke to the chief, too, and moved aside for him.

"How is she?" he asked, not her, but the paramedics.

"All her vitals checked out," said the older medic. "And she says she's fine."

"I didn't ask you what she said," Boone said. "What do you say?"

Charly looked at the medic. He didn't seem embarrassed at all. He, like most people in this town, was apparently used to their chief's gruffness. "She's okay," the older medic said. "We didn't find any issues."

"I want her transported to the hospital so they can run tests, just to be safe."

"Oh, no, Chief," Charly interjected. "That absolutely won't be necessary."

Boone looked at her. His face was as serious as if he was a doctor examining her. "I want to make sure there's nothing internal going on," he said.

"I'm fine," Charly said firmly.

She could tell Boone didn't like his orders to be questioned. He looked at the paramedics. "Give me a few minutes," he said, "and then you will be transporting her to the hospital."

"Yes, sir," the older medic said as he glanced at Charly, and then both medics moved away from them.

"I don't need to go to any hospital, Chief," Charly said. "I wasn't injured." He didn't like her speaking up, but that was tough. It was her body. Her call.

"I want you checked out," Boone said.

"But for what? I'm fine."

"Let the doctors be the judge of that," Boone said. "I've seen too many people claim they're fine at the scene, and they feel fine, only to have unchecked internal injuries that eventually do them in. Better safe than sorry."

Charly exhaled. She knew what he said was true too. But she hated doctors and hospitals!

"What happened?" Boone asked her.

"I was driving along and then this red sedan drives up behind me, riding my bumper. I go faster, I slow down, I move over, but they just kept riding me. And then, when it looks like they're leaving, they swerved toward my car, and I swerved away from their car and lost control. I ended up on two wheels and then I ran into that tree." She pointed to the tree.

Boone looked. There appeared to be a little scuff mark on the big tree, but it looked otherwise fine. Then he glanced at her car. But for a noticeable indentation on the hood, it looked okay too.

"It's just a little banged up," she said of her car, "but thank God it's still running."

"I'll have one of my men take it to the hospital," Boone said, "because that's where you need to go. And guess what? That's where you're going."

Charly stared at him. What kind of caveman was he? Did he not realize it was the twenty-first century? Did he not realize women were liberated long ago? But she knew it wasn't just a woman thing. He ordered men around too.

But deep down, she knew he was right. It was always better safe than sorry.

"Did you get a look at the driver?" Boone asked her.

Charly shook her head. "One of your officers asked me the same thing. But like I told him, It was too fast for me to see any real features. They appeared to be young, maybe as young as seventeen-eighteen-year-olds, I know that."

"They?" Boone asked. "It was more than one?"

"The driver and a passenger, yes. Both were males. Both were white. One appeared to have long hair. And they both were laughing a lot."

Boone nodded. "Okay," he said, and took her by the arm. "Let's get you checked out."

"Not in an ambulance, please," Charly said, rising to her feet as he assisted her up. "I'll drive myself there."

"You're do no such thing," Boone said firmly. Then he told the paramedics they could leave. Told one of the two uniformed officers to drive her car to the hospital where she could retrieve it after she was checked out. And then he placed her into his Ferrari.

And Chief Ryan personally drove her to the hospital.

And waited for what turned out to be nearly three hours, until all tests were run and the doctor gave her the all-clear.

But he realized, as he watched her at that hospital, that he was developing feelings for her that went well beyond the sexual. He didn't understand why, and he didn't like the feeling. It made him feel too vulnerable, as if she was pulling his strings. As if she had all the power in their twosome.

He was never going to allow that.

That was why, when the doctor told him that her tests were all negative, he didn't wait to say goodbye to her. His man had driven her car to the hospital. She had wheels to get home. He just left.

But for a man as busy as the chief to go to the hospital at all, Charly was impressed. The nurses and doctors, who all knew the chief, were too. It was a very nice gesture for him to wait around like that, they said. Some of the nurses even said, outside of the chief's presence, that he generally treated females like pieces of meat. "You must be a very inviting piece of meat," one of the male nurses joked.

But for Charly she didn't see it that way at all. It wasn't a physical thing to her: it was an emotional thing. His kindness was like a balm to her soul when she needed it the most. She was a stranger in a town nobody really wanted her in. She felt alone and isolated at home; bullied and mistreated on the job. And although she was trying to make the best out of her bad situation, and she stood up for herself at every turn on that job, it was still, even before the accident, a bad situation.

Chief Ryan was turning out to be an ally; an unlikely spark of light in her life. And even more than that the way he went out of his way to be kind to her. In her entire life, nobody had ever treated her the way he was treating her.

Nobody.

Because just like Sarge, Charly had never seen anything like it either.

CHAPTER NINETEEN

After returning to her office and working several more hours, reviewing all of the duties and responsibilities on the manifest Amos had prepared for her, she drove back to her apartment in Low Town. All she wanted was to soak in her tub and forget about her tough situation. But as soon as she turned into the complex, and made her way toward the row of one-story apartments where her apartment was located, she nearly slammed on brakes.

She couldn't believe it. That same red sportscar was parked in front of her apartment, but this time there was no mystery about it. The chief himself was standing outside of the car, leaned against it, with his muscular legs crossed at the ankle and his burly arms folded. And instead of watching her arrival, his entire focus seemed to be on a group of young black and Hispanic men sitting on the hood of their muscle car, listening to rap music, and drinking beer.

The chief, it seemed to Charly, was giving them that stare of intimidation, and she didn't like it. She sped up, parked her Nissan next to his car, and got out. She had a vanilla folder with her: homework.

"May I help you, Chief?" she asked as she walked around the front of her car toward him.

"How are you?" he asked, still staring at those guys.

"I'm fine. The doctors said all of my tests were negative. May I help you?"

Boone finally looked away from the young men. When he saw Charly standing there, looking so vulnerable it seemed to him, although he couldn't say why he felt that way, he exhaled. "Just thought I'd drop by," he said.

Charly didn't know what to say to that.

"You doing okay then?" he asked her.

She nodded. "Yes, I'm fine."

"Those guys giving you any trouble?"

Charly was offended by that insinuation. "Why would they give me trouble, Chief?" she asked him.

"Why? Because all of them have rap sheets twenty pages deep at least. From murder, rape, assault, drugs, you name it. That's why."

Charly was a little shaken by the litany of crimes he recited. She knew she wasn't dealing with choirboys, but damn. Murder? Rape? An anguished look appeared in her eyes as if that was the last thing she needed to hear.

And Boone saw that look. He hated to tell her that. But it was the truth. Porch and his boys were bad news, and he wanted them to know that he had his eyes on them. He wanted them to know that Charly Johnson was off limits.

They were fearless young men, but they feared Boone Ryan and Boone knew it.

"Stay away from them," Boone warned Charly, "and they'll stay away from you."

"What makes you so sure of that?" Charly asked him.

"Because I'm here. They know you're off limits now."

At first, Charly wondered if the chief was overstating his power over those young men. But as she looked into his hard eyes, she realized he wasn't overstating a thing. And she was pleased that he wasn't. "Okay," she said.

"Okay good," he said, and then he stood erect and began opening his car door.

Charly was thrown. That was it? He came all this way to show those boys to leave her alone? He didn't even know when she'd get there. "How long have you been here?" she asked him.

"Not that long," was all Boone would say.

"And you came by just to remind those guys that you knew me?"

"Yeah," Boone said. "Trust me, they needed to know that."

Charly nodded. She wasn't going that far to say she actually trusted him, but she appreciated him for sure. "Thank you," she said. "You came all this way for that. That was kind of you."

"Oh, that reminds me. I did come by for something else."

"Uh-oh," Charly said. "What else?" She somehow figured the something else was probably the main thing. "I don't owe you money, do I?"

Boone laughed. "Nothing like that," he said. "But I did come by to, yes, remind those fellars, but also to ask you something."

"Yes?"

"What are you doing tonight?" he asked her.

She had planned to take a bath and read a book. She could have told him that, since it did qualify as *something*. But she didn't go there. "Nothing," she said.

Boone seemed encouraged by her response. "How about dinner?"

Charly was confused. "But you've already alerted me about the kids I need to be on the lookout for."

"Not that kind of dinner," he said. He wanted to make himself clear as to what he wanted this time. "It's not about work. It's going out, hanging out, having dinner. How about dinner?"

A part of Charly wanted to run away from him as fast as she could. There was a side of him that she'd only gotten glimpses of, where he seemed so domineering and obnoxious and mean to his core that it was disturbing in its harshness. Hurt people tended to hurt people, and he seemed to be the classic hurt guy.

But there was another side to him. The side that defended her at Rita Mae Brown's house. The side that broke his own rule and allowed her to see Amos Yerkson. The side that took her to that hospital and stayed far longer than seemed appropriate. The side that was always asking if she was okay every time she saw him.

She went with that side.

"Dinner sounds good," she said.

Boone nodded. He was so pleased that he wanted to smile. But he didn't. Because as pleased as he was, he was also a little alarmed.

But when he was in, he was all in. They were going out on a real date this time. There would be no meeting him at the restaurant. "I'll pick you up at eight," he said, and got into his car before she could even bring up any *I'll meet you there* nonsense.

She fully expected him, after he got into his car, to speed away the way he did at the Browns, but he didn't. He, in fact, remained right where he was parked until she had gone inside of her home and locked her door. When she looked out of the peephole, he was just pulling off.

She leaned against that door after he had driven away. There was something about that man that was blowing her mind. Blowing. Her. Mind! But it was crazy. She was brand new in this town. She was working a job for people who didn't even want her there. And she was falling for a guy who had all the markings of another womanizer just like Darryl was? It was insane!

But she still smiled. She hadn't been on a date in years. Not once after her husband died, and hardly at all when he was living.

But she also knew she had to be real clear about what the chief of police asking her out on that date truly meant. In other words, it wasn't that serious to him and she'd better not make it serious to her. It was just a date. That was all. It didn't mean a darn thing to him in the long scheme of things, and it wasn't going to mean a darn thing to her. But at least, she also thought, it was something to look forward to.

Instead of hopping in the tub right away, as had been her plan, she hurried to her bedroom, threw open her closet door, and began searching frantically but happily for just the right outfit to wear.

CHAPTER TWENTY

"What in blazes are you doing?"

Boone Ryan was standing in his bedroom mirror staring at himself, in the fifth designer suit he had tried on. The four other suits he had tried on, reviewed in that mirror, and rejected, were tossed all over his bed. He, too, was searching for the right outfit to wear. His cousin and the mayor of Hemingway, Freddy Ryan, had walked in amused.

"How did you get in my house?" Boone asked as he continued to stare at himself in the mirror.

"I have a key, remember? You gave me a key."

"Remind me to take it back."

"What in blazes are you doing?" Freddy asked him again.

"What does it look like? I'm getting dressed."

"What's the big occasion?"

Boone didn't respond.

Freddy propped down sideways on Boone's big poster bed, his big body half lying down, and looked at the discarded suits that covered the bed. "There must be fifty-thousand-dollars-worth of clothing you just tossed aside like this. Which is saying something even for you." He looked at his cousin. "What's going on?"

But Boone wasn't ready to go there, not even with a cousin who was also his best friend. He just exhaled as if he was about to discard the suit he was trying on too.

Freddy frowned. "What's the matter?" he asked him.

"I look fat in this thing," Boone said.

Freddy couldn't believe it. "What?"

"I look fat. I don't want people to think I let myself go."

At first Freddy just stared at Boone as if somebody had kidnapped his cousin. And then he broke out laughing.

"It's not funny," Boone said.

"Sorry, but come on, Robert!" Freddy said. "When in our lifetime have you given a flip nickel about what people thought? You throw aside these ten-thousand-dollar suits like you grabbed them from a picnic table at the Salvation Army. You shower, brush your teeth, but don't even bother to comb your hair. You get a spit shine on your shoes almost every single day, but will wear mix-matched socks like it was no big deal at all. And right in front of the shoe-shine man! And you expect me to believe that you suddenly care what people think about you gaining a little weight?"

But Boone remained dead serious. He turned to the side. He smoothed down his suit coat. But no matter how he sliced it, he didn't think he was looking his best. When he really wanted to look his best.

But Freddy was also right.

Why give a damn?

He grabbed his wallet and the change he had sitting on the dresser and began to place them in his pants pockets. Then he looked at his cousin through the mirror. "How you doing?" he asked him.

Freddy smiled. "Better than you apparently." Freddy sat up. "What's up? I know you didn't ask me to drop by your house for the hell of it."

"I need you to talk to Fritz," Boone said.

Freddy was puzzled. "Fritz Hollingsworth?"

"He's the only Fritz I know."

"What you need me to talk to him about? He gave me the latest info on that killing over at the school, unlike my police chief whose job it is to keep me informed."

"I need you to talk to Fritz," Boone said again.

"What about?"

"The new dean of students over at Saint Chris. Her contract stipulated that the board of directors would select and pay for housing during her first year under their employment."

Freddy nodded. "That's the standard contract all of their senior staff gets. They're supposed to get her an apartment, or a house if they prefer. But that's up to them. What? They didn't provide housing for her?"

"They provided it alright. They got her an apartment in Low Town."

Freddy frowned. "Are you serious? They put their dean of students over there?"

Boone nodded. "That's exactly what they did. And we both know why," Boone added, looking through the mirror at his cousin again.

Freddy shook his head. "They need to cut that crap out," he said.

"You'll talk to him then?"

"Of course I will," said Freddy, frowning. "I don't play that either."

Then he continued to stare at Boone. "I saw that video," he said.

Boone glanced at him.

"Billy Ray Rogers has hired an attorney. He says he's going to file a lawsuit against the town for police brutality."

"He won't--"

"Don't intimidate him, Boone," said Freddy. "Stace already dropped the charges against him. When he does decide what he wants to do, we plan to settle out of court, if he'll take it, for twenty thousand bucks."

Boone exhaled.

"If that happens, you'll owe the town twenty thousand bucks."

"Wait on it," Boone said although Freddy knew he'd pay up.

"It'll just be two less suits you buy next year," Freddy said. "You can handle it."

But then Freddy looked as Boone sat down on the bed beside him and began putting on those expensive, well-shined dress shoes he had mentioned. "But getting back to that dean," Freddy said. "The question is," he added, "why are you so concerned?"

"Don't know what you mean," Boone said.

"I mean what I said. Why are you so concerned about where they housed her?"

"She doesn't need to be in any crime-infested area like that."

"And what else?"

"It's not safe."

"And?" Freddy asked again. He knew his cousin far too well.

"And that's it," said Boone. "Tell Fritz and that gang to do better than that."

Freddy stared at Boone.

Boone, feeling exposed, frowned. "What are you staring at me for?" he asked as he put on his second shoe and stood up.

"Who says I'm staring?"

"I say it."

"Sorry," Freddy said as he continued to stare at his cousin.

"Kiss my ass," Boone said, and began leaving out of his bedroom.

Freddy laughed. "You forgot to comb your hair," he reminded him.

Boone, at first, kept walking, which was exactly what Freddy expected him to do. He also expected him to tell him what he could do with that comb.

But then, to Freddy's total shock, Boone didn't say a word. Boone, instead, returned to the dresser, grabbed the comb, and actually combed his thick brown hair in place. Then he tossed the comb back onto the dresser, glanced at his cousin as if he dared him to say a word to him, and left.

Freddy smiled and shook his head. "Wow," he said. He'd never known his cousin to fall this hard for anybody. And he knew that was what was happening, even if Boone didn't know it himself.

Then Freddy stood up, too, and began heading out of Boone's bedroom. *Who in the world*, he wondered as he walked out, *is this dean*?

CHAPTER TWENTY-ONE

She was stepping out of her apartment just as he had gotten out of his car and was heading for her front door. Boone smiled. Most women would see a man coming but wouldn't dare open the door before he knocked. They didn't want to look desperate, was how they rationalized it. But to Boone they were just being pretentious. They knew he was coming to pick them up. Why not come on out?

But that was why he liked Charly. There didn't appear to be a pretentious bone in her nice, shapely body, he thought, as his eyes couldn't help but to trail down that body.

She wore a very nice bright-blue, form-fitting dress that showed off every inch of her curves. Criss-crossed at the top, it also showed off her big breasts. Boone realized he was getting hard just watching her.

"Hey," he said, smiling, to keep her eyes focused on his eyes and not his suddenly expanded midsection. "How are you?"

"I'm good," Charly said, smiling too. And she meant it. She actually liked the idea of going out for a change. "And you?"

"Good," Boone said. "Thank you for being on time," he added.

"Thank *you* for being on time," Charly said, since she tried to be a stickler too. They both laughed.

But as Boone escorted her to his car, he also took a peep at the young men a little further away that sat on a car smoking and drinking beer, listening to rap music, and watching them.

But Charly wasn't thinking about those guys, despite their long rap sheets. They weren't bothering her at all. Her thought was in front of her. He was the one she was most worried about, as he opened his front passenger car door for her.

She realized, when he first drove up, that he was driving a different car. It was already surprising that a policeman could afford a Ferrari. But a Mercedes too? And not any Mercedes. An elegant, black, S-class Maybach. Such extravagance reeked of corruption to Charly. "Where's the Ferrari?" she asked him.

Boone looked at her. "Say again?"

"This is a Mercedes," Charly said. "What happened to your Ferrari?"

"Nothing's happened to it," Boone said. She looked so serious, he thought. "I figured you'd have more leg room in this."

"Oh. Okay," Charly said, as she got into the beautiful automobile.

But she still couldn't get pass it. What kind of police chief, she wondered, could afford a Ferrari, let alone what looked like a nearly-brand new S-class Mercedes? Was he some corrupt cop who took graft to make ends meet? She'd be shocked if that was true. There was something too strident about the man to be in anybody's pocket. But she didn't know him like that. He could be as crooked as Darryl.

Boone, not privy to her inner thoughts, closed the door after she sat down and made his way to the driver side. When he got in, the car automatically cranked up and he looked at her. "Ready or not," he said, "here we go." And he drove them away.

But Charly felt as if he was saying a whole lot more.

Ready or not, here we go.

Why she felt that way? She couldn't say. But she felt it.

The restaurant he had chosen wasn't even in Hemingway. It was in Lexington, some twenty miles outside of Hemingway. And unlike Danley's, the first restaurant he had taken her to for their business dinner, this was elegant with a capital E.

It was a beautiful, sprawling restaurant with valet service and a roof-deck terrace. And what she liked about the chief was the fact that when the valet went to open her door, he, instead, hurried around to open it himself. And he took her hand to help her out of the car. Simple things, she knew, that any self-respecting man would do. But it had been a long time since a man had done so for her.

But they were so close as she got out of his car, that she could smell his fresh cologne and could see the beauty of his color-changing irises as she brushed past him. She was on a date with a very sexy man, she realized, as he closed the door, buttoned his Armani suit coat, and then briefly placed his hand on the small of her back as he escorted her inside the restaurant.

That brief moment evoked yet another strange feeling for Charly. It had been a long time, since before Darryl died, that she could recall any man touching her that intimately. And it felt good. She actually wished he'd kept his hand right there instead of removing it once he apparently realized he was touching her.

Once seated and their drink orders taken, the chief had to field a phone call from the station. As he talked to his guys, Charly looked around. There was a dance floor in the restaurant, and many couples had populated it. The music playing wasn't necessarily to her liking: more like elevator music to her. But those couples seemed to be having a ball.

But then a less elevator music type song came on, a Celine Dion tune, and she began to bob her head to the sound too.

Boone noticed Charly was watching the dance floor as he ended his phone call. She apparently liked to dance. He did too. But not yet. He needed to get to know this woman.

"Nice place," she said when she realized he was no longer on his phone.

"Yeah, it is. I enjoy it whenever I'm in town. Which is often."

"Oh, okay," Charly said. "You have business in Lexington?"

If partying with some of his wilder friends, and sleeping around with some of his wilder women qualified as business, then he had plenty in

Lexington. "I know some people here," was all he decided to say.

Charly understood that response. It was a non-response as far as she was concerned. Which was fine. She needed to mind her own business anyway.

"What about you?" he asked her.

She looked at him. "What about me?"

"Tell me about yourself." Boone leaned back, turned sideways, and crossed his legs. "Where are you from?" he asked her.

"Texas originally."

Boone smiled. "Really? I wouldn't have taken you for a Texas girl."

"That's because I was adopted when I was a baby, and my family relocated to California when I was something like two or three."

"Ah. Got cha. So you're a California girl."

Charly smiled. "Yes."

"A Malibu Barbie."

"Ha!" Charly said with a smile. "Not hardly."

Boone grinned. But he got right back on topic. "What's it like being adopted?"

"Not great for me."

"What do you mean?"

"I had the kind of adopted family that felt, whenever I disappointed them or disobeyed them, that they could give me back. When I married Darryl, whom they despised, they gave me back."

"That's cold," Boone said.

Charly nodded. That sounded about right, she thought.

"I know you aren't married now, but have you ever been married?" Boone asked her.

"Yes. He died."

"That's right. But how long ago was it?"

"Three years ago."

"What happened? He was ill? Got in an accident?"

"He stole money from the mob and was executed."

Boone leaned his head back. "Whoa," he said. "Are you serious?"

Charly nodded. "I'm afraid so."

"But what makes you so sure that's what happened?" he asked her.

"I was there when it happened. And because I saw his killer, he was trying to execute me too."

Boone's heart ached for her. He could hardly believe it. "You? Are you serious?"

Charly nodded. She wished she wasn't.

"What happened to the killer?" he asked. "Did he get away?'

"No. I was able to identify him in a book of mugshots. After they stopped looking suspiciously at me anyway."

"And they found him?"

Charly nodded. "They found him. There was a trial. I testified for the prosecution, and he was sentenced to Life in prison without the possibility of parole."

Boone was pleased to hear that. "Well that's good," he said.

"He died in his first year there."

Boone nodded. "That's even better. But you don't worry about any other members of the mob looking for you?"

"I was right there in L.A. for three solid years after Darryl died. Darryl was my husband's name, by the way. Nobody bothered me then. Besides, Darryl took that money. I didn't. And that killer was a hired gun. He wasn't in any mob family. They left me alone."

"Thank God for that."

Charly nodded as the waiter brought their drinks. "I do," she said.

When the waiter took their food orders and left, Boone looked at Charly. "How do you feel about all of that? Still too painful to talk about?"

Charly nodded. "Not really, no. It just never comes up. And how do I feel? I feel like I made it to the other side. I'm grateful."

"But it hasn't been easy?"

"Lord, no," Charly said as if he'd just said the understatement of the decade. "It's been hell. The Feds took everything I owned because Darryl had stolen what they claimed was legitimate, not mob money. Darryl told me it was mob money. The guy who killed him was a hit man for the mob. So go figure. But I lost it all. I had to start from the bottom again when, before Darryl died, I was heading straight for the top. It's been tough."

Boone stared at her. He could only imagine.

"What about you?" Charly asked him. "What's your story?"

"Nothing like yours," Boone said and they both smiled.

But then Boone's look turned decidedly sad. Charly wanted to ask him what was that about, but she didn't. She waited for him to tell her. But he didn't.

"Were you born and raised here in Kentucky?" she asked him.

"Yep."

"In Hemingway?"

"Yep."

"And you prefer to be called Boone rather than Robert?"

"I think so, yeah."

"Why do they call you Boone anyway?"

"They nicknamed me after Daniel Boone, the greatest Kentuckian to ever live. I used to be a searcher, my old man said, just like Boone. I could never stay anywhere too long. I was always searching."

"Although you stayed in Kentucky your whole life."

"Actually, I didn't. Like all of my siblings, as a very young man I took off to find my fame and fortune too. And I became a very successful businessman in just five short years. Very successful. But after my kid brother died, my mother needed me, so I returned home. I decided to become a cop and right the wrongs in this town, as I saw them anyway. I liked it, so I stayed."

"Ever got married? Ever had kids?"

"Never married, no."

"Kids?"

There was a hesitation in Boone. A long one. Then he answered, "No. She died."

Charly's heart dropped. "Ah, man. I'm so sorry. What's her name?"

Boone looked at Charly. He appreciated that she didn't act as if his little girl was now nameless because she was gone. "Courtney," he said. "Her name's Courtney."

Charly smiled. "That's a pretty name. I'm sure she was adorable."

Boone smiled a weak, painful smile. "She was. She was the best thing that ever happened to me."

"How old was she?"

Boone exhaled. "Two," he said.

Charly nodded and stared at him. She knew he was a hurt individual. But she thought it was a woman. She wanted to ask him how did it happen. But she waited for him to tell her.

He did.

"I was on the phone arguing with my baby's mother and ran a stop sign. A car ran into us. They tried to save her, but they couldn't. She died at the hospital."

Charly exhaled that time. "So sorry," she said, although it sounded hollow even to her.

Then Boone looked at her. He had to move on. "What about you?" he asked. "Any kids?"

Charly shook her head. She had no such hesitation. "None," she said. "Darryl didn't want any."

Boone stared at her. "Did you?"

225

Charly nodded. "Oh, yes. Plenty would do. But I wasn't going outside of my marriage."

"You wouldn't dare."

Charly smiled. "How do you know that?"

"Because I know that. You aren't the type."

Charly continued to stare at him. "Are you?"

Boone looked her dead in the eyes. "Are you asking if I've ever cheated on the various girlfriends I've had in my life? The answer is yes. I've cheated on all of them. They've all cheated on me."

That was a crushing admission to Charly.

"I forgot to warn you," Boone said. "I'm brutally honest."

Charly smiled.

"Or was that too honest for you?" he asked.

"No, I'll take honesty every time thank you. Even if it hurts."

"So what's your verdict on me? That because of my past, I'm not husband material?"

Charly laughed out loud. "Husband material? You aren't even boyfriend material!"

Boone laughed too. Although, inwardly, he felt ashamed.

And their conversation slowed.

Until Charly leaned forward. "I have a question," she said to him.

Boone looked at her breasts, and then into her eyes. He was still sitting sideways. He still had his legs crossed. "What's your question?"

"How did you come back? From what happened to your daughter, I mean."

Boone thought about it. "I don't think I ever did," he said. "You're never the same."

"No, that's true," said Charly, thinking about the trauma in her own background. "That's very true."

And then they just sat there and waited on their food as the music improved from the oldies but goodies to more modern tunes. And when one song in particular came on, an upbeat Post Malone tune called *Sunflower*, Charly smiled. It was obvious to Boone that she liked that song.

"Let's dance," he said, without asking if she wanted to, and he stood up and reached his hand out to her.

Since Charly was game, she accepted his hand. "I'm happy to dance," she said as she stood up too. "But there's one problem," she added.

"What?" Boone asked as he continued to hold her hand.

"I can't dance," Charly said.

Boone laughed. "Don't worry, kid," he said, "I'll show you the ropes."

That was funny to Charly, the idea that some white boy was going to show her how it's done. But she accepted his challenge and went on the dance floor with him.

Because the song was upbeat, she had an easier time of it. But what shocked her was that Boone wasn't kidding. That man could dance! He had moves that would put Beyoncé's dancers to shame. Charly couldn't quite keep up. She really did have two left feet. But she hung on and actually enjoyed herself.

Boone enjoyed himself, too. He was always the life of the party, and this time was no exception as other couples on the dance floor seemed to start taking his lead and trying out the same moves he was making. Charly couldn't believe how natural the chief seemed to be. It was like he was in his element.

He was a far cry from the stern authoritarian he portrayed, not only when he was working, but seemingly all the time!

But when that song ended, and a slower song quickly came on, most of the couples remained on the floor and began to slow-drag. Charly was about to leave. One song was plenty for her. Besides, slow-dragging was a tad intimate.

But when Boone pulled her back, and then eased her against him with one hand holding her hand against his shoulder and his other hand on her back, she didn't resist him. She wasn't sure if she could.

It was Celine Dion singing Diane Warren's *Because You Loved Me*, and the beat was so simple that even Charly could keep up.

> *"You were my strength when I was weak.*
> *You were my voice when I couldn't speak.*
> *You were my eyes when I couldn't see.*
> *You saw the best there was in me.*
> *Lifted me up when I couldn't reach.*
> *You gave me faith 'cause you believed.*
> *I'm everything I am,*
> *because you loved me."*

Boone pulled Charly closer and held her tighter. Charly hadn't been held that close in so long that it stunned her senses. Everything seemed so vivid. His big hand on her. His big body against her body. His breath in her ear. The rough stubble of his face brushing against the softness of her face. His cologne. *Him.*

Boone felt it too, and he was starved for affection. He was with a woman, usually a different one, almost every night. But no woman had ever felt this good in his arms. No woman had ever made him want to hold her forever. Most times, he didn't want to even say good morning to his previous ladies.

He felt as if he could say good morning forever to Charly.

It spooked him. What was happening to him? He almost released her and walked away.

But he couldn't.

He stayed right where he was.

And held her even tighter. He even closed his eyes.

"You were my strength when I was weak.
You were my voice when I couldn't speak . . ."

And no more words were said between them.

They just slow-dragged to the music, and held onto each other.

CHAPTER TWENTY-TWO

They arrived back in Low Town, at Charly's apartment, still in that quiet frame of mind. The guys were still hanging out in the complex, which didn't sit well with Boone, but he ignored them. Charly was on his mind. She was all he thought about the entire drive home.

He got out, walked around to the passenger side door, and opened it for Charly. When she got out, he placed his hand on the small of her back again, but this time he kept it there. They were still just friends. He wouldn't dare call it anything but what it was. But it still felt to him as if they had crossed some invisible line. They both still had boundaries, but the demarcations weren't as pronounced.

Especially when they walked up to her front door. A part of Boone wanted to go inside and do to her what he did to every woman he'd ever had a date with. But another part of him didn't want to mess this up. Whatever *this* was. Because it felt too good and pure.

Charly was in that category, too. On one hand, she wanted to experience the fullness of Boone Ryan. She knew a man as sexy as he was had to have some serious skills. But on the other hand, she was terrified of what would happen next. She wasn't ready for any full-blown love affair, and she was certain he wasn't. At least not the kind that she would require. Darryl cheated on her so many times, and like a fool she kept taking him back. She allowed him to treat her the way he treated her. She wasn't allowing any man to ever treat her that way again.

When she unlocked and opened her door, she looked at Boone. "Thanks," she said. "I had a nice time."

Boone still wanted in. He was so hard he was tenting. And when he moved closer and gave her a good night hug that lingered, she felt it too. He was so hard he felt like steel against her. He was so hard she could almost outline the massive size of him. And she almost faltered too.

But she didn't. She *couldn't*. Going down that road with him would be a suicide mission, when she barely survived her last attempt. "Good night," she said when they stopped embracing. She almost walked on in and closed the door, but she couldn't do that to him either. She needed him to co-sign her decision.

She could tell he didn't want to. He wanted in. But she could also tell he knew it was for the best.

Their heads overruled their hearts.

"Goodnight," he said to her. But then he glanced over at those guys again, and looked back at her. "Lock your door," he ordered her.

But he needn't have bothered. She was nobody's fool. "I will," she said as she walked on in, and closed the door behind her.

He stood there until he heard it lock. Then he headed for his Mercedes. But not before glaring at those young men again.

And when he got into his car and backed out, and was about to drive off, he felt such a burden that it alarmed him. How could he leave her in a place like this? He knew what kind of element lived there. Ninety percent were great, God-fearing, hardworking people. But that ten percent he knew like the back of his hand. He'd arrested each and every one of them before. He knew what they could do.

But Boone would be damned if they were going to do it to Charly. Or even attempt to.

Instead of leaving, he sped his car over to where the guys were hanging out. They all rolled their eyes, expecting some kind of harassment.

But Boone wasn't that kind of cop. He didn't play those kind of games. He got out of his car, walked straight to Porch, the guy he knew was the leader of the pack, and looked him dead in the eye.

"What did I do this time?" Porch asked. He had a long, well-deserved arrest record. "What did I do?"

"If you or your boys touch a hair on her head," Boone said to him, "it will be the same as if you were touching me. And nobody touches me," Boone added, stared at the rest of the gang too, and then got in his Mercedes and sped away.

Porch puffed on his cigarette. "So asshole got an asshole now. Maybe he'll stop screwing us," he added, as his boys laughed.

Then Porch sipped more beer, as his face turned to stone.

CHAPTER TWENTY-THREE

It was well after midnight when Charly finally began to feel sleepy. She was awake in bed, not thinking about her new town, her new job, her new life. She was thinking about Boone. The way he held her, mainly, but also the way he looked at her. He made her feel so special, even though she was at a point in her life when special was the last thing she felt. But he pulled it off.

She turned over, still thinking about Boone. He wasn't her usual type. She usually went for the cool black guys, not some older, white hothead like him. And the way he was so quick to arrest Amos Yerkson for a crime she wasn't at all sure he committed. To Boone Ryan, Amos lied about minor matters that could have been easily checked out. That, to Boone, proved his guilt. But in Charly's mind, that, to her, proved his innocence. He lied about small matters that could be easily checked out because he was no criminal. But Boone seemed to render judgments on people with precious little evidence.

And maybe that was why he was rendering a judgment on her, too, with precious little information about her. To him, she was just this sweet little dean. She thought, after she told him about her past and the kind of man that had actually been her type, he'd become cool to her. But on that dance floor it was just the opposite. And when they arrived back at her place, he was as hot for her as he had been on the dance floor.

She turned over again. She didn't know what to make of that man!

And she fell asleep thinking about that man, all over again.

Across town, Boone tried with all he could to fall asleep, but he couldn't get there. He tossed and turned and turned some more. But something was bugging him, and he couldn't figure out what.

He kicked the covers off and got out of bed. Naked as a jaybird, because that was how he slept every night, he went into the sitting room adjacent to his bedroom, walked behind his full-sized bar, and poured himself a drink. He looked at the clock on the wall. Just after two a.m. Charly, he suspected, was fast asleep. Charly, he knew, was why he wasn't.

He couldn't stop thinking about her!

He didn't know what it was about her. And it wasn't that she wasn't his type because he didn't have a type. He liked all kinds of women. But she wasn't his speed was more to the point, he figured.

She wasn't a party girl. She wasn't somebody he could get in bed with and hit and run with. If he ever got in bed with her, he was certain, he wasn't going anywhere. She would leave him before he left her.

And that, for a man like Boone Ryan, was a problem.

He'd never give up that much power. Not ever.

But it damn sure was tempting, he thought, as he sipped from his glass.

But something still was bugging him. He still felt unsettled. How could he do it, he wondered. How could he leave Charly at that crime-infested apartment complex to fend for herself? He felt strange when he left her, as if he was leaving a part of himself with her, but he left anyway. Now it was bugging the daylights out of him. Porch and his crew were bugging the daylights out of him.

He knew what they were capable of.

He took more sips. But he couldn't stop thinking about Charly no matter how much he drank. He walked to his floor-to-ceiling window and looked out over the lake. He paced the floor, and paced some more. But nothing helped. His concern wouldn't let up. It became so pronounced until he realized there was only one answer for it: he had to make sure she was alright.

He went back over to his bar, poured the last of his drink down the drain, went back into his bedroom, and dressed quickly. He grabbed his wallet, and the keys to his Ferrari, and took off. He would have no peace, none at all, until he made sure Charly had peace.

CHAPTER TWENTY-FOUR

When he arrived at the Scotland Arms apartments, he drove throughout the entire complex, slowly making his way toward her place. All was quiet, which he was pleased to see, and everything around her apartment looked just fine too. There was nothing to see there. Nothing to make him think that anything was amiss.

But that gnawing feeling was still there. So much so that he considered knocking on her door, to see for himself that she was okay. But he knew that could be easily misinterpreted. She'd think he was after a booty call. She'd lose a little more respect for him when the last thing he needed was to be a bastard in her eyes too.

Maybe his instinct was wrong this time, anyway, he thought. Maybe he was feeling so unsettled because he didn't end up spending the night with Charly when he never in his life took a woman out to dinner and *not* ended up in bed with her. He just needed to get a woman, that was all. He had a thick book of them. All he had to do, he knew, was to choose which one.

But having any other woman that wasn't Charly, he also knew, would be a mighty letdown.

But he also felt ridiculous to get out of his bed, in the middle of the night, just because he had some unexplained, unable-to-verbalize feeling. A whim, in other words. It was insane, and he needed to get himself away from there. He drove away from her place, and toward the exit.

But even as he approached the exit, he still felt unsettled. And suddenly it didn't feel like a whim at all. Something was wrong.

Instead of leaving the complex, he drove back through it. But nothing had changed. Nothing was amiss.

Get a grip, Boone, he said out loud. *She's okay. Besides, she's a strong woman. She can take care of herself even if something was wrong. What's your problem*? He wasn't her man, not even her lover, and certainly not her keeper. Why was he acting as if he was all of the above?

He turned around once again, ready to head for the exit once again. But as he drove away, and glanced though his rearview at her section of the complex, he caught a glimpse of something in the woods beside her apartment that happened so fast he couldn't figure out what it was he'd seen. A man, a woman, he couldn't even say. Or was it even real? Was it a figment of his early-in-the-morning whacked imagination?

But in case it wasn't, he turned around, anyway, and headed back toward her place. He felt like an unsettled fool, but he headed back.

But when he was almost to her place, he heard a sound that chilled him to his bones. A sound he knew like the back of his hand.

A gunshot.

And not just one shot, but a volley of shots in the back of the building where Charly lived.

His heart pounding, he slammed on brakes, grabbed the two loaded guns he kept in his glove compartment, and jumped out of his Ferrari. He was praying, literally praying, that it wasn't Charly's apartment. He ran toward her apartment, praying that she was okay, knowing that she wasn't.

She didn't know that she wasn't at first, until the gunfire started. She had finally fallen asleep, after many hours tossing and turning, when gunfire awakened her with such a start that she thought she was having a heart attack. She leaned up from her pillow with a hard jerk-up. And then there was the sound of her window shattering as bullets flew through it.

She didn't know what was happening, but she jumped out of bed and dropped to the floor. Then she crawled under the bed, crawling on her belly, as the hail of bullets besieged her. She could hardly believe it. How could everything go so crazy so quickly?

But she wasn't trying to seek the reason. She was trying to stay alive. And when one of the bullets ricocheted off of the lowest part of the bed, as if the gunman knew she was underneath it, she knew she had to get out of that room.

She crawled from beneath the bed and decided, just like she decided all those years ago when that hitman was after her, that she had to make a run for it. No matter what, she couldn't remain there and be a sitting duck for some crazed shooter. She had to get out.

And as soon as there was a momentary lapse in gunfire, as if the gunman was reloading, she made that run.

She got off of the floor and ran for her life, out of that bedroom. There was still no gunshots heard so she kept running out of the bedroom, down the hall, through her living room, and toward the front door. He was in the back of her apartment. If she could grab her keys off of the key rack in the living room and get to her car, she just might get away from there.

But there was no time for any of that because, just as she entered the living room, her front door was kicked open. She was just about to turn around, and run toward her back door, when she realized who had bust it open.

She'd never been happier to see a man the way she was when she saw Boone Ryan.

She ran to him, irrationally trying to tell him that somebody was shooting up her apartment, as if he didn't already know.

And then the gunfire started again, this time in the living room. Boone immediately grabbed Charly and fell, with her in his arms, to the floor. They hit the deck hard. But Boone was on top, shielding Charly with his own body, and firing back at the gunman outside. He fired and he fired and he fired. His goal was to overwhelm that gunman with as much firepower as he could muster, knowing that it might be enough to scare him off. He shot every bullet out of one gun, dropped it, and then, without missing a beat, pulled out his second gun and continued to fire nonstop.

Until Charly didn't hear another shot from the gunman. Boone was still shooting, but she didn't hear return fire. "He stopped," Charly said anxiously to Boone. "Boone, he stopped. Why did he stop?"

Boone had realized it, too. "I don't know," he said, getting off of her, "but I'm going to find out."

He jumped up and grabbed her hand, lifting her with one strong jerk. "Lock the door. Don't let anybody in but me," he ordered, and ran out of the apartment.

Charly, not about to defy the man who just saved her life, quickly did as he ordered and locked her door. Then she took shelter away from all windows.

And Boone took off, out of the apartment and around to the side. He had to secure her first. Now he needed to get that gunman.

But the gunman hadn't fired another shot. Which meant, to Boone, that his strategy of overwhelming him with shots fired back might have paid off. But he had to be sure.

When he saw that there was nobody on the side nor the back of the apartment section, he ran through the woods on the side of the complex. All he could think about was how close to death Charly had come. What if he hadn't been there? What if there was no return fire and that gunman broke her door down to get to her? Boone's heart was in agony.

But despite the agony of the what ifs, he kept running. He ran fast and furiously through those woods with his gun drawn and ready. With his heart hammering.

Although he still didn't hear another gunshot, he suddenly heard the sound of a car engine cranking up deeper into the woods. As soon as he heard it, he ran even faster. He ran so fast, getting whipped by the powerfully thick brush, that it felt as if he was running through an obstacle course. He had to lift his feet higher and higher as he ran nearly blind through the darkness and the thickets. But he kept running.

By the time he made it to where he thought he heard that car cranking up, he saw a car speeding off. The lighting from the complex was poor, but it did give the car a reddish tint, but he couldn't be sure. It was gone so quickly that he couldn't swear to any details.

And he didn't waste time trying to either. Charly was alone in that apartment. She was still at the crime scene. He ran back to Charly.

CHAPTER TWENTY-FIVE

It looked to Charly as if the entire police department was at her complex. And even though their chief had an investigation to oversee, he was sitting on the sofa right next to her. And seemingly to the shock of each and every one of his men who walked through that door, he kept his arm protectively around her waist as if he was making some statement. That she was now his, maybe? Or just that they were friends. She couldn't say. But whatever it was, she needed it.

She was still shaken. So shaken that Boone could feel that she was still trembling. Anytime she heard a loud noise, or something fell, or somebody suddenly laughed out loud, she jumped. She was not okay. She was a long way from okay. And his heart ached for her. When would this woman get a break, he wondered? When was all of this upheaval supposed to end for her? But he was mostly concerned about why in the world would somebody try to kill her?

Although Charly had that question paramount on her mind, too, she had a different question on her mind as well. "How did you know to come over here?" she asked him.

Boone exhaled, and although he didn't realize it, he leaned her closer against him. "I didn't know," he said. "I just felt something was wrong."

Charly looked at him. "You felt it? What do you mean you felt it?"

"I felt it. I couldn't sleep. I couldn't think straight. I felt something was wrong. So I came on over."

He looked at her when he realized she was staring at him. Both of them knew how odd what he had said sounded. Both of them knew how absolutely right what he said sounded too.

They both looked away.

Morley and Dontay were the two detectives Boone had assigned to the case. They both came over and sat on the coffee table in front of their chief and his friend, and they both felt uncomfortable as they could feel.

Especially Dontay. The idea that their hard-edged boss would be showing any kind of affection toward anybody was amazing to him. But to show it toward a black woman was almost shocking to him. Chief Ryan had a reputation that didn't jive with what Dontay was seeing. To the black community of Hemingway, their chief wasn't what they would call friendly by any stretch of the imagination. But since their chief wasn't friendly toward anybody, Dontay never took it personally.

Morley, who knew Boone far longer than Dontay, was also surprised by Boone's show of affection toward Dean Johnson. She was pretty, he'd give her that, and Morley knew Boone dated all kinds of ladies in his past, including black ones. But he'd never known him to make any public display of affection toward any of them. That was the shocker.

But as the evidence technicians did their jobs, and as other cops canvassed the complex in search of witnesses, Morley and Dontay had a job to do too. And they, albeit awkwardly, got on with it.

"We hate to have to ask you these questions, ma'am," Dontay said, " but we need to know who you believe might have attempted to do you harm tonight."

But Charly was shaking her head. "Nobody," she said. "I can't imagine anybody."

"Everybody has enemies," Morley said. "Are you telling us you don't?"

Dontay was surprised by his partner's brashness, but that was Morley. And Chief Ryan didn't seem to mind him aggressively doing his job.

"I can't think of any enemy that would want me dead, that's correct," Charly said. She had one, Meeker Tabloski, the man she testified against after he killed her husband, but that was it. And he died in prison.

"But what about when you were run off the road," Dontay said. "Wouldn't that person qualify as your enemy?"

"But those were just kids," Charly said. "Those were just kids out on a joy ride."

"What makes you so certain of that?" Dontay asked.

Charly looked at him. "What do you mean?"

"He means," Boone said, "that you have no way of knowing if it were kids having fun, or kids being paid to harm you."

Charly frowned. "But why?" she asked.

"Maybe that guy, the one you testified against, has a family," said Boone.

"What guy you testified against?" asked Dontay.

Morley looked at Dontay. "What is that your business?" he asked him.

"Perfectly legitimate question," Boone said, defending Dontay. "Dean Johnson's husband was killed by a mob hitman. She testified in court against him. He later died in prison."

"But he might have family members out for revenge," Dontay said, understanding now.

Boone nodded. "Right."

"Or the mob," said Morley. "If he was their hitman."

"But that all happened over three years ago," said Charly. "Why would they all of a sudden want revenge when I move to Kentucky, when they didn't want it while I was still in L.A.?"

Morley and Dontay knew it made no sense, either, but it was all they had.

Charly rubbed her forehead. Their questions were good questions, but it was all so distressing. The mob was suddenly after her? Or Tabloski's family members? It was crazy to her.

But Boone could see her distress. "Let's wrap it up, guys," he said to his men. "Dean Johnson will be available for further questioning another time."

That wasn't satisfactory to either Morley or Dontay, but they knew they didn't have a vote in the matter. They stood up, and walked away.

Boone stood up, too, and reached his hand out to Charly. "Let's get you out of here," he said to her.

Charly rose. She knew she couldn't stay there tonight. That was for certain. But she didn't exactly have money to burn on a hotel either. But she had no choice. "What about all of these shattered windows?" she asked.

"I've got a guy on his way now to repair them all. Don't worry. A couple of my guys will stay here until this place is secured. You're just not staying here."

Charly would normally find his domineering style off-putting, but not that time. She was so shaken that having a man like Boone Ryan around was comforting to her. No medicine, she felt, could relax her more than he did. "I'll grab a few things," she said, and walked away toward her bedroom.

Boone watched her walk away. He could feel her anguish all over his own body, just like he felt she was in trouble even before she was. And he couldn't figure it out. What was it about that woman, he thought, that haunted him so? He just couldn't figure it out.

But after she threw some clothes into a suitcase, and made her way back up front, Boone already was standing outside. And he was already eyeing that crew that seemed to get under his skin.

"I'm back," Charly said when he didn't seem to notice that she was standing by his side. He was too busy staring at Porch and his boys. Like most of the people in that complex, they had all come outside too.

Boone finally tore his eyes away from Porch when he heard Charly's voice. "Ready?" he asked.

"Why are you so interested in them?" Charly asked him. Surely he didn't think those guys were involved in what happened at her place.

"They're crooks and cons," he said to her as he grabbed her suitcase. "I'm always interested in crooks and cons."

He escorted her to the passenger side of his Ferrari, assisted her as she sat down in the sports car, and then placed her suitcase in his trunk. He got in behind the wheel, thought the better of it, and began getting right back out. "I'll be back," he said.

"Boone, don't confront them this time of morning," said Charly.

But Boone kept getting out.

"Boone?" she asked again, but he was already heading toward Porch and his crew.

Charly quickly unbuckled her seatbelt and got out too. She didn't know those guys like that. She'd be the first to admit that Boone knew them a million times better than she did. But what proof did he have that they had absolutely anything whatsoever to do with what happened at her place? Would it be another case of him arresting somebody based on his intuition?

But then again, she thought as she followed Boone over to her neighbors, it was his intuition that led him to come see about her in the first place. It was his intuition that saved her life.

She decided to be there, but not to dispute him in front of those guys.

And Boone didn't waste any time as soon as they approached them. "What happened?" he said to Porch. Charly could see his crew grinning, as if they expected Boone to be automatically suspicious of them. Apparently he always was.

Porch, who was leaned against his car, looked at Boone. "How would I know?" he asked him.

"What happened?" Boone asked Porch again.

"I told you I don't know. Don't you have criminals to catch? Damn. Why you always harassing me?"

"If you don't tell me what happened, I will be hauling your ass in," Boone said. "What happened?"

Charly wanted to look at Boone. She wanted to ask him if he was for real, or just joking? What evidence on the face of this earth did he have against that man?

But she held her peace. For some reason, she sensed Boone knew what he was doing. Boone was her ally, not some random guys in the neighborhood who didn't give a darn about her. Yet Boone came all the way over to her place just to check on her without even being sure that she needed to be checked on. What man had ever done something like that for her? She couldn't even count them on one hand because there was none to count.

She was casting her lots with Boone.

"I told you, and I'm gonna tell you again," Porch said, "I don't know a damn thing about a damn thing. Don't try to blame me if your hoe got enemies," he said and before Charly could say a word, Boone grabbed Porch by his collar and slammed him against Porch's own car, denting it.

"What did you say?" Boone angrily asked Porch.

"I was just talking, man, that's all."

"Apologize to Miss Johnson and do it now!" Boone yelled and slammed him again. "Do it now!"

"I apologize!" Porch said to Charly with bitterness and bite. No man liked to be manhandled, and especially not a leader like Porch.

But Charly didn't care about any apology. She wanted answers that Boone apparently felt Porch could give to them. "Who shot up my place?" she asked him. "Who tried to kill me?"

"And your ass better talk to her respectfully," Boone warned.

Porch's guys stared at Boone. They'd never known him to give a damn about any woman, let alone a black woman. He was known around town as the love'em and leave'em kind of guy. Then they looked at her. What in the world did that chick have that no other woman had ever had before?

"Now answer her question truthfully and with no bull attached, or your ass will be in lockup I assure you," Boone said.

"But I didn't do anything."

"Answer her question!" Boone ordered.

"I don't know what happened," Porch said and Boone was about to slam him again. But he spoke up. "I heard things, aw'ight?"

Charly was surprised that he was about to tell them something. But Boone wasn't. He knew all along Porch wasn't coming clean with them. "What did you hear?" he asked him.

Porch was a reluctant snitch. But to the surprise of no one since they all knew what Boone Ryan was capable of, he snitched anyway. "I heard some guy was asking around about her."

Charly was shocked. "Asking about me?" she asked.

"What was he asking?" Boone asked Porch. He needed the details first, not the man's name. If Porch gave the man's name first, the details would get too skimpy. Porch would feel as if he gave up the goods when he gave up the name. But the details, to Boone, were critical. The details would often tell who the man was.

"He wanted to know basic stuff like where she lived and did she live alone and where did she work."

"What did you tell him?" Boone asked.

"I didn't tell him a damn thing," Porch said. "That ain't my fight."

"What else he wanted to know?" Boone asked.

"Who she was sleeping with," said Porch with a sly grin. "But I didn't want to tell him that because I didn't want to implicate our wonderful chief of police." His guys laughed.

Charly was mortified. They, too, were leaping to conclusions based on little or no information whatsoever. What kind of town was this?

But Boone was too busy staring at Porch. "You're lying to me," he said to him.

"I'm not lying."

"Who was the guy?" Boone asked.

"How should I know?" Porch responded. "I'd never seen him before."

"Did he give a name?"

"No."

Boone stared at him. "You're lying," he said again.

"He didn't give a name!" Porch insisted.

But Boone slammed him against the car again. "You're lying!" he yelled.

"He didn't give a name," Porch said again and Boone, to Charly's dismay, was about to slam him again. "But I found out his name," Porch quickly said.

Charly was shocked. Boone really did know what he was doing!

"You found out from who?" Boone asked.

"That's not important," said Porch.

"What's his name?" Boone asked.

"Like I'm supposed to remember some cracker's name."

"What's his name?" Boone said angrily.

"It began with a T, aw'ight? Damn! It was like Taroski or Tanoski something like that. Tajaski."

Charly was floored. She could hardly believe it. "Tabloski?" she asked.

Boone looked at her, then he looked back at Porch.

Porch was nodding his head. "Yeah, that's it. Tabloski. Some big, ugly, white dude. Kind of look like you, chief," he added, and his crew laughed.

But Boone couldn't care less about an insult. He was too busy staring at Charly. "That's the guy?" he asked her.

She nodded her head. "That's his name. But he died in prison. Unless it's his son or somebody related to him, like you said earlier."

Boone was nodding too. "That's what it has to be," he said. Then he looked at Porch. "Did he have a first name?"

"I'm sure he did, but I never heard it."

"When did you talk to him?" he asked.

"Just after she got in town," said Porch, motioning toward Charly.

That surprised both Boone and Charly. "Did he come here to this complex to talk to you?"

"No."

"Where did this conversation take place?"

"Some guy I know hooked us up."

"What guy?"

"I'm not telling you that," Porch said defiantly.

"What did your friend tell you?" Boone asked.

"He told me that this guy was asking questions about one of my neighbors and would be willing to pay me good money if I answered a few of his questions.   So I met him in the parking lot at Walmart, and answered his questions."

"I thought you said you didn't answer his questions," said Boone, catching him in a lie.   "I thought you said it wasn't your fight."

"It's not. But the money was right. I answered his questions."

Boone turned around. When he saw one of his uniforms staring his way, he motioned him to come over. The young officer ran over.

"Yes, sir, Chief?" he asked.

"Cuff him, frisk him, and haul him to the station," Boone said.

"You gonna arrest me anyway?" Porch asked. "But I cooperated!"

"And you're going to continue to cooperate downtown," Boone said.   Then he looked at the cop. "Let him go through every mug book we have. He needs to identify a guy named Tabloski.   You run a check on that name too."

"Yes, sir. Then let him go, sir?"

"Not a chance," Boone said.

Porch was shocked. "Why not?"

"When you give me the name of the guy who put you in touch with Tabloski, then you can go. If not, you'll be held for obstructing a police investigation. For withholding vital information."

It was all bull and Porch and his crew knew it. Charly knew it, too. But Boone ran that town.

But she also knew where Boone was coming from. This was a matter of life and death. Porch needed to give them that name of his friend so they could get more information on Tabloski. Besides, she was still too shaken by what happened at her place, and by the fact that the horrors of her past seemed to be catching up with the horrors of her present, to be worrying about Porch's well-being and safety. He had information to give. He needed to come clean. Her life just might depend on it.

That was why, when Boone said, "let's go," she didn't hesitate. She needed to be with him as much as he wanted her to be with him.

She got in his Ferrari, and they drove away.

Ready or not, here we go.

CHAPTER TWENTY-SIX

And man, Charly thought, did he drive. He didn't slow down until they were turning onto a long, winding driveway that led up to what looked like to her to be nothing short of a mansion. A very beautiful, colonial-style mansion. She looked at Boone.

"What is this?" she asked him.

"My house," Boone said as he slowly drove further up the winding driveway.

But Charly was stunned. "Your house? What do you mean? You *live* here?"

Boone smiled. He knew she would be surprised. As far as she knew, he was just a cop. "That's right," he said. "I live here."

"With your family?" she asked.

There was a hesitation in Boone. He used to want a family, but after Courtney's death that seemed like an impossible dream. "No," he said. "Just me."

"And you own it?"

"That's right," Boone said and looked at her. "That's alright, isn't it?"

Charly didn't know what to say to that. Because, honestly, she wasn't sure if it was. She leaned back and looked at the massive home again. Not too much intimidated her. When she was married to Darryl she lived in a nice house too. But it wasn't a mansion! She'd never been driven around by a man who owned a mansion. And it was intimidating. She either had a very crooked cop on her hands, or a very wealthy one.

"That's alright, isn't it?" he asked her again.

"Depends," she finally responded.

"On what?"

"How it was obtained," Charly said, and then looked at Ryan.

Ryan nodded. He liked that she questioned it. Not one of his other women ever had because they didn't give a damn. They just loved that he had it going on like that. But Charly, as usual, he thought, was different. "It was legally obtained," he assured her. "I told you I was a successful businessman."

"What was your business, I guess I should have asked?"

"Oil," Ryan said.

That surprised Charly. "*You* were an oil man?"

"I went to Texas, made my fortune, and then took the money and ran. But don't worry, dear," he said to Charly, patting her hand, "I despise crooked cops."

Charly smiled. "As do I," she said, reassured. Not just by his words, but by the fact that his hand remained on hers. "I can't see how a cop named after Daniel Boone would be crooked anyway," she added, and Boone laughed.

Charly also couldn't see how a man who would come to her rescue in the middle of the night simply because he *felt* she was in danger, could be either.

Boone stopped his car at the top of the driveway, got out, and walked around to the passenger side. When he helped Charly out, he immediately placed his hand around her waist, as if he wasn't letting her out of his sight. She also noticed that he was looking around, as if he wanted to make sure whoever had gunned for her hadn't followed them to his place.

They walked together to the trunk of his car, pulled out her suitcase, and then, with his hand still on her back, made their way across the sidewalk and into his big, stained-glass double doors. He remotely disarmed his home with a key fob, and then closed the door behind them.

But oddly to Charly, as soon as that door closed, and he remained beside her, she felt safer. And it was a unique kind of safe too. As if she was finally at home, or something akin to that kind of place. It was the strangest feeling.

"This way," Boone said, and began walking her up the sweeping staircase.

"It's very grand," Charly said as they walked.

"Are you trying to say I'm not?" Boone asked.

"Oh, no, I'm not trying to say it. I *am* saying it," Charly said definitively and Boone laughed. She also noticed, as he was laughing, that he squeezed her too.

When they made it up to the second floor landing, Boone escorted her into what looked like a master bedroom. "This is your room," he said.

"But I don't want to put you out of your own bedroom," Charly said.

"You aren't," said Boone. "All of the rooms look like this. Mine is right down the hall that way."

"Oh, okay," said Charly. She felt a little embarrassed to think that he was giving up his own bedroom, but she felt she played it off well enough.

He sat her suitcase on the bed. "Just holler if you need anything at all," he said.

She nodded. "I will." But then she just stood there.

Boone watched her as she stood there. He could see the tightness of her body. He could see the anguish in her great big eyes. He could see the pain all over her pretty face. And his heart went out to her. He went to her.

As soon as Boone walked up to her and placed his arms around her, Charly broke down. She cried in his arms. "When will it end?" she asked him. "Every time I think I have a new beginning, all I have are new problems. Or old problems coming back. When will it ever end?"

Boone held her tightly. She might have been saddened by the events of that early Sunday morning, but he was pissed. He was the bastard. He was the one who deserved problems like the kind she had to deal with. But she was the one getting the blowback. Over and over again. He could feel her pain.

He felt it so much so that he decided to share it, too. He lifted her into his big arms, carried her out of the guest bedroom and into his master bedroom down the hall. She was so busy sobbing that she didn't realize what he was doing. Not even when he pulled back the covers on his bed and laid her onto it. Not even when he walked around and got in the bed too.

It wasn't until he pulled her into his arms, into a big bearhug lying beside her, did she realize what he had done. But instead of being afraid or uncomfortable or even uneasy, she was pleased. She didn't think she could have been alone. She knew she didn't want to.

And Boone didn't want her to. He held her for hours. He held her until she fell asleep in his arms. He held her all night long.

CHAPTER TWENTY-SEVEN

The next morning, Charly woke up alone. After adjusting her still-sleepy eyes, she realized she was still in Boone's bedroom, in Boone's bed, but he was nowhere to be found. She still was fully clothed, which meant he behaved like a gentleman in her hour of distress, thank God, but she missed his nearness. It was the dawn of a new day, but that old baggage was still weighing her down.

She got out of bed and left his bedroom. When she made it back to the guest room he had earmarked for her, she locked the door, took a quick shower in the adjacent bathroom, brushed and gargled with what she had packed in her suitcase, and dressed. It was Sunday and she had every intention of going to church, so she wore a well-fitted bright blue dress with stitching across the shoulders. The faculty at Saint Christopher's were required to attend Saint Christopher Church, and sit as a united front upfront in the church, and she aimed to do as her contract required. She was not Episcopalian. She was actually a Baptist girl who'd always attended Baptist churches. But she was also a rule abider. Despite the turmoil in her life, and what happened to her at the complex, she wasn't about to lose her job.

The problem was: how was she going to get there? Chief Ryan had done enough for her already. He rescued her from a would-be assassin. He invited her into his home. He held her in a way that allowed her to get one of the best night's sleep she'd had in a long time, the first time ever a man had gotten her in his bed without wanting more than just to cuddle. What more did she want from the man?

A ride to church, that was what, she thought, as she made her way downstairs. And also his protection, too, because whoever attempted to take her out was still out there himself. He'd already saved her life. She needed a man like Boone.

And when she made it downstairs, and saw that the man was in his kitchen cooking breakfast, she felt as if she was in a dream. A man cooking breakfast for her? Maybe that was taking it too far, she knew. He was probably cooking it for himself. But it was still a sight to behold.

"Good morning," he said as she entered his gourmet kitchen.

"Good morning."

"You look pretty," he found himself saying as his eyes roamed down the length of her sexy dress. But then he immediately felt odd. He'd never been an affectionate man in his life. But around her, he was behaving as if that was the only way he could be.

Charly didn't find it odd at all. "Thank you," she said, and quickly moved on. "Smells good."

"That's good to know," he said, happy to move on too. "I'm glad you approve."

"I haven't tasted it yet," Charly said with a smile and Boone, as he was prone to do at the least of her jokes, laughed out loud.

"What is it?" she asked him as she sat at his center island.

"Ever hear of Burgoo?"

"Bur *who*?" Charly asked and Boone laughed again.

"It's a stew," he said.

Charly smiled. "A stew for breakfast? Are you serious?"

"Oh, very serious," Boone said as he spooned out a bowl full for her, a bowl full for him, and sat both bowls on the island beside each other. He sat beside her.

"I must admit I've never had stew for breakfast."

"It's a staple of the Ryans of Kentucky. My mother fed six boys on this stew."

Charly smiled, they said grace, and then ate up. She immediately began to fan her mouth.

"What's wrong?" he asked her, smiling as he did.

"Stew with a kick," she said. "What is that?"

"Just some chili peppers," he said as if it was no big deal.

But Charly was floored. "Boone!" she yelled and pushed him. "For breakfast?!"

Boone was laughing. "Just keep eating it. You'll get used to it."

Charly took another smaller spoonful, and then another one, and then soon, she was actually enjoying the spicy kick. She smiled. "You're right," she said.

"Told you so. It's really good."

"You cook all the time?" she asked him.

"Cook? Me? Never!"

That surprised Charly. "Never? Then why did you all of a sudden decide to cook this kind of elaborate breakfast this morning?"

Boone was a little sheepish, but he told her the truth. "I figured you'd like it," he said.

Charly didn't know what to say to that. And soon neither one of them seemed to know what to say. And the burden of what happened, and why she was at his home to begin with, took root again. They ate in silence.

Until Boone's phone rang. He pulled it out and answered quickly. "Yeah?"

It was Morley. "We got a name, Chief."

"From Porch?"

"Yes, sir. A few hours in the brig does wonders for one's memory."

"Who?" Boone asked.

"Dalbert Lee."

Boone was floored. "He said Dalbert was the friend who told him about Tabloski?"

Charly looked at him.

"Yes, sir," Morley said. "And he knows where Dalbert's been holing up too."

Boone could not have hoped for more. "Where?"

"You know that trailer park behind those projects on Rollins?"

"Just a few trailers back there, but yeah," Boone said.

"That's where our boy Dalbert has been in hiding. At least according to Porch. And I know he won't lie. He knows you'll throw the book at him, not to mention your fists, if he even think about lying to us."

"Keep him in custody until his story checks out."

"Yes, sir."

"And what about Tabloski? Any info on him?"

"Nothing. Meeker Tabloski died in prison and there's no mention of any children or a wife or nothing like that. So we don't know who this Tabloski could be. Maybe a brother or something, or a nephew. Or the name could just be a coincidence."

"Yeah and I'm Oprah," Boone said, and Morley laughed.

"How your girl*fri*," Morley started to say and then quickly caught himself. "I mean, how's Dean Johnson?"

Boone glanced at her. "She's okay," he said.

"So how do you want us to play this Dalbert game? He wasn't at that last trailer park we got a tip about. How do you want to play this one?"

"More lowkey," Boone said. "Who all knows now?"

"Just me and Dontay and Sarge."

"Keep it that way," Boone said. "We'll meet in about an hour at the spot."

"Heavy armor?"

"Heave armor, but just the four of us."

"Got cha, Chief," Morley said. "We'll see you there," he added, and ended the call.

"What about Dalbert Lee?" Charly asked.

"He was the friend Porch claimed introduced him to Tabloski."

"Dalbert Lee again. There has to be a connection," Charly said.

"Oh, there is," Boone said, standing up. "But what that connection could be is a mystery to me."

"Me too," said Charly, standing too. "So we'll meet up with your men in an hour you said?"

Boone looked at her. "What you mean *we*?" he asked.

"I want to be there too," Charly said.

Boone frowned. "Are you out of your mind? You want to be there? There's no way I'm letting you anywhere near Dalbert Lee, or any other lowlife like that."

"But he may know who tried to kill me, Boone."

"I know that."

"And I can't stay here alone."

"I know that too. You aren't staying here. Let's go," he said, and didn't wait for her to agree.

CHAPTER TWENTY-EIGHT

They drove to a sprawling ranch near the outskirts of Hemingway where a massive R in a circle was etched prominently into the gate. Charly assumed the R stood for Ryan. She assumed it was yet another one of Boone's properties.

Until they made the long trek up a dusty dirt road to the main home at the end of the drive, and an older white woman was on the old-fashioned, elongated porch watering potted plants.

Boone stopped the car and removed his seatbelt. "Who's that?" Charly asked as she removed her belt too.

Boone hesitated, staring at the woman. Then he exhaled. "My mother," he said, and got out of the car.

As he walked around the car to open the passenger side door, Charly didn't know what to make of that. His mother? He brought her to his *mother's house*? How in the world was this woman going to feel about him bringing some stranger lady to her house? How did Charly feel about coming to a man's mother's house when their own relationship wasn't even defined yet?

But it wasn't as if Boone was giving her a vote in anything. He wasn't. He was behaving as if he and only he had a say in her life right now. And in a way he did, she felt, while that gunman remained at large. But she also knew as he opened her door and held her hand as she stepped out, that she'd put a stop to it if he got out of hand.

By the time Charly had stepped out, the woman on the porch had stopped watering her plants and was now just standing there, staring at the two of them. And she didn't look all too pleased either. Which wasn't unusual in Charly's world. Boone and Amos Yerkson were about the only two people who showed her immediate kindness in the nearly two-and-a-half months that she'd been in Kentucky. Why would this woman be any different than most?

"Hello, Stranger," the woman said to Boone as they made their way toward the steps.

"Hello, Mother," Boone said, walked with Charly up the steps and kissed his mother on her rosy cheek. The woman had to be in her sixties, with long gray hair, a beautiful face, and hard eyes like Boone.

But then Boone said: "This is Charly. She's going to stay here until I get back." Then he turned to Charly. "Charly, this is my mother," he said. "I'll be back." And then, without saying another word, Boone hurried down the steps, got into his Ferrari, and sped back down the dirt path and out of the gate.

Charly was mortified. The idea that she was left with yet another offensive person that didn't want to be bothered with her either was becoming too much. And she was his mother? Way too much.

Charly and Mrs. Ryan looked at each other. Charly might have felt mortified, but she didn't display it. All Mrs. Ryan saw was a tall, elegant, completely in charge black woman. And, for some strange reason Boone's mother couldn't even fathom, she liked Charly immediately.

But all Charly saw was contempt on the woman's face. But she smiled, anyway, and extended her hand. "My name is Charlene Johnson," she said. "But everybody calls me Charly. Nice to meet you, Mrs. Ryan."

Mrs. Ryan continued to stare at Charly. "You're that new dean," she said.

"Yes, ma'am," Charly responded.

"The one that was shot at in the wee hours of the morning."

"A blunt assessment of a very traumatic event," Charly said, "but yes."

But Mrs. Ryan was still staring at Charly as if she was sizing her up. "Well," she finally said, as if she'd reached a conclusion. "He's never brought one of his women here before."

"Oh, no ma'am, I'm not one of his," Charly started saying, correcting Mrs. Ryan, but Mrs. Ryan didn't give her a chance to finish.

"If he brought you here," Mrs. Ryan continued, "then you must be special to him. Which means you're special to me. Come on in, Charly," she said, and began heading for the entrance door. "I'll get my rifle and lock up. He expects me to protect you."

Get her rifle? Seriously? Charly didn't know what to make of that tough old lady. Her words were kind, but her eyes weren't. They still looked hard as steel. But she welcomed her into her home despite her son's unceremonious way of introducing her. Charly went on inside.

Boone and his men went on inside too. Morley kicked the door to the trailer open and Boone, followed by Dontay, barged on in. Sarge remained in the van down the street, ready to come and swoop them up if need be.

But as soon as the door was kicked open, a mad scramble of the people inside ensued, and gunfire erupted. Boone knocked Dontay down and fired on the man who was about to fire on Dontay. The man fell down. Then Boone and Dontay and Morley fired on several other men, who were firing and running toward the back of the trailer, attempting to get away. Boone shot another one, and Dontay got one in the leg, as they ran after the men. Women were in that trailer, too, they realized, and they had to be careful. But Boone was determined to get his man this time, women or no women. Besides, those women had to know what kind of pill-pushing scum they were dealing with. They assumed the risk, too, as far as Boone was concerned.

That was why, when he followed the man he came to collect toward the furthest back room in the entire double-wide, where two women were also in that room, Boone didn't hesitate. The guy was about to jump out of the window. Boone fired his gun beside that window, almost hitting one of the women and barely missing the man.

But it was just a warning shot anyway. The next one would be spot on. "Stop or I'll blow your head off!" Boone yelled at the man, his gun aimed squarely at the back of the man's head. Both women were sitting up in the bed screaming, which could have been a major distraction, but Boone wasn't distracted at all. He'd know Dalbert Lee a mile away, and he wasn't flinching this time. He had his man.

Dalbert Lee, the largest dealer of drugs in all of Hemingway, dropped his gun, lifted his hands in the air, and turned around.

"Assume the position you lowlife piece of trash," Boone said, and Dalbert, knowing the drill too well, dropped to his knees, laid down prone, and spread eagle.

Dontay ran into the room. "You okay, Chief?" the young cop asked his older boss. Then he smiled when he saw that they finally caught their man. "You don't have to answer that," he said as he stared at Dalbert. "I know you are."

But if Boone thought he was going to have a difficult perp in Dalbert Lee, he was mistaken. "I didn't kill Rita Mae," Dalbert said.

"Who said you did?" asked Boone as Dontay cuffed him.

"I was paid to get info on that lady. That's all I had to do with it."

This interested Boone even more. "On what lady?" he asked him.

"That new lady. That dean. Your woman."

Dontay glanced at his chief. Boone didn't even bat an eye. "What info you were paid to get?"

"Everything I could. He wanted me to call her and set her up, and I told him I did, but I didn't."

"Set her up how?" Boone asked.

"After his hired gun didn't kill her in Low Town like he was supposed to, he contacted me. Told me to set up a meeting for later tonight. I was to tell her that if she wanted information on who tried to kill her, she can meet me in the back of Danley's after it closes at eleven. And she had to come alone and tell nobody. Especially not you."

"Midnight tonight?"

"Yes, tonight. Did I stutter?"

Boone hit Dalbert upside his head, causing Dalbert's long hair to flap. "Get smart again!" Boone yelled, "and I'll kick your ass next time!"

"Alright, man, you don't have to brutalize me! I saw that video. I saw what you did to Billy Ray. It's a crying shame for a cop to act like that."

"Who paid you?" Boone asked him.

"This creep named Tabloski."

Tabloski. That name again. "He's the one who thinks she's coming to meet him tonight?"

"That's right."

Boone exhaled. "Why does he want her? What did he say?"

"He was jawing on about how she snitched on his old man and sent him to prison, and how his old man died in prison, and how she was good for nothing and all that kind of bull. I don't know. I didn't care! I just know he paid me to set her up. So I told him I did. I figure if I can hide out from you, I could take his money and hide out from him too."

Boone walked closer to Dalbert. "If your ass is lying to me, it'll be the last lie you ever tell. You understand me, Dalbert?"

"I understand. I know you're a bastard. You ain't got to tell me twice."

Boone exhaled. To know that Charly wasn't just theoretically a target, but a target in fact, was a horrifying proposition for him. He had to stop this Tabloski in his tracks. "Get a crew out here to keep him and his men right here, under house arrest with full guard," Boone said to Dontay. "Keep him here until I get Tabloski. Then have them haul his ass to jail."

"Yes, sir," said Dontay.

CHAPTER TWENTY-NINE

"Charly's not your given name," Boone's mother said. "Or is it?"

Charly smiled. "No, ma'am. Charlene is my given name."

"That's right, you did give me your real name when you had the courtesy to introduce yourself. Unlike my irascible son. We call him Boone, but we just as well have called him Tarzan. *Me Tarzan, you Jane*. That's how he communicates you know."

Charly smiled, but didn't respond. She wasn't about to even pretend to diss the man who saved her life, and who had given her shelter when she needed it the most.

She and Boone's mother were sitting at a big kitchen table inside the main house on the Ryan ranch. Boone's mother had made coffee and they both were taking sips. There was also a rifle sitting on the table just in case.

"For the record," Boone's mother said, "my name is Barbara Ryan, but everybody calls me Babs. So I know what it's like to have a nickname too. So let's make a deal. If I can call you Charly, you can call me Babs. Unless you utterly hate your nickname."

"It wasn't my choice, as you said," Charly said, " but I'm okay with it."

"My sentiments exactly," said Babs and sipped more coffee. But she kept staring her expressive eyes at Charly.

Charly felt as if she was being assessed: is this person good enough for my beloved son? Although, Charly knew, she and Boone hadn't even gotten to that point of knowing what their relationship was themselves. Right now, as far as she was concerned, they were just becoming friends. Friends with feelings, she'd admit. But friends.

"How do you like Hemingway so far?" Babs asked her.

"Not so much so far," admitted Charly. "But time will tell."

"No, it won't," said Babs. "I've been here all my life and I'm not crazy about it either."

Charly smiled until the sound of the front door crashing open startled her, who, admittedly, was still shaken from what happened at her own apartment. She jumped.

Babs didn't flinch. She just stared at Charly. "That'll be *my* old man," Babs said. "I know his entrance like I know my name. Back here, Duke!"

Charly felt more at ease when Babs explained who it was, but since the man didn't respond, she wasn't going to relax until she saw him for herself.

When the big, tall man entered the huge kitchen, looking like an older version of Boone himself, Charly did relax. Down to the sexiness and gruffness combined together, there was no doubt about it: this man was Boone's father.

"You're up early enough," Duke said to his wife as he plopped down at the kitchen table, staring at Charly.

"Where have you been?" Babs asked him.

"I had to take care of my horses. Where do you think?"

Charly saw Babs give him a look that made clear she didn't believe him, and then she sipped more coffee. There was a tension between the two of them that a knife couldn't cut.

But Duke already seemed to have his sights on Charly. "You're that new dean," he said to her.

"Yes, sir."

"The one who got shot at."

"Yes, sir."

"You're pretty. Not the prettiest, but pretty."

Charly glanced at Babs. "Thank you, sir," she said.

"Got meat on your bones like a lady supposed to have. I like that."

"Meat. No meat," said Babs. " When did that matter to you?"

Duke laughed. "You got that right! But if I had a preference, it'll be a dame just like you, sweetheart," he said to his wife and pinched her chubby arm.

Babs swatted his hand away, but Charly could see her smiling.

"So what are you doing at my kitchen table?" Duke asked Charly.

It sounded so harsh, but Charly didn't flinch. "Boone brought me," she started saying, but Babs cut her off.

"That's Boone's girlfriend," Babs said.

"Actually, I'm not," Charly started saying, but Duke cut her off.

"His girlfriend, eh?" Duke said. "I've never in his entire life known him to bring a girlfriend around us."

"Me either," said Babs.

"You must have something awfully special between those two legs of yours," said Duke.

"Duke!" Babs yelled.

Charly couldn't believe he would be that disrespectful. "Please don't talk to me like that, sir," she said to him.

"You're at my kitchen table telling me how to talk?" Duke shot back at her.

"Yes, sir," Charly said. "If you're going to talk that way to me, I am. And I can certainly get away from your table, and your house, too, if you prefer."

Babs smiled. That was how to handle a joker like her husband!

Duke stared at Charly. "Got gumption, do you? Good. That's what Boone needs. We raised him to be hard because we had a hard life at that time. We raised all our kids to be hard. Not hard-hearted, but hard."

He continued to stare at Charly. "I like gumption," he said. "Boone needs that. But don't take it too far, young lady, or I'll have to rein you in. And it won't be pretty. Nobody in this county talks to me any kind of way. You won't either."

Charly stared at him. She was about to get up and leave, but she didn't want to disrespect Babs.

"But you're right," Duke said. "I shouldn't have been so honest. I apologize. I assumed you were accustomed to brutal honesty if you're my son's girlfriend."

"I'm not his girlfriend," Charly said firmly. "Boone and I have only known each other for a couple months."

"So what?" Duke asked. "Guys and gals are having cyber relationships these days. They're getting married the same day they meet face-to-face for the first time!"

"I understand all of that, sir, but Boone and I--"

"Make an interesting couple," Duke said. "You aren't his usual type, I'll tell you that. I thought he liked them younger, and smaller, and, if I may be brutally honest again, whiter."

Charly found herself smiling. "Yes, that's true," she said. She reached that very same conclusion when those two women came to their table at that restaurant. "But I'm not his type because I'm not his girlfriend."

"You are his girlfriend," said Babs. "You just don't know it yet."

Charly couldn't believe she said that. She didn't know it yet? What was that supposed to mean? But then the front door crashed open again, and a loud, unfamiliar voice was heard.

"Where's everybody?"

"Back here, Freddy," yelled Duke.

When Freddy Ryan entered the kitchen, all Charly saw was a nice-looking man in a nice-looking suit. "How's everybody?" he asked as he hugged Duke's neck and walked over and kissed Babs on the cheek.

"What are you doing here?" Babs asked him.

"I thought you'd have breakfast on the table by now," Freddy responded as he took a chair, turned it backwards, and sat down in a straddling manner, facing the table. "Where's the beef, Babs?"

"On your be-hind," said Babs, and Freddy and Duke laughed.

Then Freddy looked at Charly. "It doesn't take a genius to know that you must be that new dean," he said, extending his hand.

"Yes, I'm Charlene Johnson," Charly said, shaking his hand. Finally a normal guy, she thought.

"I'm Freddy," Freddy said. "These two knuckleheads are my aunt and uncle. Don't let them scare you away, alright?"

"It'll take more than our tongues to scare her away," said Duke. "She's got gumption."

"She's going to need it hanging around you two," Freddy said. "How do you like Saint Chris so far, Charlene? Can I call you Charlene?"

"Or Charly if you prefer," said Babs. "Charly's her nickname."

"Charly?" Freddy asked, getting permission from the source herself.

"Yes, that'll be fine," Charly said. She liked Freddy immediately.

"He's the mayor," said Duke.

"Oh, really?" said Charly. "That's very impressive."

"Don't be too impressed," said Duke. "He might be the mayor, but he's not a very good one."

Freddy laughed. "Still getting my sea legs," he said. "I'll improve."

"He's the reason you're here," said Babs to Charly.

Charly was confused. "He's on Saint Chris's board of directors you mean?"

"Don't remind me about that board," said Babs. "But no. He told that board, however, that this town had to diversify."

"They needed more blacks in positions of power, in other words," said Duke. "The blacks in town were Freddy's margin of victory, mainly because all of his women voted."

Charly found that an odd reference. "Excuse me?"

"Don't mind him, Charly," Freddy said.

"He likes black women," Duke said.

"And you don't?" asked Babs. "That's news to your son and daughter."

Duke gave Babs a hard look. Even Freddy seemed to tense up. Charly didn't know what that reference meant, but it was apparently a low blow to Duke.

"You didn't have to go there," Duke said.

"You didn't, either, all those years ago," said Babs. "But you went there. Not once, but twice. A son *and* a daughter. Don't you talk to me about where I didn't have to go. You've already been!"

Duke looked at Charly. "As I was saying," he said to her, "Freddy here as a thing for black women. He just loves them. And they have a thing for him. He's in bed with the blacks, literally and figuratively, and he wants more of them in leadership roles. Not his women, per se, but black women in general. He's in bed with the blacks you see."

Charly wasn't sure if she loved Duke's use of the term *the blacks*, as if they were a monolith community, but he said he was brutally honest and she most definitely believed him.

Then he looked at Charly again. "I heard about what happened," he said. "I'm glad you weren't harmed."

"Thanks to Boone, I wasn't. He was there."

"Yeah, I heard that," said Freddy. "What, he was spending the night or something?"

"Oh, no! It was nothing like that."

"No? I thought you were Boone's girlfriend."

Where were they getting this from? "I'm not his girlfriend," Charly said yet again.

"You aren't? Really?" asked Freddy. "Has anybody told Boone?"

They all laughed at the table. Charly smiled and sipped more coffee, but she didn't get it at all. Was Boone telling them something he hadn't yet bothered to tell her? Or were they, as she suspected, taking too little information and running with it?

Whatever the reason, she refused to go along with what was an obvious lie. They were just getting to know each other. As far as Charly knew, that was all they were doing.

Freddy would be gone, Babs and Charly would have prepared breakfast for themselves and Duke by the time Boone returned. Charly had hoped to go to church, and so had Babs, but Duke made clear they all were going to stay put. They didn't know if the person who tried to take out Charly had been caught yet. "Boone didn't bring her here for nothing," he said. "He expects us to protect her. And we shall."

They were all sitting on the porch, in rocking chairs of all things, with the rifle at the ready, when Boone's Ferrari turned into the long dirt driveway and began speeding toward the wraparound porch.

Charly was so happy to see his return that she got up from her seat and walked up to the porch railing, waiting for him.

Babs touched Duke on his arm. "Not his girlfriend indeed," she whispered to him.

He smiled. "Oh, she's got it bad," he whispered back.

CHAPTER THIRTY

Charly didn't know what Babs and Duke were whispering on about, and she didn't care. She was too happy to see Boone in one piece. She knew he had to go on a dangerous mission.

When he got out of the car, she couldn't help it. She made her way down the steps. "You okay?" she found herself asking him.

She'd never know how happy Boone was to see her walk down those steps. His heart leaped with joy as he was driving toward the porch and he saw her get out of her seat to greet him. It was a happy, unfamiliar feeling that he liked a lot. He was amazed at how quickly she was growing on him.

"I'm good," he said as he closed his car door. "I hope my parents haven't given you too many fits."

Charly smiled. Boone understood that smile. "I knew you'd be safe here, that's why I brought you here. They're good people once you get used to their ways, which aren't so great."

"I understand. And you're right: they'll take some getting used to. But they've been kind to me, I have no complaints trust me."

Boone smiled and placed his hand on the small of her back. "Good," he said.

"How did it go?" Charly asked him.

"We got Dalbert Lee in custody," he said.

"That's a good thing," Charly said.

"Yes, it is. We also found out what Tabloski is up to."

"So he's not a ghost?"

"No ghost. He's the son of the man who killed your husband. He thinks he's going to be meeting you tonight at Danley's after closing time. Around eleven."

"Meet me? Why?"

"He paid Dalbert to set you up. Dalbert told him he contacted you and told you he had some information to give to you about who shot up your place, and you agreed to meet him at Danley's tonight. Only he wasn't going to be there. Tabloski will be there with plans to take you out."

Charly was spooked. "Goodness," she said.

Boone rubbed her back. His parents were staring at them. But Boone's sole focus was Charly. "It'll be okay," he said. "You'll be right here under the protection of my folks, and me and my men will meet Tabloski ourselves."

"Oh, Boone, that'll be so dangerous!"

"I'm a cop. I can handle danger. But I can't allow him to harm you. I won't allow that. Meeting him is the only way. You'll have to stay in the lion's den a little while longer."

Charly smiled. "I wouldn't call it that."

"With my old man around? Yes, you would."

She nodded. "Yes, I would."

"But don't let him disrespect you, Charly. He'll never respect you, if you let him get away with any of his nonsense. You understand that?"

She nodded again. "I do, yes,"

"Come on," he said, and began escorting her back up the steps. It wasn't lost on her, nor his parents, that he did not remove his hand from her back.

"Welcome back," Babs said with a smile. Charly could see that Boone was the apple of her eye.

"Thanks," said Boone. "Thanks for looking out for her."

"Is it over?" Duke asked.

Boone shook his head. "Not until later tonight."

"So we get to keep her all night?"

"Until I return, yes."

Duke exhaled. "And I planned to skinny dip tonight. Oh well!"

Babs shook her head. "Ignore him, Charly," she said.

But when Boone and Charly sat down in the bench seat together, and Boone folded his legs and kept his hand around her waist as if he was protecting her, not from the forces from without, but from his parents within, Duke didn't let up.

"What I don't understand," he said, "is how in the world could you allow your woman to live in Low Town like that? That's insane, Robert!"

"That had nothing to do with Boone," Charly said. "It's the apartment the board selected for me. It's a part of my contract."

Babs shook her head. "That board," she said. "They should be ashamed of themselves."

"Freddy's supposed to be working on it," Boone said. "He's going to talk to Fritz."

That was news to Charly, but she wasn't going to put Boone on front street with his parents.

She, instead, allowed them to small talk all morning long, and she just listened.

CHAPTER THIRTY-ONE

On purpose, Boone and his men arrived late at the scene. An SUV was already there, and Boone was careful to be driving Charly's vehicle, since that was what Tabloski would have been expecting to see.

"They're in place," Boone said to Morley and Dontay, who were bent down in the backseat. "I'm going to be seen as soon as I get closer to that SUV, so I need both of you to be ready to fire as soon as I give the word. If these guys mean to shoot it out, that's what we'll do. No hesitation, just do it."

"Yes, sir," said Dontay.

"You know I will," said Morley.

"But only on my call or I'll kick your ass, Mor," Boone said.

Dontay smiled. "That won't be necessary, sir," Morley said.

But all of them were tense as Boone inched his way toward that SUV.

"Okay, I got a read," Boone said. "Three men. One behind the wheel, and two on the backseat.

They're locked and loaded I can tell by the way their arms are positioned."

Then Boone swerved his car. "They saw me and their preparing to fire!"

The first shot missed. "Now!" he yelled and Morley and Boone jumped out of the backseat and began firing, with Boone positioning the car as their shield.

The men in the SUV were firing back, but the driver was backing up, trying to get away. That was when Boone jumped out of the car, too, and began running toward the retreating SUV and firing as he ran.

"Stay behind that car!" he ordered his men. "Back me up!"

Morley and Dontay didn't expect anything less from Boone. He never wanted to put his men in harm's way. He would take the bullet if any of them had to take one.

That was why they were firing at that SUV, backing up their boss, as if their lives depended on it. They'd go through the fire for Boone.

But they didn't have to, because Boone had already taken out the driver, causing the SUV to begin driving wildly as it was still backing up, and the two men still alive were firing at a disadvantage. That driverless SUV was swerving and knocking them around.

But it was just the advantage Boone needed, and he took it. He stood still, and aimed and fired. He took out one man, and then the other one, and then he, Dontay, and Morley began running toward the SUV.

"Wait!" Boone yelled, pulling Dontay back when he attempted to run in front of his boss. "There may be others inside," he warned. "We don't want an ambush."

Boone stayed in front, as they kept their guns aimed and made their way to the SUV. Boone was even looking beyond the SUV, just in case.

But it wasn't necessary. When he finally pulled open the door of the SUV, and they all looked inside, there was no need to worry. There had been three men inside, and all three were dead.

Boone holstered his gun, checked for ID, and identified the ringleader.

"So that's Tabloski," Morley said.

"That's Tabloski," said Boone when he pulled the driver's license out of Tabloski's wallet. "Romney Tabloski, the son of Meeker Tabloski. The son of the man who killed Dean Johnson's husband."

Dontay exhaled. "He looks like a chump," he said.

Boone smiled, and then laughed. He liked Dontay. Besides, he was just happy that the man who wanted Charly dead was no longer a threat to her.

Later that night, thrilled that the threat was over, they arrived back at his place. It was just after midnight and they both were tired. They headed upstairs.

Boone kept his hand around her waist as they walked up his stairs. He kept taking glances at Charly, as if he needed to see if she felt the way he felt. But nothing in her body language gave it away. But he was feeling something powerful.

When they made it on the second floor landing, and up to the guest room, Charly did her customary turn. "Good night, Boone," she said to him.

"Sleepy?" he asked her.

"Very. You?" she asked him.

"I'm tired. Don't know how sleepy I am."

"Thanks for taking care of Tabloski," Charly said, heartfelt. "And for keeping me safe while you were at it."

"Anybody who can endure my wonderful parents can endure anything," he said.

Charly smiled. "Spending all day with them and most of the night, I think I'm getting to know them a little better."

"Your verdict?"

"Good people, but tough."

Boone smiled. That was exactly right. "Yes," he said. "Brutally so."

"Like you," said Charly.

"I would have thought I was more diplomatic, but okay," he said.

"You and diplomacy?" Charly shook her head. "Don't think so, Boone, sorry."

He laughed. And found himself moving closer to her. And it was no fluke this time: she could just feel his heat.

And that was why she knew she'd better get away while she could. "Anyway," she said, "good night." And she moved to close the door.

But Boone's strength was already gone. She had moved too late. Because, as she was closing the door, he placed his big shoe in the doorway and prevented the closure. Charly looked at him.

He moved even closer to her, staring into her eyes. He placed his hands on her arms. "If you will have me," he said to her, "I would like to spend what's left of the night with you."

Charly didn't expect him to be so blunt about it, but given that Ryan nature, she wasn't surprised by it. But would it be the right call for them to make? "Are you sure?" she asked him, searching his eyes.

"Oh, yeah," Boone said without hesitation, rubbing her arms. "I've never been surer about anything in my life. I want to make love to you. I *need* to make love to you. Please."

It didn't sound like begging to Charly, although Boone knew that was exactly what it was. He was doing something he'd never done before in his life: begging a woman to sleep with him.

He'd beg all night long for Charly.

But he didn't have to. She wanted him too.

That was why she stepped aside, and allowed him to step into the guest bedroom, and close the door.

Then he leaned against that door, pulled her into his arms, and began kissing her with such passion that she felt as if her entire being was melding with his.

They kissed long and they kissed hard. He wrapped her into his arms and couldn't stop kissing her.

She placed her arms around him, too, and couldn't stop kissing him.

They were too old pros afraid to go down that road. But the feelings were too strong now. It was a road they had to go down.

Until Boone finally stopped kissing her, and rubbing his tented pants against her. He lifted her up, and carried her to the bed.

CHAPTER THIRTY-TWO

Charly woke up alone in bed. She looked at the clock on the wall. It was two minutes after six. School started at eight. She had good time.

But she was still wet between her legs, which only served to remind her of Boone, and she found herself just laying in that bed smiling.

It was the best lovemaking experience she'd ever had in her entire life. And just thinking about it, she wanted to be with him again. But she knew that was an impossibility. She loved being with him, but she wasn't losing her job over being with him.

She got out of bed, showered, and then got herself dressed for work. Not her best attire. She only had what she had placed in her suitcase, so she opted to wear a pair of slacks and a tucked in shirt. To make it look more professional, she placed on the small, white cardigan sweater she also had with her.

When she made it downstairs, she could smell the food cooking in the kitchen. That same stew he had given her the day before. And she was ready to eat it.

"Good morning," she said jovially as she entered the kitchen.

"Well good morning," Boone said, happy too, as she walked in. She looked so radiant to him that his heart leaped with joy. *This was his woman*, was what went through his head. *This was his woman?*

She gave him the best sex he'd ever had, but it was more than that. He'd been having sex with women all his life. Charly was the first time he made love to a woman. Charly was the first time he couldn't wait to be with that woman again. Charly was the first time he felt that he could be with that woman for the rest of his life.

It was a terrifyingly happy feeling.

"I thought you'd never get up," he joked.

"Quit lying," she said, "it's early still."

Boone laughed.

"Stew again?" she asked him.

"You seemed to like it toward the end."

"I did. It's a good pick'em up for early in the morning."

"That's the reason my parents always fed it to us too. We were boys and they weren't about to raise no sorry men."

"But I thought your mother said something about a daughter," Charly said.

Boone looked at her as he plated the stew. "Oh, they mentioned them," Boone said.

"Them?" Charly asked.

"My stepsiblings. My father's love children from a woman who was not his wife."

Charly was surprised. "Oh, I see." Then she remembered what they were talking about when that conversation came up. "Are they African-American?" she asked.

Boone nodded. "They are. Their mother is a doctor over in Lexington. I was a teenager when it happened."

"And your mother stayed with him?"

"Oh, yeah. That wasn't his only indiscretion then and to this day. It was the only indiscretion that produced children."

Charly shook her head. "Men," she said.

"Don't put me in that category," said Boone.

"You? Oh, those two women were just a figment of my imagination?"

Boone looked at her. And for the first time, Charly realized what it all meant. She'd just slept with a man who could very easily break her heart. She'd just slept with a man who all but told her he didn't know what being faithful to one woman meant. What had she done???

The alarm in her eyes startled Boone. And he knew exactly why she was suddenly so fearful. He had to reassure her! "I'll never do that to you, Charly," he said to her.

Charly looked at him. He stared at her. What man didn't say that to her, and then turned around and cheated on her as if it was what she deserved. Why should he be any different?

She stood up. "I think I'm going to get to the office," she said. "My car is still at your parent's home." Boone had brought it there after they took care of Tabloski and company. "Can you drop me over there?"

"I can, but I want you to drive my car."

"Your car? Why? I have a car."

"You're with me now. You aren't driving that."

Charly stared at him. "Boone, what are we doing? I can't take another heartbreak."

"I'm not going to break your heart," said Boone.

But Charly still wasn't convinced. She'd heard that too many times before as well. "What are we doing?" she asked him again.

"We're trying each other on for size," he said. "We're seeing if it can work."

"I have serious trust issues," Charly said.

"As do I," said Boone.

"I'd be crazy to fall for somebody else when it nearly killed me the last time."

Boone frowned as he thought about his little girl and how she died. "Me too," he said.

But Charly was still unsatisfied. "What are we doing, Boone?" she asked him yet again.

He put down the stew pot and made his way to her side. "We're trying, Charly," he said. "We're giving it a shot. We're trying to see if we can beat the odds and get a second chance at love."

Tears appeared in Charly's eyes. Boone pulled her into his arms. "Don't cry, darling. Please don't cry. It'll work out. I believe it'll work out."

"But how can you be so sure?"

Boone stopped hugging her and looked her in her eyes. "Because I'm usually the problem," he said. "I'm not going to be the problem."

Charly smiled. It was a sweet thing for him to say. And then she gave him a peck on his lips. But he wasn't into pecks when it came to Charly. He pulled her back into his arms and gave her another long, passionate kiss. So long, and so passionate that Charly knew that they would end up right back in bed again if they weren't careful. So she had to be. She had the most to lose.

She pushed back from him. "We can't," she said. "I'll be late for work."

Boone let out a hard exhale. He wanted to be with her again, there was no doubt about that. His erection proved that. But he knew she was right. "Tonight," he whispered in her ears.

She smiled. "Trying to get me dick-whipped?" she asked him.

"Oh, I already got you there," Boone said with a grin. "You were dick-whipped from the moment I put that whipping on you."

"Boone!" Charly laughed, hitting him playfully. Talk about brutally honest!

"What I want to get you," said Boone with a serious look on his face, "is Boone-whipped. Because," he added, "I'm already Charly-whipped."

Charly stared at him. Was he really? Was this man for real for the long haul, or for right now?

She didn't know, and she knew falling for a man like Boone Ryan was quite the risk. But she knew she had to take it.

She smiled. He smiled. And he pulled her into his arms once again.

CHAPTER THIRTY-THREE

Boone walked Charly to his Ferrari. "The Ferrari?" she asked. "I thought for sure you was going to let me drive the Mercedes."

But Boone was already shaking his head. "Nope," he said. "Some people in this town knows I drive that Mercedes. They all know I drive this Ferrari. They know this is my car. I want them to know that you're my woman now. I want no ands, ifs, or buts about it. You belong to me. You're driving the Ferrari."

Charly felt as if she was some kind of queen the way he said that. "You want the people of this town to know that I'm your woman," she asked, "or do you want the *women* of this town to know that I'm your woman?"

"The women, yes," he admitted, "and any man who has any designs on you. Especially the men."

"You needn't worry about that," Charly said, getting in the car.

"You needn't worry about those women," he said, helping her get in.

After she was behind the wheel, he showed her what was what. "You can drive a stick, right?"

"No, Boone," she said sarcastically. "I'm just going to figure it out as I go along." He laughed. "Of course I can drive a stick or I wouldn't have gotten in this car, boy!"

"Okay, okay," he said, still smiling, "don't take my head off."

Then they looked at each other. "Be careful," he said, and kissed her. It lingered, but only just. He knew they had jobs to get to.

But then he pulled out a small pistol and handed it to her.

"What's this?"

"Ever shot a gun before?" he asked her.

She nodded. "Yeah. After I testified at Tabloski's trial, a cop on the force used to take me to the range and he taught me how to use one. In case the mob or somebody came after me. I used to carry one with me everywhere I went."

"Do the same with this one," he said to her.

She looked at the gun. Then at him. "I thought Tabloski was dead."

"He is."

"The threat isn't over?"

"It probably is," Boone said, "but just in case."

Charly understood his concern. And she gladly took the gun.

"Kentucky is an open carry state, so don't worry about getting in trouble. I'll have that gun registered to you."

"Just like that?"

"Just like that," Boone said.

"A perk of being the boss?"

"You got it."

"Well, I'm not the boss. I've got to get to work and get there on time."

He waved at her as she drove away. He'd never felt prouder to have somebody representing him the way Charly represented him. She was, in his eyes, the very definition of classiness. And sexy? There was nothing sexier to him than to see her driving his car. He liked it. It made a statement, he felt.

He kept watching her until she was clean out of sight. His men would be shocked by his behavior, because he was shocked too. That was why he got into his truck, and sped off too.

Tabloski was gone, just as he told her, but he couldn't stop wondering if the threat was over. Why he wondered it, he couldn't say. But that pesky gut of his started bothering him again.

CHAPTER THIRTY-FOUR

When Charly drove into the Dean of Students parking spot at Saint Christopher Academy, everybody in that parking lot was staring at her. That was Boone Ryan's car, and they knew it. What in the world, they all wondered, was she doing behind the wheel?

They'd heard about the shooting, and how Boone just happened to be to her house at the time, but they still couldn't believe he'd be that interested in her. He wasn't that interested in anybody else, why would he be that interested in her? It was baffling to them.

But when Charly stepped out of that car, she wasn't thinking about their prying eyes. She smiled at them, said hello to the few she knew by name, and made her way toward the school's entrance. But if she were to be honest with herself, it felt good. By letting her drive his car, Boone wanted to make a statement to all of those in town who would doubt his allegiance to any woman, and particularly to her, and she had to admit it was working like a charm. Like a bludgeon over their heads.

Charly was never the showoff type. She kept her head down and got her work done. That was how she rolled. But to be Boone Ryan's woman, as he called her, felt awesome.

She didn't rub it in, however. That wasn't how she rolled either. She made her way into the building as if it was any other day. She let her high-held head, her high-stepping feet, and that Ferrari do the talking for her.

But she had only made it to the main office, and was asking Minnie Fennel to pull up the absentee list from last week, when both of them heard a bloodcurdling scream that seemed so far away, but was so loud it seemed as if it was right in their own eardrums. And then they heard many screams, even louder screams, and the sound of students running.

Minnie ran to the office door and locked it, as if there was no one else on that campus, but Charly ran behind her and pushed her away. "There're students out there!" she cried. "What are you doing?"

Charly quickly unlocked the door and as soon as she did, students ran into the office as if their lives depended on it. "Go to the back!" she yelled to the students as they ran in. "Go to the back!"

And all of them obeyed as if, for the first time in their lives, they were happy to be ordered about, and ran toward the back where the principal and vice-principal, and Charly's offices were. Amos was still in jail, and Dr. Dorsett never arrived to work that early, so nobody was there but Charly. She was, by default, the senior staff in charge.

And she took charge, grabbing the gun Boone had given to her out of her purse so fast that the purse spilled all over the floor. Then she ran out of the office and into the hall. Minnie had run in the back with the students, but Charly knew she couldn't hide back there.

"What's happening?" she was asking the students who were running past her, but none of them could answer. They were running for their lives.

Charly never dreamed she'd be running to trouble. That wasn't her on any given day. But these were kids. She had a gun. She had no choice.

But when she ran toward where all of the students were running from, and she saw what they were running from, she stopped in her tracks. She could hardly believe it.

And then another door opened, and the students that had been in the gym came rushing out, and the stampede was on.

CHAPTER THIRTY-FIVE

A chair flew all the way across the squad room and crashed through the window, shattering it so completely that the cops sitting anywhere near that window had to jump up and move out of the path of the flying glass.

But that glass was the least of their worries. Boone Ryan was pissed and he wasn't holding back. "How in the world could this happen?" he was asking them. "He was booked yesterday and already he got out?"

"Looks like it might have been a processing error, Chief," said Sarge.

"Processing error my ass!" Boone shot back. "What are talking about? I had him under house arrest until Tabloski was handled, and he didn't escape then. But when we bring him to the station and put him in one of my cells, then he escapes? How in the world did that prisoner escape? How in the world is that even possible?"

Boone was beside himself with anger, as nobody could answer his questions. "Nobody's leaving this building until I get answers," he said. "He escaped? Are you kidding me? As long as it took me to find that asshole, and you're telling me he escaped? I want an accounting of every man's time from the moment he was brought to this station up until this very moment. I want cameras seized. I want phone records. I want laptops seized. Nobody in or out until I find out how the hell did this happen!"

The phone was ringing, but nobody dared answer it.

"Answer that *got*damn phone, what's wrong with y'all?" Boone yelled, and Dontay quickly answered the call.

"When was the last prisoner check?" Boone asked Sarge.

Sarge looked at the logs. "Six-fifteen this morning."

"And he was there?"

"He was there. Joby said he laid eyes on him and everything."

Dontay stood up. "Chief?"

"What was he doing when Joby laid eyes on him?" Boone asked Sarge.

"Chief?" Dontay said again.

"He was asleep in his cell," said Sarge.

"Chief?" Dontay said yet again and Boone yelled, "*What*?!"

"There's been a shooting at the school, sir," Dontay said.

"A school shooting?" Sarge said, jumping to his feet.

"At Hemingway High?" Boone asked, hoping that it wasn't the other school.

"No, sir," said Dontay. "At Saint Chris. And sir, there's a fatality."

Boone's heart dropped. And he ran out of that squad room.

"Dontay, you and Morley go with him," Sarge ordered since Boone didn't bother to do so, and Dontay and Morley began hurrying out too. "I'll get the cops on patrol over there too."

But after Sarge put the call out for cops in the area to get to Saint Chris, he sat behind his desk and exhaled. First they have a prisoner escape. Now this? "Lord, don't let it be that gal," Sarge said.

The cop nearest to his desk looked at him. "What gal?" he asked.

"That dean," Sarge said. "Who else? You think he's mad now, let somebody harm that dean."

The cop looked at another cop. Neither one of them had any idea what Sarge was talking about. But the other cops in that squad room knew exactly what Sarge was talking about.

Boone was the first law enforcement officer to arrive on campus, but Dontay, Morley, and several patrol cars were right behind. He ordered the patrol officers to set up a perimeter outside, while he, Dontay, and Morley ran inside of the school. Boone was asking any faculty in sight, or any of the students still on campus about one person and one person only: "Where's Dean Johnson?" he kept asking. "Have you seen Dean Johnson? Is Dean Johnson okay?" He had been praying for everybody to be okay, but he was especially praying that she was not harmed. That she was not the fatality Dontay had mentioned.

But nobody had a clue where she was, or where anybody else was until one teacher pointed further into the guts of the school, and said he last saw her there.

Boone's heart was hammering as he ran in that direction. It was exactly where he DID NOT want Charly to be because everybody was pointing in that same direction when he asked them where the action was.

The action, according to everybody, was in the cafeteria. And when Boone and his men made it to the hot zone, they realized that it was not an active shooter on campus, as had first been reported, but a dead body on campus, just like Rita Mae's situation. But this time, Boone quickly realized when they saw the body, the victim was the elusive Dalbert Lee, the very man Boone had arrested the day before. The very man Boone had learned not an hour earlier had escaped from his jail.

And his body, lying in a pantry inside the cafeteria and discovered by another cafeteria worker, was what all the fuss was about.

And then Boone saw Charly.

She was further over in the cafeteria, consoling the cafeteria staff, when he first laid eyes on her. As a precaution, to his relief, she held that gun he had given to her in her hand. And he couldn't help it: he left Dalbert's body and made a beeline for her.

When Charly saw Boone hurrying his way, she broke free, too, and hurried to meet him. When they made it up to each other, they both wanted to fall into each other's arms. Boone, especially, was just that relieved that she was okay. But they were consummate professionals. They didn't touch.

Besides, Boone was looking at the tiny nip on her forehead. "What happened?" he asked her.

"They found a body," she said, but Boone pointed to her forehead.

Charly touched it. "Oh, that," she said. "Some students were hysterical and knocked me down, but I'm alright. I just can't believe there's another dead body on this campus."

"Neither can I."

"And some of these workers are saying it was Dalbert Lee's body, but I know you arrested him yesterday."

Boone nodded. "Yeah, I did," he said. "But that is his body."

"Does this mean the threat isn't over?" Charly asked him.

Boone exhaled as an anguished look appeared on his face. "That's what it looks like," he said. And when that same anguished look appeared on Charly's face, he couldn't help it. He was angry that Dalbert's escape and death meant that the threat was not over, and he was relieved that she was okay. He was angry that she might still be in harm's way, and relieved that at least for that moment she wasn't. He pulled her into his arms.

Charly knew she should have resisted his pull. Students shouldn't see their affection. But she couldn't resist Boone. He was, once again, the balm she needed. She melted in his arms. At that moment, they didn't care who saw them.

And later that evening, when they made it to Boone's house, they were both so emotionally spent that they headed straight upstairs. Boone investigated the crime scene, while Charly had to make sure all of the students had gotten home safely and that all of the complaining parents had been reassured. She also ordered the guidance counselors to be on hand tomorrow morning, along with grief counselors, to help students deal with yet another tragedy on their campus. The school would remain closed that extra day, the board decided, and the counseling sessions would take place at the adjourning Saint Christopher church, instead of the school. Charly had to spearhead that entire effort.

Now all they both wanted to do was go to sleep.

But Boone wasn't about to sleep alone. When they made it upstairs, and Charly broke away from him to head to the guest room, he pulled her back to him. "That's not your room anymore," he said to her.

"Actually," she said to him, "I thought I would be going back to my own apartment today."

But Boone was already shaking his head. "You aren't ever going back there, except to get your things."

"What are you saying?" Charly asked him. She was alarmed on a different level. She wasn't about to live with him. She wasn't about to make it that easy for him. She needed her own space, her own life, or a man like Boone Ryan would consume her. "I'm not living with you."

"I understand that," Boone said. "But you aren't living there. We'll find an apartment for you. I'm not saying you have to stay here. But you aren't staying there. I am saying that."

Charly had been with some domineering men in her life. Darryl was one of them. But she'd never been with a man quite like Boone. His domination was never about him. His domination was always about what he felt was best for her. He was looking out for *her*.

"Come on," Boone said, nudging her toward his bedroom.

Charly smiled. "You're a smooth operator, Robert Ryan," she said.

"And you aren't?" he asked, and Charly laughed.

But when they made it into his bedroom, and he fell across the bed bringing her on top with him, their levity was gone. Boone smoothed the hair out of her face. He stared into her big, pretty eyes. And then he kissed her. And then he held her, pleased to have her safe and sound and with him.

They would eventually shower together, and then pull back the covers and get in bed. They still needed rest. It had been too emotional a day. But their nearness, and their flesh against flesh, was too much for them to resist.

They made love that night, too, but only just. Because mostly they held onto each other. Mostly they took solace in knowing that two people who thought happiness had come and gone for them, just might beat the odds.

They might not have to go it alone after all.

CHAPTER THIRTY-SIX

The next morning while Boone was upstairs dressing, Charly was downstairs preparing the kind of breakfast she was accustomed to, and it didn't involve stew. Bacon, eggs, and toast were on the menu that she cooked from. And even Boone appreciated the smell of bacon in his house.

But then his doorbell was ringing as he made his way downstairs, prompting him to immediately pull out his gun. Nobody came to his house uninvited. It just wasn't done in Hemingway. But a lot of things, Boone also realized, were changing in his town.

Charly was out of the kitchen and coming up behind Boone when he peeped out of his peephole. She realized he had his gun at his side, which only reminded her of the danger that still lurked around them, and then he relaxed. And opened his door. But he kept that gun at his side.

When Charly realized the man at the door was the guy with the dreadlocks who had been at Rita Mae Brown's family home, she relaxed too. But not entirely. Why would he be coming there?

"What is it?" Boone asked him.

Dreadlocks glanced at Charly. "May I come in?" he asked.

"No," said Boone firmly. "What is it?"

"I heard they shot Dalbert," Dreadlocks said.

"Who shot him?" Boone asked.

"His boss is who I'm willing to bet."

Boone and Charly both frowned. "His boss?" Boone asked. "Who's his boss?"

"Lester P," said Dreadlocks.

"Lester Pataki?" Charly asked before Boone could. "You're saying the vice-chairman of the Saint Christopher board of directors is a drug dealer's boss?"

"That's exactly what I'm saying," said Dreads. "Lester P always been Dalbert's supplier. He runs the drug trade in Hemingway. You wanna know how that opioid crisis got so bad around here, look no further than Lester P. He got those doctors to prescribe all of that Vicodin and oxycodone and all of those pain killers to drug addicts like it was cotton candy at the fair. He's the man you need to arrest."

"Why didn't you mention his name when you were talking to me at Rita Mae Brown's house?" Boone asked him.

"Cause I knew your mind was already made up," Dreads said. "You had Amos Yerkson behind bars. Like most cops, the case was closed as far as you were concerned."

"Why didn't you mention his name to me?" Charly asked him. "My mind wasn't made up."

"But you didn't have the power to do nothing. I figure you hook up with Dalbert, he'd tell you what you needed to know. Instead you hooked up with Chief, and let him tell you what you needed to know when he didn't know squat either."

"Watch it," Boone said to him.

"I'm just telling you what I know," said Dreads.

"And how do you know this?" asked Boone.

"I'm not gonna lie, I used to send clients Dalbert's way, okay? I used to do that, sure I did. And Dalbert wanted me on his payroll. He's the one who told me about Lester P. But I wasn't going out like that," Dreads said. "People wanna poison their systems, fine. But I'm not selling that poison to them."

"Anything else?" Boone asked him.

"Nall, that's it."

"Don't leave town," Boone said. "I may need to talk to you again."

"Where I'm going?" Dreads asked as he turned to leave.

"And Malcolm," Boone said, calling him by a first name Charly didn't know herself.

Dreads turned back around. "Yeah?"

"Why would you come all this way just to tell me that?"

"Because Dalbert pumped that poison into Rita Mae's system when I told his ass to let her be. Now he's dead and nobody's gonna pay for her death? That's why I came here."

Boone nodded. He was going to tell Malcolm to never come to his home uninvited ever again, but he didn't want Charly to think less of him. They needed the info he gave to them. That was why he remained silent as the young man left.

Boone closed and locked his door. Charly looked at him. "You believe him?" she asked.

"About Pataki? No," said Boone.

"But how would you know if he's telling the truth or not?" Charly asked. "He sounded convincing to me."

"He was convincing alright. He convinced us of his lie. But my experience tells me Pataki's not that kind of guy."

"Or that you made up your mind that Amos is Rita's killer, and therefore you aren't interested in any other scenarios? I hope that's not the case."

Boone was a little hurt that she would think of him that way. But he realized their relationship was still brand new. They were still getting to know the heart and soul of each other. "I'll check it out," he said. "But in the meantime," he said, pulling her into his arms, "you, young lady, will be going back to my parents' home."

"I can't. I've got to be at the church. The grief counselors are coming, and Dr. Dorsett put me in charge of spearheading the effort."

"Okay," Boone said, proud that she was taking the bull by the horns. "Good. But I'll take you there, and I'll pick you up. I do not want you to hang outside under any circumstances. You understand me?"

She nodded. "I understand that you think you're the boss of me," she said with a smile on her face.

"I think it?" he asked her, kissing her. "No, ma'am. I know it!" She laughed. He slapped her behind and stared at it as she headed back to the kitchen and to their breakfast.

CHAPTER THIRTY-SEVEN

Boone's truck stopped outside of the law office of Les Pataki. Dontay Culpepper, whom Boone asked to ride shotgun with him, got out on the passenger side. Dontay felt honored that the chief would ask him to accompany him, and not one of the more seasoned vets. But he was realizing what the seasoned vets already knew: Boone was always giving Dontay the choice assignments. Boone always had Dontay accompanying him. To the veteran cops it wasn't fair. He should get in line like they had to. But to Dontay, it was God's grace. He lived his life in faith and trust and hard work. It was paying off for him.

Les Pataki's secretary allowed them passage into Les's office, and neither one of them accepted his offer to have a seat. And as usual, Dontay thought, his boss was no brownnoser. He got down to business and told Pataki exactly why they were there.

And Pataki was insulted. "It's a bald-faced lie!" he said. "I've never been involved in any drug trade or drugs of any kind in my life!"

"Then why did your name come up?" Boone asked.

"How should I know? Somebody's lying on me!"

"Or you aren't telling me the whole story. Perhaps if I take you downtown, you will."

"Downtown? You mean *arrest* me?"

Boone nodded. "Interrogate you, and yes, if I'm not satisfied that you're coming clean, arrest you."

Pataki couldn't believe it. He had to sit down before he fell down. This could get out of hand! "Okay," he said.

Dontay was surprised. He was going to come clean? Really?

"Tell me," Boone said.

"I'll admit I had her, too, but I never gave her any drugs or anything like that."

Dontay looked at Boone. Did he miss something? But Boone was puzzled too. "You had her too?" he asked.

"Yeah. Every powerful man in this town had her, Chief, except maybe you and your cousin. But we all had her. Not just me!"

"Are you saying Rita Mae Brown was a prostitute?"

"Of the highest order, yes," said Pataki.

"And many men in this town had her?"

"Many men in this town, yes," said Pataki.

"Including Amos Yerkson?" asked Dontay.

"I don't know about him. I'm not sure if he could afford her."

"Who did she work for?" Boone asked.

"Who was her pimp, you mean?" Pataki asked.

"Yeah. Who?"

"Dalbert Lee, the guy the found dead yesterday. Who else? He had a string of girls on his payroll. He didn't just deal drugs. He dealt women too. Only everybody wanted Rita Mae. I would have never killed her. And anybody claiming I was a drug supplier is telling a lie. A big, fat lie!"

Dontay looked at Boone. Pataki was damned convincing, he thought. But Boone was trying to put the pieces together. And then Pataki's desk phone rang. He answered. When he hung up, he addressed the chief.

"I've got to go," he said.

"Where?" the chief asked.

"There's an emergency board meeting at the church."

"Oh, yeah?" Boone asked. "About what? Dalbert's death?"

"Not in a manner of speaking. It's about Dean Johnson. But Dalbert Lee's death has something to do with it."

Dontay looked at the chief. The chief was staring at Pataki. "What about Dean Johnson?" he asked.

"With everything that's been happening since she came to town, it seems they're good and ready to get rid of her," Pataki said. "And I don't disagree with that," he added. "That lady is bad news with a capital B."

Dontay expected the chief to rip into Pataki for speaking so ill of Dean Johnson. Dontay certainly wanted to give that arrogant so-and-so a piece of his mind. But Boone remained calm. He wasn't about to show his hand to that bastard and give that board all the more reason to fire Charly.

"Go to your meeting," he said. "We'll talk again." And then Boone, with Dontay on his heels, walked on away.

But as soon as they had gotten back into Boone's truck, and were driving away from Pataki's law firm, Boone was making a call of his own. He needed heavy artillery. He needed somebody to beat back that board on Charly's behave, and he needed them now.

Because one thing he knew for sure: nobody was taking Charly away from him.

CHAPTER THIRTY-EIGHT

The main auditorium of Saint Christopher Church were filled with students and grief counselors and Charly had been on her feet since her arrival. Students were gravitating to her, because they knew she was the one faculty member that looked out for them yesterday. She was the one faculty member that didn't run and hide to save her own skin, but put herself in harm's way to make sure they were safe. There was no school shooter the way they had thought. But that dead body still spooked every one of them, and they were there in force, to get whatever coping mechanisms those counselors could give to them.

That was why, when Dr. Dorsett pulled their dean aside to speak with her, they looked flustered. Charly was the students' example. They wanted to know, in a time of crisis like that, where did she find that courage. Why didn't she run and hide too?

"I hate to disturb you," the principal said to her, "because the students seem to be taking to you like fish to water. And I like that. But the

340

board is here, Charly," he said with a look of regret in his eyes. "And unfortunately, they're here about you. They wish to see you."

Charly could feel her heart beginning to pound as soon as Dr. Dorsett stated that the board meeting was about her. But she had work to do. If they were going to fire her, it wasn't going to be today.

"As soon as I finish directing these kids, I'll go in there," Charly said and turned to leave.

But Dr. Dorsett stopped her. "Charly," he said, and she turned back toward him. "This isn't a debatable point. A majority of the board members are here, which means they aren't just meeting about you. They're going to vote about you. You need to get in there and defend yourself. But whether you do or not, you still have to drop everything right now, and go in there."

Charly stared at her principal. He was actually a good guy, from what she'd seen of him, but unlike Boone, who called out bad behavior on every turn, he stayed in his lane. Hiring and firing was the job of the board of directors. He was going to let them do their job, regardless of how he felt about her.

And unbeknownst to Charly, Dorsett was really digging her and her work ethic, and her principles, and, if he were to be honest, her very sexy, very voluptuous, smoking-hot body. She was growing on him.

Charly knew, after that shootout at her place, that she was on borrowed time. Somehow she knew the board would find a way to blame her for what Tabloski's man tried to do to her. But she also thought her work would speak for her. And her colleagues would speak for her. But if not even her principal was willing to go against the board, why would his underlings?

She gave him the clipboard with the names of the grief counselors and how many students they had spoken with so far, and made her way into the back conference room inside the church.

"Have a seat, Miss Johnson."

Fritz Hollingsworth, the board chairman, was the first face she saw, and the only voice she heard. He was at the head of the table and had invited her to take a seat at the opposite head of the table. Other members of the board, including Margaret Ackroyd and Mark Kerchup, were also there. The vice-chairman, Les Pataki, to Charly's surprise, was there too.

Charly wondered if Boone had gotten a chance to speak with Pataki, and how did that go, but she had not heard from Boone. Besides, she wasn't all that certain if this sudden board meeting didn't have everything to do with Dreadlocks' allegations against Pataki. Allegations the board might also be blaming on her. Whatever the reason for the get-together, she did as she was ordered, and sat down.

"We won't beat around the bush, Miss Johnson," Fritz said. "We, as a unit, have decided to terminate your contract. Effective immediately."

Charly knew it was coming, but it still stung deep. This unlikely place, Kentucky, needed to be her soft landing. It wasn't. She'd had nothing but setbacks since she arrived in town. But she was getting in a groove. Students were coming around. And even some faculty members were tolerating her better.

And Boone.

She and Boone were trying to make a start.

Things, she thought, were looking brighter for her.

Now this.

"May I ask why I'm being terminated?" she asked Fritz.

"Where do we begin," said Margaret Ackroyd. "The list just keeps getting longer."

"For starters," said Fritz, "you and your now-deceased husband were once the target of an assassin."

Charly frowned. "I was not the original target," she said. "But you knew all about that, and what happened to my husband, and how I testified against his killer, when you hired me. And you hired me anyway. How could that suddenly be the reason you terminate me?"

"Because you were the target of another assassin's bullets," said Margaret. "That's how!"

"If we keep you around," said Fritz, "we could be putting our students in harm's way."

"Although," said Mark Kerchup, "the people responsible for that shootout at your apartment have been terminated themselves, by out crusty chief of police. So I don't see the point of this firing myself."

"There's more," said Fritz.

"Much more," said Margaret, giving Mark the crude eye.

"You didn't attend church on Sunday the way you are mandated to do so."

Charly was dressed to attend. She had no idea Boone would get a lead on Dalbert Lee and have to leave her at his parents ranch for her own protection. But they knew all of that too she was certain. The reasons just didn't matter to them.

"You also had a gun yesterday at school," said Fritz. "A gun," he added, "which the board had not approved to be on campus."

Charly could have defended herself there, too, telling them that the chief of police had given her that gun. But she knew they didn't care. The writing was on the wall. They wanted her as far away from their precious school, and by default, their town, as they could get her.

They could force her away from their school but, until she found out where things were going with her and Boone, she wasn't leaving their town.

Boone, she thought. He was rich like they were, and had influence too. But he was nothing like them and they knew it. Nothing he could say to them would persuade them. Charly knew that.

"May I at least be allowed to stay until the end of the day," she requested, "until after the grief counselors leave?"

Fritz looked at Margaret, the real chairman of the board, Charly thought, and she gave her tacit approval. "Yes," he said. "But then you must leave and not return. We will provide you your final paycheck immediately, and a plane ticket back to L.A. if you so desire."

"No thanks," Boone said as he suddenly appeared at the conference room door.

Everybody looked in his direction, including Charly. She knew he couldn't reverse their decision, but his support was like a shot in the arm for her.

But she and the board quickly realized that he was not alone. He came with his own support. Namely his cousin the mayor, and his mother Babs. Charly was shocked. What was she doing here?

But, to Charly's shock, all of the board members rose to their feet when Babs Ryan, walking with a cane, walked in.

"Mrs. Ryan," said Fritz, "what are you doing here?"

"What are you doing here?" Babs asked Fritz as she, Freddy, and Boone walked further into the room. Boone looked over at Charly, and she could tell he was worried and pissed, but they both kept their distance.

"We're conducting a board meeting," said Margaret.

"A meeting," Freddy asked, "or a firing?"

Fritz swallowed hard. "Both, as it happens," he said.

"So you want to fire Charly," Babs said.

"That's correct," said Fritz.

"Why? Because she won't kiss your ass?"

"Why, we have never!" said Margaret.

"Shut up, Maggie," said Babs.

And Margaret, to Charly's shock, did shut up. She thought Margaret was a member of the power family in the county. Apparently she thought wrong. Looked like the Ryans were the power family in that county.

But Babs continued. "Answer my question, Fritz," she said. "Is it because this young lady won't cow-tow to your nonsense and kiss your ass? Is that why you have this sudden need to fire her when you just hired her a few months ago?"

"It's for lots of reasons," Fritz said. "None of which concerns my rear end, thank you!"

"I am a lifetime board member," Babs said. "My father, along with your father and yours, too, Maggie, were the founding members. But Duke's father was the Executive Chairman of the founding members, which makes him, and me after I married him, lifetime executive chairmen of this board. We and we alone have the power to overturn votes."

Boone looked at Charly. He knew she'd be shocked, and she was.

"Why on earth would you want to overturn us?" asked Margaret. "You don't even know this woman!"

Babs exhaled. She was leaning on her cane. "My arthritis was going haywire this morning. I wondered why. It usually don't bother me like that on sunshiny days. But it was bothering me this time. Then I got the call from my son."

Boone called her? How did he even know, Charly wondered?

"I don't attend board meetings," Babs said to the group, "as all of you know. Have no idea what's going on. I don't attend meetings because, frankly, I can't stomach any of you. But when Boone told me what this particular meeting was about, I could not believe it. Somebody tried to kill Dean Johnson, and you were blaming *her*? Are you kidding me? Do you think I'll sit idly by and let you idiots fire a woman because somebody was out to get *her*?"

"Is it because we're firing a woman," Margaret asked, "or your *son's woman*? Is that why you're so concerned? Is that what got you off of that ranch?"

"I overrule the firing," Babs said. "That's what got me off of that ranch!" And then she took her cane and headed back out of the door she had come through. Freddy, smiling, followed his nail-tough aunt.

Charly wanted to jump up and run to her she was so happy. But she curbed her enthusiasm. Because Boone was curbing his, as if he didn't want to rub it in. And since he knew that board far better than she did, she took her cues from Boone.

But when the board excused her, they could only admonish her at best: "Clean up your act," Fritz said, "because Babs Ryan won't always be your savior." But she didn't feel vindicated. Like Fritz Hollingsworth said, it was more a reprieve than an exoneration. But she'd take it.

Boone was waiting for her in the hall, leaned against the wall. He smiled when she walked up to him. "Thought you were a goner, didn't you?"

"You know it," Charly said with a smile of relief. "Thanks. I didn't think you knew this meeting was even taking place."

"I was at Pataki's office when they called him," Boone said. And then Dr. Dorsett walked up.

"Congratulations, Charly," he said to his dean.

"Thanks," Charly said with a smile.

"No thanks to you," Boone said to Dorsett.

Dorsett was accustomed to Boone's brutal honesty, so he ignored him. "Why don't you take the rest of the day off," Dorsett suggested to

Charly. "I don't want you to incur the ire of that board another second. I'll see you at the office tomorrow."

"What about the students?"

"They're fine. Get you some rest. They'll need you more tomorrow, when they're back at the scene of the crime, than they need you today."

Charly thanked her principal, and Dorsett, giving Boone a hard look as if he was suspicious of the chief, walked away.

Then Charly and Boone began walking too. "I guess I'll head over to my place," she said to Boone.

"Nope," he said to her.

"To at least get some fresh clothes, Boone," she insisted.

"Nope," he said again. "You're hanging with me. And I can't get over to Low Town just yet."

"Then where are you going?"

"To find out why Malcolm, or Dreads as you call him, would have lied on Les Pataki."

"How do you know he lied?"

"Because I knew it all along," said Boone. "I was just making sure."

"Do you always go by your first instincts?"

"Always."

"What were your first instincts about me?"

"That you were hell on two legs," he said, "but worth it."

Charly smiled, and then laughed.

But then Boone's look turned serious. "Pataki did tell me something interesting about Rita Mae."

"What?" Charly asked. "That she was a hooker?"

Boone stopped walking and looked at Charly. "How would you know that?"

"Come on, Boone. Amos was interested in her wellbeing. Dreads was interested in her. I pegged Amos as a man with an unhealthy sexual appetite, not a man with a bloodlust. He didn't kill her, is my impression, but he did other unsavory things to her. The same for Dreads. Dreads was pointing the finger at others to keep that spotlight off of him."

Boone stared at Charly. He was impressed. But he wasn't going to give her the big head. "Smart ass," he said, Charly laughed, and they headed out together.

CHAPTER THIRTY-NINE

Dreadlocks lived on a backroad where houses were miles apart, and Charly began to feel queasy. "What if this was the plan all along," she said to Boone. "To lure us back here."

Boone smiled. "Malcolm knows not to try that with me," he said.

"You've known him a while?"

"Ever since he was a kid knocking old ladies in the head and stealing their purses."

"Really? Dreads is like that? I didn't take him for a thief."

"Because he isn't anymore. That's when he was a kid. He's still a criminal, but his crimes tend to be of the domestic variety."

"Fights with girlfriends?"

Boone nodded. "You got it," and then he turned into the driveway of one of those small houses. "We're here," he said.

But he turned and looked at Charly. "You wait here."

That made no sense to Charly. "Wait here?" He was the one who wanted her at his hip.

"Let me make sure nothing's weird. Then you can get out."

Charly nodded. She couldn't help but appreciate a man who was always looking out for her best interest first. It was so new to her that she didn't quite know how to handle it. "Okay," she said, and Boone got out of the truck.

But as soon as Boone walked across the dirt yard and up to the front door, that same door flew open and Dreads came running out.

"Get him!" he was crying, holding his stomach. "He shot me! He shot me!"

"Where is he?" Boone yelled as he pulled out his gun.

"Inside," Dreads said as he ran toward Boone's truck. "We got to get out of here!"

"Charly, drive!" Boone yelled, as he ran into the house.

Charly was already getting behind the wheel of Boone's truck before Boone told her to go, and she waited until Dreads jumped into the truck's cab.

But to his amazement, she still didn't go.

"Drive!" Dreads yelled. "He told you to drive!"

But Charly hesitated. She wasn't going to leave Boone there to die! She didn't drive.

Inside, Boone was aiming his weapon toward every corner, every crack, every crevice in that small home. But he didn't find the shooter. He ran toward the backdoor, opened it, aimed, and looked out too. But no shooter.

He ran in the back rooms of the house, and aimed at every corner in those rooms too. But no shooter.

But when he ran back up front, he realized what he had missed all along. It was the house. The house was pristine. There was no sign of any kind of violence whatsoever, let alone a shooting!

And then he realized what else he had missed.

Blood on Malcolm. There was no blood on Malcolm. And now, he was with Charly.

"Charly!" Boone cried, and ran out of that house faster than he had run into it.

When he realized Charly was still on the driveway, he felt better. But as soon as he saw his truck, he saw Malcolm rising up, with a gun in his hand, and aiming it through the window of the cab. He screamed Charly's name when he saw Malcolm aiming that gun directly at her head.

"Charly!" he screamed and aimed his own gun, ready to fire, but Charly, God love her, he thought, turned around and beat him to the punch. She fired once at Malcolm. She mostly missed, but she was able to graze his shoulder just enough that he dropped his gun and grabbed that shoulder.

And Boone pounced. He ran down those steps and over to his truck so fast he looked like a ninja to Charly. But however he looked, she was glad he was okay and coming her way.

Boone jumped onto the back of that cab, grabbed an already injured Malcolm, and beat what his old man called the snot out of him! He punched him and punched him. The idea that that bastard would try to kill Charly kept him punching him.

Charly stayed behind the wheel, and was looking back and watching it all. She'd never condone violence and especially not police brutality, but she was condoning it that day. When she had looked through her rearview mirror and saw Malcolm raise up that gun toward her head, she had a split second to react. A split second to lift her gun, turn and fire. She fired awkwardly, because of the urgency, but it was enough to stop him from firing. But that was too close for her to be comfortable. She would have beat his ass, too, if she was in that cab with Boone.

Boone finally grabbed him up as if he was a rag doll, and pointed his gun directly at his nose. "Tell me all you know," he ordered him. "Tell me now!"

"He made me say Dalbert did it," Malcolm cried. "He made me say Dalbert killed Rita. He made me say Pataki was Dalbert's boss. He made me say it!"

Boone didn't ask who yet. He wanted all Malcolm had to tell him.

"Why did you try to kill Charly?"

"Who's Charlie?"

"Dean Johnson," Boone said. "Why did you try to kill her?"

"He said I had to. He said they'd kill me if I didn't do it."

"Who said that?" Boone asked him.

"Amos," said Malcolm.

Boone was shocked. So was Charly. "Amos?" Boone asked. "Why would Amos tell you to kill Dean Johnson?"

Malcolm was shaking his head. "I don't know. He's the one who told me to say Dalbert killed Rita Mae. He's the one who said they'd kill me if I didn't do everything he said."

"Who'd kill you?"

"The same people who killed Rita Mae."

Charly was shocked. Amos really was involved in Rita Mae's death?

Boone stood erect in the cab of his truck. "If you're lying, you're dead," he said to Malcolm. Then he thought again about how Malcolm could have shot and killed Charly. "Bastard!" he said, and punched Malcolm so hard that he knocked him unconscious.

CHAPTER FORTY

If his men thought he was going to sit the dean in his office while he went to confront Amos in the cells, they were mistaken. Even Charly was surprised after he booked a now conscious Malcolm and told her to come with him.

His men were staring at both of them as Boone held Charly's hand and walked with her down the corridor that led to the cells, and then all the way down to Amos's cell.

Amos was standing, as if he was expecting them, when they walked in.

"Hello, Miss Johnson," Amos said cheerfully when Boone unlocked his cell. "Hello, Chief," he said with less vigor.

But it didn't matter because, as soon as Boone entered the cell behind Charly, he rushed up to Amos, grabbed him with both hands, and threw him against the wall. Then he kept Amos's head smushed against that wall. His mouth was almost touching Amos's wax-filled ears.

"Who's behind it?" Boone asked Amos.

"I don't know what you're--"

"I don't wanna hear that bull!" Boone yelled angrily. "Who's behind it?"

"Behind what?"

"You want to play games? *Got*dammit," Boone said, pulling out his gun and forcing it into Amos's mouth, "let's play games! Let's play *kill that bastard*! Wanna play that game?"

Amos was saying something, but the gun was in his mouth. Boone removed it. "Talk, dammit! Talk! Who wants Charly dead?"

"They were just supposed to scare her," Amos said. "That's all it started out as. It was a jealousy thing, you see. You couldn't be happy, and you were showing interest in her. So they were hired to run her off the road. That's all that was about. But Rita Mae was the main thing."

Charly glanced at Boone, and then looked back at Amos. "What do you mean?" she asked him.

"Rita Mae had to die. She wanted Rita Mae dead."

"Who wanted Rita dead?" Charly asked.

Amos didn't say.

Boone jacked him up again. "Answer her!" he yelled.

"My niece," he said. "And what she wants, she gets. She's been rich and spoiled her whole life. My brother, her father, died an early death trying to give her everything she wanted. And I shielded her too. When I came to Hemingway, nobody even knew I was related to her, because I wasn't a sort of person with means. She was ashamed of me. And I wouldn't reveal our relationship either. I've always shielded her too."

"Who's your niece?" Charly asked.

Amos hesitated. Boone was about to jack him up again, but he spoke. "Monica," he said.

Boone frowned. "Monica?"

Amos nodded. "Yes. Courtney's mother. The woman you used to purport to love. *That* Monica."

Charly was shocked. Was he talking about the mother of Boone's deceased child? She looked at him.

But if she was shocked, Boone was stunned. "Monica?" he said to Amos.

"She said Rita Mae had to die."

"Why would Monica want Rita Mae Brown dead?" Boone asked him.

"Because Rita knew, " Amos said.

"She knew what?" asked Boone.

"She found out it wasn't an accident."

Boone and Charly looked at each other. Had they missed something? Then they both looked at Amos. "That what wasn't an accident?"

"Courtney's death," Amos said.

Charly frowned. Boone's heart nearly stopped beating. "What?" he asked Amos. "What are you talking about?"

"Monica planned it all," Amos said. "She knew you'd get angry that night and drive off like you always did. She knew how to push your buttons. But she figured you'd let her get the baby out of the backseat like you always had before. But that night you sped off with the baby still in the backseat. You wouldn't let her get that child."

"And?" Boone asked, still barely able to breathe.

"Monica had it all planned out. She would get the baby, you would drive off angry, and that SUV would T-bone you and take you out. That was the plan. The lady driving that SUV was paid to take you out. But you had Courtney in your vehicle. Courtney wasn't supposed to be in your vehicle!"

Charly could hardly believe it. She looked at Boone. He looked outright ill. "What are you saying?" Boone asked Amos. "Are you saying?"

"It was murder," said Amos. "Monica had plans to have you killed for all that cheating you did to her. She hated you. If she couldn't have you, nobody was going to have you. But she killed her own child instead."

"Oh, God," Charly said, covering her mouth. She was in agony for Boone!

Boone was still too stunned to feel anything. He was still staring at Amos. "You're telling me that Monica hired somebody to take me out that night, but instead . . . Instead . . ." Boone couldn't say it.

"Instead, they took Courtney out. Yes," said Amos. "Courtney died in that car crash, but you lived. It was Monica's worse nightmare."

Boone literally stepped back. Charly moved closer to him, and placed her arm around his waist.

"Where is she now?" Boone asked Amos.

"She's in hiding," said Amos. "She's in the same place she's been in since Courtney died. She's in hiding pulling all our strings."

"Where?"

"A long path off of Beaumont Road. She won't open the door for anybody but me."

Boone stared at him. There was only one answer for that. "Let's go," he said, "because that bitch will be opening that door."

He cuffed Amos and then unlocked the cell. Then he looked at Charly. "You come too," he said.

"I want to, of course," Charly said. "But are you sure?" It sounded like so much family drama to her. So personal.

But Boone was sure. "She tried to kill me three years ago," he said. "She tried to harm you three days ago. I'm sure. Besides," he added with pure anguish in his eyes, "I need you with me when I confront that . . ." He attempted to contain his anger. "I need you with me."

When he said those words, Charly squeezed his arm and didn't hesitate. She went with Boone.

CHAPTER FORTY-ONE

Boone's truck, followed by Morley and Dontay in an unmarked police car, made their way to Monica's place. It was a long drive down a long, winding pathway even after they turned off of Beaumont. In Boone's truck, they rode in silence. Boone behind the wheel of his pickup, Amos in the middle handcuffed, and Charly riding shotgun.

Boone didn't know how to feel. He was angry, mostly, but also sad. Sad for his daughter. Sad for Charly. Sad that he didn't let Monica take their child that night the way he usually did. But he had had it with her using their daughter as a bargaining chip. He wasn't allowing that anymore. He wished to God he had allowed it that night.

Charly could feel his anguish. She leaned forward so that she could see him beyond Amos's body. "You okay?" she asked him.

Boone glanced at her and attempted to smile for her sake. But he wasn't going to lie to her. "Hell no," he said.

Charly understood.

"It could get dangerous," he said to her.

"Monica isn't going to do anything with me present," Amos said to them.

"But how would you know that?" Boone asked. "She had Rita Brown killed. She had Dalbert killed. She wanted Malcolm to kill Charly. And she's not dangerous?"

"She's not! She just didn't want it all exposed."

"She didn't want what exposed?" Boone asked. "The fact that she had our daughter killed?"

"She didn't tell you to run that stop sign," Amos said.

"By your own admission," Charly said to Amos, "that SUV was going to crash into him whether he ran that stop sign or not. She killed their daughter. There's no dressing that up."

"Right," Boone said, nodding his head, although nothing was going to take away the guilt he still felt.

But then Charly looked at Amos. "How could you be a party to her madness?" she asked him. "Especially after she had Rita killed."

Amos let out a hard exhale. "She's my niece," he said. "I'll do anything for her."

Charly stared at him. "Even kill?"

Amos just stared forward. His silence said it all. Boone and Charly glanced at each other, and shook their heads. Some people, they knew, could pick up and put down morality like they were picking up and putting down trash. They continued to ride in silence.

"How much further?" Boone finally asked Amos.

Amos looked around. "Couple hundred yards," he responded.

Boone pulled over and stopped his truck. Dontay and Morley stopped their car just behind Chief's truck. All of them got out. Morley and Dontay walked over to their chief.

"Amos and I will go the rest of the way on foot," Boone said.

"How far is it?" Morley asked.

"Couple hundred more yards he says. But even if it's further, hang back."

"Yes, sir."

"Charly, you're going to stay back here with Morley and Dontay."

He could tell Charly didn't like that decision.

"At least until I can get control of the scene," Boone added. He preferred her with him, too, but he wasn't going to risk her life.

Charly understood and nodded. "Okay," she said. She wasn't about to make the situation any more stressful for him than it already was. Morley and Dontay were stunned he had brought her this far to begin with.

"Once the perimeter is secured," Boone said, "I'll radio for you guys to come in."

"Yes, sir," said Dontay.

And then Boone walked Charly to the unmarked patrol car, and put her in the backseat. Dontay and Morley got up front. And then Boone grabbed the arm of the handcuffed Amos Yerkson, and they began their journey to Monica.

The small wooden house was a little closer than the two football field distance Amos had said was the distance away, but regardless, they weren't walking straight on. Because Boone was taking no chances. They walked through the woods. A method, Boone hoped, that would keep them undetected by anybody in that house.

Oddly, Boone thought as they walked, it was peaceful out there, and beautiful. But looks, he knew, given who lived out there, could be deceiving.

"When you get to the front door," Boone told Amos, "announce yourself. Get cute and you won't have a chance to get cuter. I have men out there, and I have Charly out there. I'm not risking their lives, you understand?"

"Yes, Chief, I understand. Just don't hurt her. She's been hurt enough."

Boone looked at Amos. "*She's* been hurt enough? Are you kidding me? What about my daughter? What about Rita Mae Brown? Think they've been hurt enough?"

"Just don't hurt her," Amos said again as if Monica was all that mattered to him.

But when they finally made it to the front door, Amos obeyed Boone's command and announced himself. "It's me, Monnie!" he said loudly. But there was no response.

"Monnie? They let me out. It's me, Uncle Amos. Open up!"

There was another pause, then the sound of a woman's voice: "It's open," she said.

When Amos reached for the doorknob, Boone whispered in his ear: "Go in slow," he said. Just in case the bitch saw them coming, he wanted to add. But Amos had already opened that door.

And as soon as he opened it, a shotgun blast at close range ripped through Amos's chest, exploding it with blood and guts, and he immediately fell straight back.

Boone had his gun drawn, and had been ready to confront whatever was on the other side of that door, but Monica's shotgun was right in his face too. "Drop it, you bastard," she said with a voice dripping with bitterness. "Drop it!"

And Boone, knowing that she definitely had the upper hand, dropped his weapon.

But further back, and as soon as they heard that gunshot, Charly was anxiously yelling for them to go, go, go, and Dontay was already shifting the gear to Drive, hitting the gas, and speeding toward that house. Charly's heart was hammering.

But as soon as the car made it to the house, and Morley yelled for Charly to wait in the car, and as he and Dontay hurried out of the car, a voice over a loudspeaker was suddenly heard. It was Monica's voice.

"I have your chief at gunpoint," she said. "Get out of the car, drop your weapons, and come in. If you don't do exactly as I said, I will kill your chief. And if you don't believe me, look what I did to my uncle!"

They saw the body in the doorway. They saw the blood. They didn't see their chief.

"You have five seconds," said Monica. "Drop your weapons and come in now!"

Then there suddenly was another gun shot, causing Charly, who remained in the dark-tinted unmarked car, to drop down in the backseat.

"The next shot will be Boone's head," Monica said and Dontay and Morley looked at each other.

But they continued to resist. They needed proof of life. What if she had already killed him?

"Tell those fools, Chief," Monica could be heard saying, as if she knew why they were hesitating.

"Do as she says," Boone yelled over the loudspeaker. "Morley, Dontay: do as she says."

It wasn't lost on neither one of them that he didn't mention Charly's name. He wanted her to get out of there alive, or at least to go and get some help. But as soon as they heard their chief's voice, they knew they had to do what Monica said. They dropped their weapons and began making their way to the house.

When they got inside, they realized it was no trick. They had to step over Amos's dead body to get inside, and that was when they saw Chief Ryan. He was standing further into the home, with Monica pointing her shotgun at him. And with that shotgun she was directing them to go stand beside their boss.

Once they did, she relaxed. And smiled. "I knew it would come to this," she said happily. "I knew Uncle Amos would snitch and bring you here. I knew he would. To save his own hide. What did you promise him, Boone? His freedom if he turned me in? Is that what you promised him?"

"I didn't promise him a damn thing," Boone said. His singular focus was on his men and Charly, and how in the world was he going to get them out of this situation alive.

"You promised him his freedom in exchange for bringing you here to me," Monica said, refusing to believe him. "You've been a liar all your life," she added.

"What are you going to do?" Boone asked her.

"What's my game plan, as you used to love to say? My game plan is to do to you what I tried to do to you three years ago. When you took Courtney away from me. When she died when it should have been you!"

Monica calmed back down. "Then you had the nerve to fall for that teacher, or whatever she is. How dare you fall for that bitch!"

"Why did you try to kill her?"

"I didn't try to kill her. I didn't have to. Her enemies had tracked her down. They were trying to kill her. Until you killed them. I told Uncle Amos she had to go too. And like always, he saw to it. He loved me, you see." She glanced at his dead body. "Foolish man."

"But to think that my precious baby was dead, and that you were going to find happiness? Over my dead body!"

"Why now?" Boone asked her, staring at the woman he never loved. "I've been around this town for three years. Why now? Because Charly came to town?"

She stared at him. "You don't know, do you?"

Boone stared at her. "Know what?"

"He died."

"Who died?"

"Herman."

Boone was lost. "Who's Herman?"

"Herman Witherspoon. Courtney's father. Her *real* father."

Morley and Dontay looked at their chief. But Boone was still lost, still looking at Monica. "What are you talking about?" he nervously asked her.

"Rita Mae was blackmailing Amos. He was sleeping with Rita, you see, and he told her everything about it. He told her how I tried to kill you. He told her how you weren't Courtney's father. He told her everything! And she was going to go to you, and tell you. She was going to have me arrested for murdering my own daughter if we didn't pay up. So I told Dalbert she had to go. She was his pimp, or whatever they call'em now. He could handle her."

But Boone was still at that point when she declared Courtney was not his child. "It's not true," he said. "Courtney was *my* daughter."

Monica smiled. "You wish! You've never fathered anything, and if I have anything to say about it, you never will! And I knew it all along. We had broken up when I got pregnant. When we got back together, and the baby came early, I paid my doctor to claim she was premature. But she wasn't. She was right on time. But I was so in love with your sorry ass. I wanted you to be her father, when Herman would have been so much better at it. But I was so selfish then."

Boone was too stunned to speak. But it didn't matter to Monica. She was ready. She was ready to end this now.

"Herman died. The only man who ever loved me died. He's why I never went after you. He's why I kept my sanity when my baby was killed. But then he died. And you were still alive and trying to fall for some new bitch. It was time for you to go."

And before Boone or Dontay or Morley could react, she aimed her shotgun dead center at Boone and was just about to squeeze the trigger.

But another trigger was squeezed. By Charly. Who stood in the doorway. And this time, she had both hands on the gun. This time she wasn't going to be grazing anybody. This time, she fired and hit.

Monica, stunned that she'd been shot, looked at Charly. Boone knew it would take more than one bullet to take that bitch out. He knew it like he knew the back of his hand. Which meant Charly was in mortal danger. And he didn't hesitate.

Boone dived, grabbed his gun from the floor, and turned and fired repeatedly on Monica just as she was firing on Charly.

His bullet caused Monica to fall back, and for her bullet to go astray, as his firepower overwhelmed her and she finally dropped dead.

Charly's legs went wobbly and she fell against the doorjamb. Dontay and Morley ran to Monica, to ensure the witch was dead, and Boone hurried to Charly, to ensure she was okay.

She wasn't. She was shaking like a leaf. But as he pulled her into his big arms, he knew she would be. Eventually, he knew, his girl was going to be just fine.

EPILOGUE

They had eaten until they were stuffed: Babs and Duke, and Boone and Charly. The four of them at the Ryan ranch, on the back patio, enjoying good music over the stereo system, good company, and a wonderful Saturday night cookout.

But Babs had been dozing for some time, and Duke, it seemed to Boone, was itching to go check on his cattle. Or, as Babs and Boone both believed it to be, to go check on one of his women.

Boone used to be angry at the way his mother accepted their father's bad behavior. But now it was as much a part of their marriage as the air they breathed. Infidelity had been a part of their marriage since he was a kid over forty years ago, and it continued to be to this day. His father was an unfaithful man. Outrage, Boone learned a long time ago, was a waste of energy.

Besides, he was just like his father.

"Come on, Babs," Duke said, rising from his chair and helping his sleepy wife to her feet. "Let's get you to bed."

"I can get myself to bed, thank you," Babs said, her stubborn streak refusing even now to go along with the charade. She knew what her husband wanted: get her in bed so he could go and get in somebody else's bed. Boone knew it too. And Babs wasn't going to pretend she as if she didn't.

She pushed him aside. "Goodnight Charly," she said to Charly. "Good night, Boone." And then she gave her husband a side eye, and headed inside of their home.

"That woman," Duke said as he shook his head and watched her leave the patio. But then he exhaled as he continued to watch her. "That woman," he said again, "is the best thing that ever happened to me."

Boone and Charly both looked at him. But he just stood there, staring after his wife still, even though she was clean out of sight.

Then Duke exhaled again. "Guess I'll be going to bed too," he said.

"To bed," Boone asked, "or to check on your cattle?"

Duke looked at his son. His son stared at him. They both knew the game. "To bed," Duke said, then said his goodnights, and headed inside of his home.

Boone was stunned. That was a first, he thought. But he had other things on his mind. He had Charly on his mind.

But she stood up and started dancing, swaying to the music, with a glass of wine in her hand.

Boone, smiling, got up too. "You're right," he said, as he removed the glass from her hand. "You're the worse dancer ever!"

Charly laughed as he sat her glass on one of the tables and pulled her into his arms. The song playing wasn't even a slow song, but they slow-dragged to it anyway. And then a slower song came on: Jeffrey Osborne singing *On the Wings of Love*. When that song came on, Charly laid her head on Boone's shoulder.

And they slow-dragged even slower.

Until Boone had to say it. He leaned back, causing her to look at him as he looked into her eyes.

"Charlene Johnson," he said, "will you do an old dog like me a favor and be my lady?"

Charly smiled. "Oh, Boone," she said, "I already am."

Boone's heart leaped, and he smiled, too. "We just might pull this off, Charly," he said to her with great sincerity.

She nodded. She understood what he meant. "We might," she said, and then laid her head back on his shoulder.

And they danced.

"On the wings of love,

up and above the clouds;
The only way to fly,
is on the wings of love.

On the wings of love,
only the two of us
together flying high.
Flying high
upon the wings of love."

Like lovesick teenagers, they danced all night.

Visit

www.mallorymonroebooks.com

or

www.austinbrookpublishing.com

for more information on all titles.

ABOUT THE AUTHOR

Mallory Monroe is the bestselling author of well over
one hundred novels.
Visit
mallorymonroebooks.com
or
austinbrookpublishing.com
for more information on all of her titles.

Made in the USA
Middletown, DE
05 November 2019

78015545R00227